CW00670003

Other works by M. L. Buchman: *(* - also in audio)*

Action-Adventure Thrillers

Dead Chef

One Chef!
Two Chef!

Miranda Chase

*Drone**
*Thunderbolt**
*Condor**
*Ghostrider**
*Raider**
*Chinook**
*Havoc**
*White Top**

Romantic Suspense

Delta Force

*Target Engaged**
*Heart Strike**
*Wild Justice**
*Midnight Trust**

Firehawks

MAIN FLIGHT

Pure Heat
Full Blaze
*Hot Point**
*Flash of Fire**
Wild Fire

SMOKEJUMPERS

*Wildfire at Dawn**
*Wildfire at Larch Creek**
*Wildfire on the Skagit**

The Night Stalkers

MAIN FLIGHT

The Night Is Mine
I Own the Dawn
Wait Until Dark
Take Over at Midnight
Light Up the Night
Bring On the Dusk
By Break of Day

AND THE NAVY

Christmas at Steel Beach
Christmas at Peleliu Cove

WHITE HOUSE HOLIDAY

*Daniel's Christmas**
*Frank's Independence Day**
*Peter's Christmas**
*Zachary's Christmas**
*Roy's Independence Day**
*Damien's Christmas**

5E

Target of the Heart
Target Lock on Love
Target of Mine
Target of One's Own

Shadow Force: Psi

*At the Slightest Sound**
*At the Quietest Word**
*At the Merest Glance**
*At the Clearest Sensation**

White House Protection Force

*Off the Leash**
*On Your Mark**
*In the Weeds**

Contemporary Romance

Eagle Cove

Return to Eagle Cove
Recipe for Eagle Cove
Longing for Eagle Cove
Keepsake for Eagle Cove

Henderson's Ranch

*Nathan's Big Sky**
*Big Sky, Loyal Heart**
*Big Sky Dog Whisperer**

Other works by M. L. Buchman:

Contemporary Romance (cont)

Love Abroad

Heart of the Cotswolds: England
Path of Love: Cinque Terre, Italy

Where Dreams

Where Dreams are Born
Where Dreams Reside
*Where Dreams Are of Christmas**
Where Dreams Unfold
Where Dreams Are Written

Science Fiction / Fantasy

Deities Anonymous

Cookbook from Hell: Reheated
Saviors 101

Single Titles

The Nara Reaction
Monk's Maze
the Me and Elsie Chronicles

Non-Fiction

Strategies for Success

Managing Your Inner Artist/Writer
*Estate Planning for Authors**
Character Voice
*Narrate and Record Your Own Audiobook**

Short Story Series by M. L. Buchman:

Romantic Suspense

Delta Force

Th Delta Force Shooters
The Delta Force Warriors

Firehawks

The Firehawks Lookouts
The Firehawks Hotshots
The Firebirds

The Night Stalkers

The Night Stalkers 5D Stories
The Night Stalkers 5E Stories
The Night Stalkers CSAR
The Night Stalkers Wedding Stories

US Coast Guard

White House Protection Force

Contemporary Romance

Eagle Cove

Henderson's Ranch*

Where Dreams

Action-Adventure Thrillers

Dead Chef

Miranda Chase Origin Stories

Science Fiction / Fantasy

Deities Anonymous

Other

The Future Night Stalkers
Single Titles

ABOUT THIS BOOK

When a crashed helicopter could start a war—Miranda Chase is the woman to save the day.

When the fastest and most powerful helicopters in the US Army's fleet start falling out of the sky, autistic air-crash genius **Miranda Chase** *and her team of NTSB investigators are called in.*

One crash leads to another and they are fast entangled in a Chinese conspiracy to start a war over Taiwan. Only Miranda's team can stop the trade war from becoming a real one.

PROLOGUE

SIX MONTHS AGO

OUTSIDE THE CRIPPLED AC-130J GHOSTRIDER GUNSHIP, TWO men wearing the only two parachutes were falling through the midnight darkness toward life.

Inside there was only death.

US Air Force Colonel Vicki "Taser" Cortez stared at the inside of the jump door she had just closed, blocking her own chance of survival.

Except she wasn't any of those labels anymore.

If she set foot back on US soil, she'd be stripped of rank and court-martialed along with every other person on this plane. Too guilty to ever plea bargain a lesser sentence. Leavenworth for life. For what this crew had done, they might bring back the firing squad.

The sick joke was, she wasn't even Vicki Cortez. That was just the name on the identity papers her mother had bought when they'd slipped across the Mexican border a lifetime ago. A name she'd since associated with bank accounts, pensions, and security clearances that properly would belong to a dead girl.

With the two civilians off the plane and parachuting to safety, and the Ghostrider yawing drunkenly through the last of its death throes, there was nothing left to do.

No one left to be.

She pulled the challenge coin from her pocket. A cast metal coin, the very first one every handed out by her commander after he made general. It was a sign of his respect, and the honor of it had been her anchor for nineteen years.

Nineteen years she'd spent following General JJ Martinez on his quest. A man of perfect integrity.

He had fought for what was best for their country—his country, not technically hers.

And when blocked one too many times despite their combined efforts, the three-star general had taken on the battle himself.

Had it been a failure?

The shuddering of the deck through her boots would argue for that. The highly modified C-130J Ghostrider was damaged past any ability to land. Two hundred million dollars of stolen aircraft was in its last minutes of life.

The main gun mounted in the middle of the cargo bay, the 105 mm howitzer, had exploded and was still on fire. Through the small round view-glass in the jump door, she could see that both portside engines were also now burning. Fuel pouring from the shrapnel-punctured wings caught fire even as it streamed out.

Yet tonight they had destroyed four major drug cartel strongholds along the south side of the Mexican border. Hundreds had died beneath the barrage of this gunship. Millions, perhaps billions of dollars of drugs had burned as well. It wouldn't stop the flow, but it would cripple it while each cartel fought an internal battle to establish new leaders now that so many had been executed.

Perhaps it would finally force the United States and Mexico to do something useful together.

Perhaps not.

But all that was over.

All that was left to do was to die.

There would be no landing in Arizona's Sonoran Desert —impact with the terrain was imminent.

A day ago, even a few hours ago, she'd have gone to sit by the general and await her fate.

But Jeremy Trahn had shown her something before she'd strapped him into the last parachute and shoved him out the jump door to safety. Against his sweet nature, he'd helped her. He hadn't killed. But he'd shown her how to, and she'd done it without compunction.

While being her prisoner, he'd also improvised a weapon that would have blinded her, would have stopped the general—but hadn't used it. The unused weapon and a final kiss were the last things he'd given to her.

Yet he'd given her more.

An anger.

A fury!

The plane slid hard across a pocket of turbulence, slamming her against the closed bulkhead door. She could *feel* the plane's will to survive as the damaged wings caught air and stabilized despite all the damage done to it.

Why couldn't *that* have been her life?

Instead, for nineteen years she'd been the general's weapon, unleashing all the blackness coiled within her chest at his command.

His Taser.

Go find out what's really happening at Lockheed on this project and fix it.

Track down whoever is blocking this initiative and have them court-martialed for being an idiot.

She had done everything except kill for him.

Until the cartels' headquarters tonight.

Taz didn't know if it was funny or sad. For the nineteen years she'd been in the military, she'd never killed anyone.

During her youth in the ghettos of Mexico City and later as a teen in San Diego, she'd been lethal with a knife. She'd never hesitated to serve justice as executioner—wasting no time with judge and jury. All that had ended the day she'd walked up to the Air Force recruiter to escape that life.

And now, she was again *not* military—for the act of stealing this brand-new plane and eradicating with prejudice the leadership of four Mexican drug cartels. Those very acts had severed her from her decades of dedicated service.

Now? She wasn't even the general's Taser anymore.

The only thing that remained truly hers was the nickname "Taz."

If Jeremy had done anything, it was to offer her a glimpse of an alternate life.

Taz glanced around for the general. He'd gone back up to the C-130J's cockpit. She could see his back as he sat rigidly upright in the jump seat behind the pilots, watching them fight the already lost battle to retain some control of the landing. The AC-130J Ghostrider was going down hard no matter what they did.

Only now did she understand that the general had taken her life as surely and carelessly as she'd given it to his service. He'd never abused her, but he'd *used* her without mercy or a second thought.

She flexed her wrist and felt the Benchmade Phaeton drop-blade tactical knife she always wore there.

No.

Another hard yaw threw her to the deck hard enough to knock some sense into her. The hull's metal groaned as forces torqued the airframe one way and then another. There was no need to take the general's life; the plane would do that for her.

The weapons console was useless now. All of the Ghostrider's bombs had been dropped—all of the ammunition fired. The explosion of the very last round had killed both the big howitzer and the wing. Only the HEL-A laser remained, but its aiming cameras had been burned away. Nothing left to shoot at anyway.

Two of the gun crew members who'd survived the initial explosion of the M102 howitzer stared blankly at the shattered weapon. The three others were dead or dying on the narrow walkway around the gun.

Jeremy's lesson.

Of them all, that's the one that counted.

And it was so simple...

Live!

And the safest place in a plane crash?

Aft.

Taz sprinted for the tail, racing upslope against the steep dive of the C-130.

An inch under five feet, she was small enough to slip through a gap under the Bofors 40mm autocannon.

The pair of surviving gunners still hung on beside the ruined howitzer, taking no action to save themselves.

Squeezing between them and the big gun, the hot metal of the breech burned a line along her shoulder, but she ignored the pain.

The AC-130J's rear ramp had been fitted with vertical bomb launch tubes. No seats back here. Maybe, if she braced herself against the tubes and the tail broke away on impact, she'd have a chance.

The gunners had been snapped out of their lethargy by her passage. In moments they'd squeezed in to either side of her as the dying plane flailed and twisted toward the hard earth. The g-force pressed the three of them more tightly together than if they were having a threesome.

It was dark back here. Almost safe. The red night-fighting lights by the gun barely reached the launch tubes. Just enough that she could see the wide eyes of the man pressed chest-to-chest against her.

A sickening lurch.

"There goes the wing," the one behind her gasped out.

She'd helped recruit them to this final mission, but now couldn't even recall their names.

In a death spiral now, inevitable with only one wing. Not even being in the tail would offer any safety.

She clutched the general's coin to her chest for luck.

Luck?

General Martinez would welcome death come to find the warrior at last.

Well to *hell* with that.

Before the first spiral was complete, before she had a chance to throw the coin away, before the twisting momentum became unsurvivable, the plane slammed into the ground.

TAZ REMEMBERED ONLY FLASHES OF WHAT CAME NEXT.

The impact.

The curious soundlessness of the fuselage ripping away from the tail—the hull skin shredding, the cross-connecting beams shearing.

A clear view as the fuel in the remaining wing exploded, pulverizing the main fuselage—too loud to be called a sound.

The gaping mouth of her chest-to-chest companion as he was burned alive by the flash of fire blasted into the now open-ended tail section. She was small enough, or he big enough, that she remained tucked safely in his heat shadow—saved from the worst burns by yanking her flight jacket over her hair and face.

The final shudders of the man behind her as his neck was broken when slammed against the launch tubes.

No more slide and tumble, the tail came to rest in a shallow arroyo filled with sand and tumbleweeds.

Claw her way out from between two corpses.

Tumble onto the night-cool sand.

No longer a US Air Force colonel.

Crawling.

No longer the general's feared right-hand Taser.

Crawling with no thought but...away.

No longer Vicki Cortez.

All of her past selves dead in the flaming wreckage.

Another hard explosion behind her—she didn't bother turning to see—assured her that her body wouldn't be missed.

She was north of Nogales.

In the Sonoran Desert of Arizona.

Once more in *los Estados Unidos*—north of the border.

Once more an illegal with no identity.

Just as she had at eleven years old, she set her guide by the North Star and kept moving.

Clear of the wreckage, clear of the likely search perimeter, she buried herself in the cool night sand and slept.

When she woke, it was...again? ...still? night.

The general's coin remained clutched in her hand. The lone remnant of her past. Rather than dumping it in the sand, she jammed it into her pocket.

She continued north.

Taz hadn't expected to survive this operation, hadn't expected to want to, or she'd have emptied her bank accounts. Now all she had was the emergency fund that was never off her person.

In Tucson, she bought a new identity. Colonel Vicki "Taser" Cortez of the United States Air Force became US citizen Tanya Roberts.

The clean social security number and identity came from a crooked mortician and a corrupt medical examiner who took most of her funds between them for *not* reporting Tanya's recent death. Tanya was buried as Jane Doe—death by mugger.

No family.

Nothing in "her" apartment worth keeping or pawning when Taz checked it out, except for a phone with no contacts or recent calls other than work, and a set of car keys. Tanya had been a true loner, and perhaps even welcomed death. Perfect.

Taz replenished her funds by emptying out Tanya's meager bank accounts, and she was done.

As Tanya, she was now legally five years younger—which was closer to her true age. She'd actually joined the Air Force at fifteen straight out of high school after her first name change had aged her three years. Now, her ID declared she was thirty-two instead of Vicki's thirty-seven, or the thirty-four she actually was in some half-forgotten reality.

With her size and looks, she could have safely dropped ten years instead of just the five.

A week and a hundred miles later, she filed for a legal name change in Phoenix. Somehow, having the same name as a tall, redheaded, 1980s Hollywood sex-kitten actress just seemed too unlikely. She also wanted as clean a break as possible from anyone seeking the dead Tanya Roberts.

Flores was her original family name, left south of the border when she was eleven. She took that back for her mother's memory.

Her birth name was meaningless. In the Air Force she was always Taz or Cortez. But Jeremy had called her Vicki when they'd made love.

Made love.

She'd had sex when she cared to, but there was little question that mere sex wasn't something Jeremy Trahn understood.

And he'd proven the difference to her, much to her surprise.

She wasn't Vicki to anyone except Jeremy. So, she kept both her family name and nickname, and, for luck, the name that Jeremy had called her.

The Motor Vehicle Department clerk hadn't even looked

at the picture on Tanya Roberts' old driver's license before issuing her one under her new/old name, which had saved the five hundred dollars she'd had folded tight and ready. They'd switched over the vehicle registration at the same time. Social Security had accepted the name change with the court order and new ID; they gave her a fresh card just as painlessly.

With no plan beyond survival, Tasia Vicki Flores pocketed her new identity, climbed into "her" rusted-but-running 1997 Toyota Corolla, and left Phoenix to follow wherever the North Star led.

1

"YOU'VE GOT TO BE KIDDING ME." JEREMY LOOKED AT THE card he'd just drawn.

"Your poker face sucks. You know that, right?"

"So helpful, Mike." The game's rules kept evolving, but there was no question that the B-1B Lancer bomber was the greatest suck of an airplane card—and truly appropriate for such a sad aircraft. When he'd taken Miranda's list of aircraft and remade them into a card deck, he'd arranged them by coolness factor. Actually, by how he guessed Miranda would grade each one before making a few adjustments of his own.

What he hadn't planned on was how often he drew the deuce of combat planes. This definitely required some rethinking.

"Whatever," he laid down the card and rolled his dice. He needed at least a four to keep the plane aloft.

A one.

He augered in. Too many total crashes, and he was out of the game before it had really begun. The game needed some *major* rethinking.

While the others battled it out, he headed to the kitchen.

Miranda's island home still wowed him every time they were invited here. The big house, built of stone and timber off the land, looked like a smaller version of the grand timber lodges that were dotted all over the Northwest.

It had been built as a hunting lodge perched in the center of long and slender Spieden Island. In the 1970s it had been made into a big game resort with hundreds of imported species. The zebra and other African imports were long since removed, which was too bad as he'd like to have seen them up close. But deer, sheep, and hundreds of exotic bird species still populated the island, though they were no longer hunted. Two miles long and half a mile wide, it was half conifer forest and half grassy meadow completely surrounded by a steep, rocky shore.

The August sunset, striking reds and golds over Vancouver Island across ten miles of Puget Sound, seemed to fill the house to bursting. It warmed the fir-clad walls to a luster almost as warm as the fire crackling in the beach-cobble hearth.

He fished a beer out of the fridge, then leaned back against the maple-and-cherrywood island to watch the others. The big kitchen filled this whole end of the great room, definitely a cook's kitchen. On a good day, he could make Toll House chocolate chip cookies—by following the recipe on the back of the bag.

Mike was the real cook of the team, and he always made it seem like so much fun when he was doing it.

Miranda often ended up as his assistant, even though they all were on her team. She spent almost as much time putting everything perfectly back into place as she did cooking, but her autistic nature seemed to like doing that, so she too enjoyed herself. The rest of them were a disaster in the kitchen and were typically banned.

The others were gathered around one end of the vast oak-slab dining table that could easily seat twenty in the middle of the room.

The team wasn't invited here often, but he looked forward to it every time.

With a cry of triumph, Holly slammed down a card atop one of Mike's. "That'll teach you to stick your aircraft up my business, mate." Her Australian accent was running thick tonight, so she was clearly enjoying herself. The fact that she and Mike had been sleeping together for the last six months "but we are *so-oo* not a couple," seemed to only enhance her glee in attacking him at every turn.

Their constant battling seemed to suit them, but that wouldn't be his choice.

Miranda and Jon were also a couple, though he'd never been comfortable with seeing them together—even on opposite sides of the card table. She was the best plane-crash investigator in the entire NTSB, and Jon...really wasn't. He was a nice guy, but Miranda deserved better.

That he himself got to work with her was beyond cool. And that she now trusted him to draft many of the team's reports was simply unbelievable.

She always added things he'd never thought to, of course, but still she let him create those first drafts. If he could just be half as good as her someday...

Yeah, that was never going to happen.

Mike tossed his cards into the middle of the table with no sign of the frustration that Jeremy knew he would've shown, instead offering an easy laugh. He then rose from the table, circled to Holly, and leaned down to really kiss her.

Instead of shoving him away as she usually did, she grabbed him by the neck and kept him pinned in place. When Mike finally broke free, they were both smiling like a couple of lunatics, as if somehow convinced they each had just won their battle.

"You two have serious issues." Captain Andi Wu, formerly of the Night Stalkers and now the last and newest member of the team, gathered up the deck and began shuffling.

"Like you and the sheep!" Holly shot back.

"Somebody coulda warned me."

"Nope," Mike, Holly, and Jon said practically in unison. Miranda sat quietly as she usually did during banter, just watching the others.

When Andi had stepped down from Miranda's sleek little Cessna Citation M2 jet onto the grass runway, a mouflon sheep had nosed forward to sniff her. Standing a meter high at the shoulders, it hadn't had to strain to sniff her face-to-face. Its great horns curved almost a full circle around to its jaws.

Andi's yelp had spooked the sheep, making it bolt and sending her stumbling backward until she landed in the grass.

His own first run-in with the island's big sheep had been far less dramatic, and at a safer distance, so he shouldn't feel superior. But he did.

It still wasn't fair how Andi had just stumbled into being part of the team. But there she was, dealing out the cards, then leading the attack on Jon now that he and Mike were out of the game. Like it was women against men or something.

Jeremy had worked for years to make sure he had every

necessary credential. Dual masters in Fluid Dynamics and Advanced System Topology Modeling from Princeton—which he'd managed when only two years older than Miranda herself had earned her two masters degrees at twenty.

And despite a dozen big-firm offers, he'd applied only to the NTSB, hoping that he might at least *meet* Miranda Chase someday. That he'd been assigned to her team was still the best day of his life.

Whereas Andi? She'd been thrown out of the military—because of PTSD according to Mike, which meant honorably, but still. And while Jeremy had taken and aced every single course at the NTSB Academy, she'd completed less than half before she'd been assigned to Miranda's team out of the blue.

Keeping Captain Wu from edging into his skills area sucked.

Ever since the sabotage and explosion of a CH-47F Chinook had almost killed the team on their second major crash investigation a year ago, he'd been preparing for when they'd investigate another helicopter crash. He'd spent much of his spare time since then studying their mechanics and aerodynamics so that he could step in when Miranda finally got called to investigate one. He'd made sure he knew more than Holly, which was hard, or Mike, which wasn't.

Nothing against Mike. He was the human-factors specialist so he knew very little about the aircraft themselves. Holly covered structures. His own niche was systems, and rotorcraft had a lot of those.

Then they'd finally had their first major rotorcraft crash, and Andi had swooped in from the 160th Night Stalkers—

the Army's secret helicopter regiment—like some sort uninvited ringer for the opposing team.

Now there she was, laughing with the group as if she actually belonged. Jon merely shrugged when Andi knocked him out of the game as well.

Mike, who'd hovered to watch the round, thumped Andi on the shoulder, then came into the kitchen area.

"Thinking mighty hard there, Jeremy." Mike fetched his own beer. "Good thoughts, I hope."

Jeremy blinked. "Uh, not so much."

"Not good, my young Padawan. That's not like you. Besides, thinking cheerful thoughts is much more fun."

Jeremy tried to remember back a year to when he, Mike, and Holly had become Miranda's new team. He'd been...naive.

"I was like some overeager puppy dog back then, wasn't I?"

"Back when? Oh, before our unasked-for trip on Taz's Ghostrider? Yeah, you kind of were." Mike ruffled his hair.

Jeremy batted Mike's hand aside, but Mike just laughed.

"My, how our boy has grown." Then he pulled out a big skillet. "Everything changed all at once, didn't it?"

Jeremy just grimaced.

While Mike rubbed allspice, salt, and pepper over a row of chicken breasts, he had Jeremy slicing onions, carrots, and a red bell pepper. Before Jeremy was done, Mike had the chicken sizzling in oil and had begun doing something with thin-sliced jalapeno peppers in a boiling sugar-and-vinegar mix.

He made it look so easy. But when Jeremy tried to remember Mike's cooking later, it just turned into a blur.

Sure enough, in moments Mike was wielding a knife like

it was another piece of his arm. Minced onions and garlic were soon sizzling in a heavy pot.

"Mexican rice."

Which just reminded him again of Taz. He didn't even know where in Mexico she'd been from.

"You never got closure," Mike's voice was suddenly serious. "That must be hard. When I lost my parents, at least I got to go to the funeral. I was nine, so what did I know, but it was a chance to say goodbye. Still, it's been six months since she went down, Jeremy. Got to start letting go at some point."

Jeremy took the onion and garlic skins to the small composting crock. At least he knew how to do that.

How to survive the memory of Vicki Cortez?

How to *not* see her every time he closed his eyes—her plane impacting the desert not two miles from where his parachute had landed? How to not feel and hear the explosion, so violent that he'd felt the shockwave across the wide stretch of barren desert?

That he couldn't seem to do.

2

Jeremy sat in the second-story library with the lights off, watching the moonlight creeping across Miranda's island. The deep couch faced southeast through the great half-circle window. It rose from knee-high until it curved nearly to the cathedral ceiling.

The many radial panes seemed to offer different views of the world, despite the glass being well aligned. Slices of light slipped over the face of the bookcases, highlighting one section, then another. None clearly enough to read, but prior inspection had taught him what was there: a massive section about aircraft, a smaller one about codebreaking, and a collection of novels exclusively on those two topics. Sections on gardening, construction, and the wildlife that lived on her island were almost afterthoughts.

Sitting here at night was like looking through the nose of a librarian's starship. Except instead of just stars, the world lay painted in a moonlit monochrome of meaningless shapes.

Sixty miles that way were his parents and sister. Asleep,

perhaps dreaming. Another day of software design ahead of them.

Tomorrow for him?

It all depended on Miranda's phone.

If it didn't ring, Holly would spend time checking over the metallurgy reports on the F-16 training accident. Mike would review interview tapes of a Bombardier Q400 that had smeared itself down the length of SeaTac airport's runway, yet without a single fatality. For himself, he wanted to reprocess the audio files from the Q400's flight recorders. There were background sounds he still wanted to identify but it would take some effort to extract.

Jon would hover around Miranda distracting her, which never boded well.

Andi would...he didn't know what.

If Miranda's phone rang, there'd be a new accident. A new launch for the team. A new investigation to pile atop their on-going investigations.

He wanted the answers. He and Miranda shared that; they both wanted them *now.*

But for most incidents it was the slow, methodical study that removed variables and only eventually drove the focus toward the final solution. And even when the solution was found, there were the recommendations to consider to avoid it happening again.

"I like watching the night from here when I can't sleep." Miranda's voice was soft but it still surprised him. He hadn't heard a single squeak from the plank flooring as she'd approached. Of course, she'd lived her whole life here and would know where every single one was.

"Why can't *you* sleep?"

She settled on the far end of the couch, pulling a quilt

over her lap. "There haven't been five guests in the house at once since my parents died. I was thirteen. I can *feel* everyone like a weight. Not a bad weight, but it makes it hard to breathe."

"I've never lived alone. Living in the dorms at Princeton, I had a single the last year, but that doesn't really count with thirty-four other people on the floor and communal dining." Was that why he was sitting here? To feel what it might be like to be alone?

No.

But he also didn't know why he was awake long enough to watch the Douglas fir moon shadows shift through thirty degrees—two full hours. The deer and sheep were bedded down. The only shadows he'd seen interrupting the still night had been a pair of owls. Not even a late-night ferry. And they were facing the wrong way to spot any cargo ships heading up the Haro Strait to Vancouver.

"How could you stand it?" Miranda's voice was disembodied in the darkness, almost as if he was asking the questions of himself.

"The people? I never really noticed. Our family was close and always busy. We lived in a townhouse near the Microsoft campus. Lots of other kids: daycare, computer clubs and camps. I never thought about it much."

"Did you have a lot of friends?"

Jeremy shook his head. "I skipped a couple of grades along the way. Not as many as you, but I didn't fit in anywhere after that. Never even had a girlfriend. There was a girl who was really nice to me when I graduated high school. But that was kind of it until..." No. He wouldn't finish that sentence.

Miranda didn't ask.

Jeremy couldn't even explain it to himself. He'd met Colonel Vicki Cortez less than thirty hours before her death. When Mike offered his sympathy, he didn't know what to do with it; it had no logical place to connect. Yet she had done something to him, even if he couldn't understand what.

Miranda's silence was thankfully just that.

Together, they sat and watched the moon shift the shadows some more.

3

This was the way to travel.

Taz sat on the tail ramp of the CH-47D Chinook helicopter and watched the night-black forest go by. She'd never thought to fly in a military aircraft again, even if it was just Army National Guard.

The Chinook was the military's primary heavy lifter rotorcraft. Sure, the Navy's CH-53E Super Sea Stallion could lift more, but they also had a nasty habit of falling out the sky and killing another platoon of Marines.

She'd take the twin-rotor Chinook any day. They almost never went down, unless they were shot. Even then, they were incredibly tough.

Her hotshot wildfire crew had been called up from southern Oregon to a nasty burn on Washington's Olympic Peninsula. The firefight was in the rugged mountains above Port Angeles along the northernmost shore of the state. The achingly dry summer had turned the entire place into a giant tinderbox.

It was late in the season, they'd been on the verge of

cutting her and the other seasonal firefighters loose, but the Washington wilderness had decided it still had one good burn to go.

They'd crammed into the team's pair of ten-seat hotshot buggies and driven through the afternoon and evening to get to the town of Port Angeles at midnight. The ARNG had been waiting to immediately airlift her team of twenty to defend the Hurricane Ridge Visitor Center. The lone access road was on fire at either end. Airlift was the only way in or out.

She rubbed at the calluses on her hands. Physical work was something she'd left behind for nineteen years after Basic Training. Even after five months with the hotshots, her hands ached. But it felt good to be doing something physical after all these years. No power plays. No national crises. Simply good, hard work.

As the flight humped over the first ridge, the landscape glowed—lit from within by firelight. Bright smears of red and gold peeking through wind-torn rents in the obscuring smoke. Where the smoke hid the terrain, it was luminous with the raging fires it masked.

The Chinook was so powerful that it didn't have to claw to make the mile-high climb. It was as smooth a ride as a C-130 Hercules transport plane. *I'm going this way.*

She liked its muscley attitude.

So much of her life she'd been just that—the unstoppable force. At least in the halls and offices of the American defense system.

Her life was so different now that she barely recognized it. For over a month after the Ghostrider crash had "killed" her, she'd just drifted north from Phoenix. Sleeping wild and seeing places she'd only ever heard of. The Grand

Canyon, Monument Valley, Mesa Verde…she'd just played tourist.

Taz had spent so much of her life on the move that sitting still didn't work for more than a few hours behind the wheel. Picking up some decent hiking gear at a pawn shop in Flagstaff, she took to the hills and trails wherever she went. The farther she got out in nature, the better she felt.

Chance had placed her in Southern Oregon at Pearsony Falls Park on the first day of the testing for the Rogue River Hotshots. One of the crew bosses laughed when she asked if she could join the test. Hard to begrudge him, she stood eight inches shorter and forty pounds lighter than either of the other women among the thirty hopefuls. Half the team were regulars, which meant there were only ten open spots. Didn't matter to her, she was just looking for something new to do for a few days.

She'd waited him out.

The superintendent had shrugged as if it was no skin off his back if she wanted to join them for a bit of a workout.

Tasia Vicki Flores had lasted about an hour into those tryouts. After she came in well ahead of the pack on the first hike, her old nickname of Taz resurfaced. But she was no longer the general's Taser. It was a hundred percent her now.

As for the physical testing, what had started out as an amusing diversion had turned into a brutal ten-day trial that had fit her down to her boots. Hiking a forty-pound pack across three miles in ninety minutes was about physical toughness, the kind she'd spent a month building up during her own explorations of the Sierra Nevada. Digging organic debris off a fireline in hour thirty-six was about mental toughness. Spending nights "coyote"—sleeping wild—was what she'd already been doing anyway.

She earned her place, did the work to earn a Red Card, and became a seasonal wildland firefighter on a crew of twenty other hard-headed hotshots. One other woman made it through. The crew boss who'd laughed at her asked specifically to have her on his crew.

You're tenacious. Facing a fire, I like tenacious.

For five months they chased burns up and down the hills until she was in the best shape of her life.

And she belonged.

Taz glanced around the Chinook helicopter's cargo bay. Every one of the crew was more familiar than anyone had ever been in her life other than General JJ Martinez.

She knew that Jeff had a husband in Sacramento who didn't understand his need to fight fires half the year, but made it work. Jeff felt guilty all the time, calling fire his "evil mistress", but this was his eighth season.

Clare had been married twice, both times to firefighters, and had been well on her way to a third firefighter before deciding it would be better to go hotshot herself. *First thing I've gotten right in years.*

Taz had slowly fabricated a past.

A San Diego childhood.

Living with a Lockheed Martin engineer in El Segundo, California, then DC, to explain how she knew so much about aircraft and the nation's capital.

Catching his cheating ass with a Congressional aide, resulting in her wandering road trip in her beater Corolla.

It hadn't held together all that well until she let slip a few words about a barely avoided court-martial. Of course, implying her fictitious lover's trial—not the one she'd avoided herself by conveniently "dying" in the Ghostrider's crash without ending up dead.

She became a woman with a shadowy past, which actually made her story more acceptable to the rest of the crew. No one here to recognize Colonel Vicki Cortez. Outside the Pentagon, that wasn't much of a worry.

Yes, she'd take the present any day.

4

MIRANDA WATCHED THE NIGHT.

She'd always found it soothing. Everyone asleep. No demands on her attention. The shadows and the quiet dark the only thing in her life that moved slowly enough to not totally derail her from her own thoughts.

If Mother or Father had known about how many nights she'd spent here, they'd never said anything. Usually it was Tante Daniels who found her here in the mornings and shooed her back to her room with no one the wiser.

There had been a stillness about her that Miranda had appreciated while growing up, even if she hadn't understood it.

And then, nineteen years ago, the world changed. Or, more accurately, *her* world changed.

Tante Daniels, Miranda couldn't even remember her not living on the island, had brought her here to this same couch.

You're about to turn eighteen, Miranda. There are things you need to know.

Yes, that her parents had died five years ago, and the world they'd left behind was not one iota less confusing than it had been before their deaths.

You've completed your bachelor's degree.

And she'd be returning to the University of Washington the next week to start the dual masters program she'd chosen to prepare her for investigating plane crashes like the one that killed her parents.

And then Tante Daniels had dropped her bomb.

I'm not just your governess. I was your therapist for a decade before your parents died.

Now that she was an adult, Tante Tanya Daniels—Tante was "Aunt" in German, even though they weren't related—said it wasn't ethical for her to treat Miranda without her knowledge.

The truth had felt like a betrayal at first.

Not family, not governess, not friend—therapist.

Ever since she was twelve, Miranda had been only too aware of what was happening to her. She'd found all of the test results in her mother's desk shortly before she died.

Moderate-functioning ASD—Autism Spectrum Disorder.

Subject requires extensive therapy if ever to be even a marginally functioning member of society.

Severe learning and sensory disadvantages.

The list had been long, and each one had been an overwhelming dagger in her heart.

It was Tante Daniels who had helped her turn the blade long before Miranda knew that's why she was nearly fulltime on her parents' island.

Prove them all wrong. I know we can do it together.

And they had—*Miranda had,* as Tante Daniels kept

insisting she say. She'd finished high school by the time most of her contemporaries were entering it.

The pressure hadn't eased since—ever?

She looked over at Jeremy, who had slipped lower on the couch.

In seventeen years of investigating crashes, starting with her own crash while en route to start at the NTSB, she'd always carried the burden alone.

Her teams had shifted over the years, and even on this one, each member was only skilled at certain aspects.

Holly understood the mechanical structure of aircraft and could project backward from the crash debris to estimate what forces had been applied to damage an aircraft.

Mike best understood the one thing she herself understood least: people.

Jon was...

...was her lover, asleep in her bed even now.

Major Jonathon Swift of the US Air Force Accident Investigation Board was a skilled investigator. But his skill was as much in managing a team of experts as it was in doing any aspect of the investigation himself. She'd tried to teach him, but he just didn't see the clues even when they were spread so clearly across a debris field.

As well as understanding rotorcraft intimately, Andi Wu had proven herself observant in ways that Jon had proved himself incapable of. She also communicated the eccentricities of the American military in ways no one else on her team could manage. A pilot's view, but useful nonetheless.

And then there was Jeremy.

She'd come to rely on him like no one since Tante Daniels.

If he said something was accurate, there was no need to question the result. She always checked everything he did. Not because she expected to find anything, but rather it was the only way she had to make his findings real in her own mental picture.

"Jeremy?"

He didn't respond to her whisper. He must have fallen asleep.

If she could clone herself, it would be him.

If she dared to have a child—with a nine-fold increase in likelihood of an autistic parent having an autistic child, she didn't—it would be a younger version of Jeremy.

She and Tante Daniels had found their way from therapist, through betrayal, to friendship.

"Will you be my friend, Jeremy?" she whispered into the darkness.

He didn't answer, but she could always hope.

Miranda rose and draped Tante Daniels' quilt over him. They'd designed and sewn it together. Lessons in planning and cooperation that, she now saw, had also included companionship.

Then she returned to bed, to lie awake beside Jon, listening to the so-full house until the dawn came and she could start the next day.

5

Taz grabbed her gear and hustled off the Chinook's rear ramp. Twenty hotshots streamed after her. They dumped their packs in a big mound on the back meadow behind the Visitor Center. The grass had been mowed for a hundred meters around the structure, making it barely boot deep. That would be helpful if the firefight came down to a last-ditch effort.

They rushed back aboard to grab chainsaws, five-gallon cubes of saw gas and water, pumps, firehose, and a couple days of food, creating more piles of presorted gear with the ease of a long summer's practice. The helo's three crew chiefs leant a helping hand.

The Chinook was a sweet bonus, being able to bring all of their gear with them. Usually it was limited to what they could carry on the long hike to a fire, backed up with occasional airdrops.

She couldn't wait to get started.

Max had promised her that he'd teach her to really run the saw. She could hack down a tree but Max was a sawyer-artist with Gertrude, his twenty-four-inch, six-horse Stihl. He'd also made it clear that he absolutely wanted some serious sex with her. Not as a price of teaching her, he just wanted her.

Jeremy, wherever he was—probably back in DC where she'd originally kidnapped him—was little more than a memory as far as her body was concerned. But he remained an uncomfortable memory because he'd changed her in some way that she still didn't understand.

Taz had never been one to dwell on the past, but he wouldn't fade away.

Maybe Max would clear him out of her system. Even if he didn't, she had no doubt it would be fun. Another new concept in her life.

She dropped the last thirty-pound cube of fuel next to his saw. Max was five-ten of muscled hotshot, wearing sweat- and smoke-stained Nomex. It was a good smell. A real one. Not fresh showered and over-cologned like the men in the halls of the Pentagon.

"The answer's yes, Max." She kept her voice low.

"That's damn fine news, Taz!" He always had an easy smile, but now a bright grin lit his face as he looked down at her. "That gives me some serious motivation to kill this burn fast."

He held up a palm and she high-fived it hard, their leather gloves slapping together loudly.

Others in the crew looked over. A few laughed knowingly.

Taz hustled to get her own gear sorted and in order.

Yeah, not a lot of secrets on a hotshot crew. But after a lifetime of secrets and security clearances, that was a nice change too.

As the helo lifted clear, the moonlight revealed an amazing sight.

The Hurricane Ridge Visitor Center was perched on the edge of a four-thousand-foot drop down to a shimmering river valley far below. It should be shimmering with moonlight, not blood-red with reflected firelight, but still, it looked amazing.

Beyond the deep river valley, six- and seven-thousand-foot peaks shone in the moonlight. Vast swaths of wild forest, traversed by only the occasional hiking trail or logging road, swept up to rocky pinnacles.

"Normally be some snow up there, even now," Max told her as he stuffed a trio of aluminum liter flasks of fuel into his pack.

She did the same. Everyone on a hotshot team always carried a liter of saw fuel even though the team only had two sawyers. Better to run out of drinking water than saw fuel.

"Really bad drought this year, looking at Mount Olympus. Barely has a glacier left at all."

"Right, I forgot you were a local kid."

"Grew up just that way about thirty miles."

Even as he gestured to the east, the moonlight broke clear of the smoky haze and the top thousand feet of the entire ridgeline shone fairy-tale white.

It wasn't the sort of view she'd seen from San Diego or DC.

"Not planning on introducing me to your family, are you?" Max didn't seem like one of those crazed, over-committing types, but it was always good to know.

"Shit, woman! All I'm talking about here is sawing and sex."

"My kinda burn."

And his smile was back.

As they cached some gear and prepared what they could carry to the line of attack, she couldn't stop looking over at those magnificent peaks.

It also meant that she was the only one who saw the departing Washington Army National Guard CH-47D Chinook helicopter fall from the sky.

6

CAPTAIN JACK "THE PIRATE" SPAHR LOVED BEING A WEEKEND warrior. Army National Guard was typically about doing your monthly weekend and helping out with the occasional flood relief. In exchange he got to fly a twenty-million-dollar helo for the fun of it.

Being called up to fly bucket brigade on a forest fire for a few weeks just made it all the sweeter. And it sure beat the hell out of the unexpected six-month tour of Afghanistan they'd pulled in his first year. That had been a brutal shock but he'd been one of the lucky ones. Made it home little worse for wear.

Still, those had been hard days.

He'd been married less than a year then, kid on the way. His brother'd had to take over both their jobs in building their first major apartment complex. And Chinooks had been getting shot out of the skies right and left over there in the early days of the dustbowl.

This was a piece of cake by comparison.

"Thanks for the ride," the hotshot crew's superintendent called over the headset.

"The pirate crew of the *Black Pearl* was glad to have you," Captain Jack called back.

There was a snort of laughter, then the man was gone. The *Black Pearl* might be painted blah-tan, but that didn't matter to devoted fans of *Pirates of the Caribbean.* And his daughter's first big crush had been Johnny Depp.

Jack waited for his crew chief to confirm that the fire crew hadn't left anything behind. Wendy always made the weekend a pleasure. She was seriously funny and definitely enhanced the scenery. He might be married but he wasn't blind.

"They're out, Cap'n Jack. But they scuffed up my pretty deck something awful." Wendy's "pretty deck" couldn't look more battered even if the hotshots went after it with their fire axes. The old CH-47D had been built in 1984 and stood strong through a lot of hard service since.

Easing up on the left-hand thrust lever, he lifted the big Chinook back into the sky.

They'd come in over the wide meadow to the northeast of the Visitor center, but the fire was digging through the trees to the west. After ranging over many rugged miles, the forest stopped at the western edge of the Visitor Center's parking lot.

"We promised them a report of what's coming their way."

Jack and his crew were the only ones still able to fly. All of the other flight teams on the fire had already flown their full duty day and were on mandatory crew rest. Wasn't a fire boss on any burn who didn't wish for a way around Army Regulation 95-1. His was the only crew flipped to evenings and nights in case of emergencies. Fire bosses did their best to avoid emergencies, so they'd spent a lot of time just shuttling around supplies and personnel. Didn't bother him. Night flying was the best. If the hotshots needed easy access to the fire, Cap'n Jack and his merry band were glad to give it.

Doing some extra scouting for them was just another great reason to stay aloft.

Turned west, once they were high enough to see, the answer of what was coming their way was pure hell.

And there wasn't a thing he could do to help them until dawn. He might be nighttime qualified over a fire, but actually fighting a fire at night was a clearance he didn't have yet.

His copilot began calling the details back to the hotshots' crew boss.

"A heavy head roughly three hundred meters wide is two kilometers out and moving slow."

Which was going to accelerate fast if the winds picked up in the morning as predicted.

"The flanks appear to be spreading more south than north."

Meaning it was going to plow straight on into the Visitor Center rather than passing safely north. Jack would make sure the crew slept in their gear tonight in case the hotshots needed an emergency extraction. Barely ten miles away in Port Angeles, they could be aloft in three minutes and reach here in five more, despite the mile-high climb.

He was low enough over the head of the fire that he could feel the heat coming through the clear window that ran from his knee down to his feet.

7

WHAT CAPTAIN JACK SPAHR DIDN'T KNOW WAS THAT THERE was a hundred-and-fifty-foot hump in the terrain masked by the heat of the fire's core. Also, he was originally from Massachusetts and simply didn't think about the fact that Douglas fir trees could grow to three hundred feet, over thirty stories. Back home, a tall tree topped out at five stories.

Climbing the rocky knob, the fire had slowed and intensified. The wildfire's typical core temperature of fourteen hundred degrees rose. The inferno concentrated as it climbed up the knob and began cooking a "King of the Forest" Douglas fir that had first fought for this perch before Columbus was born.

At over two thousand degrees, a tree doesn't burn.

The interior superheated faster than the bark and outer layers of pitchy wood could carbonize and turn into ash. The sap vaporized, creating an overpressure deep inside the wood so intense that the tree simply shattered.

The upper forty-seven feet of the Doug fir launched skyward like a roman candle.

The CH-47D Chinook had survived two tours in Afghanistan—one flown by Captain Jack Spahr and his crew—another tour in Iraq, and another during Operation Desert Storm back in 1991.

Over the last thirty-five years it had rescued flood victims, delivered post-hurricane humanitarian aid to six states and four countries in Latin America plus Mexico, and spent thousands of hours on training flights.

Tonight, the Chinook was flying in relative safety six hundred feet over the treetops of the burning forest. If the exploding Douglas fir had been at the height of the rest of the forest, the flaming spear of treetop would have fallen harmlessly back to the ground before it could climb that high.

But the extra height of the humped-up knob of basalt elevated the tree fifteen stories higher.

If it had been only ten, the helicopter might have survived.

It wasn't.

If the section of tree trunk had launched a tenth of a second sooner, the only damage would have been a hole punched through the still-lowered cargo ramp. Crew Chief Wendy Dravitz, sitting on the ramp to watch the burning forest but thinking about splitting some nachos and a margarita at the bar with her new guy—they'd met during the eighty-mile "Idiot" loop of the Passport to Pain bicycle ride on Vashon Island—would have died instantly, pierced by the burning trunk. But she would have been the only one. There would be a funeral and a new cargo ramp.

Instead, the six hundred and ninety-seven pounds of flaming tree trunk speared aloft less than an arm's length beyond the end of the ramp.

Wendy's night vision was blotted out by the still-flaming trunk as it struck the rear rotor.

The Number Two blade was sheared off cleanly nine feet from the tip.

The sudden loss of two hundred and twenty-five pounds from the end of one of the three thirty-foot-long blades severely unbalanced the rotor head. The stress of the imbalance bent the rotor head and sheared the aft synchronizing driveshaft, allowing the rear rotor to spin freely.

Several things happened so close to simultaneously that their order didn't matter.

When the rear drive shaft sheared, the pair of powerful Lycoming T55 turboshaft engines fed the entirety of their ten thousand horsepower into the forward rotor.

Without the balance of the counter-rotating rear rotor, the engine's full power was instantly translated into a massive lateral torque on the frame. The rotational force slammed in hard enough to snap the necks of both pilots and two members of the flight crew. They didn't live long enough to even feel the pain.

Crew Chief Wendy Dravitz's position, sitting cross-legged on the lowered cargo ramp, saved her life from the initial disaster.

When the tail of the dying Chinook whipsawed sideways, she was actually left behind—suddenly airborne.

Her vest's three-meter Monkey Tail safety line, which would keep her attached to the helo against any normal fall, snapped along with three ribs and her left arm.

What happened next was of no consequence to Chief Dravitz or the crew.

The area swept by a Chinook helicopter's front and rear

rotors overlapped in fixed synchronization so that the blades would intermesh without colliding. Without the aft synchronizing driveshaft, the massive sixty-foot-diameter free-wheeling rear rotor—spinning at nearly four rotations per second—utterly destroyed first itself, then the main rotor.

With both rotors shattered, the fifteen tons of the CH-47D plummeted toward the ground.

In freefall, Chief Dravitz fell alongside the dying helo for a five-second eternity, fully aware of what was happening to her.

The ground was close enough that she stopped caring before the end of the sixth second after the impact by the tree.

8

Every inch of Taz's body ached.

Because the only other "rested" aircraft presently on the fire had been a spotter plane, it was left to the hotshots to scout for survivors. The spotter had pinpointed the GPS coordinates of the wreckage. The helo had passed over the fire and crashed in the Black—the burned-over area behind any forest fire.

In her typical role as team scout, Taz had been sent looking.

No one else could cover rough terrain as fast as she could. Twice now, her life had depended upon her ability to cross hard desert. In DC, her one solace had been to run. In the Pentagon's gym, in marathons, even ultramarathons. She rarely won—her career just hadn't allowed her to train at the very top level—but she was rarely out of the top ten.

Most people thought her size was a disadvantage. But she also weighed less and had never blown a knee, unlike so many heavier runners. Her muscle-to-mass ratio was exceptional. And she liked to think that her determination was off the charts.

It hadn't taken long for the hotshot crew to realize this, and she'd become the team scout. She could reach an overlook, give them a clear idea of what the burn was doing before it crested some ridge, and get back to help faster than anyone.

Last night it had sent her wide around the flanks of the fire, in some places up above the timberline to be safe. Her extreme fitness wasn't helping her as much as she'd like at the moment. Almost all of tonight's scramble had been over a mile high and strained her lungs to their limit. The Rogue River hotshots were based below a thousand, so her acclimatization sucked.

Once safely clear of the fire's flanks, she'd had to circle back over a kilometer to reach the helicopter's resting place.

The first thing she found was the snapped-off length of rotor blade.

That was all she needed to see to know the crew's fate.

In 2011, "Extortion 17"—also a CH-47D Chinook—had been shot down by the Taliban in Afghanistan. Five crew members (Reserve and National Guard), eight Afghanis, a war dog, and twenty-five Special Operations Forces—several of them rumored to be SEAL Team 6 veterans of the bin Laden raid—had died instantly. It wasn't the rocket-propelled grenade or the crash that had killed them as most people thought. The RPG hadn't hit the fuselage, it had hit the rotor. What killed them all was the abrupt slam as twenty tons of heavily loaded helo suddenly decided to spin like a child's top.

She wrapped some orange flagging tape around the scorched trunk of a nearby tree, then tracked down the helo to make sure. The Chinook hadn't crashed, it had shattered. Verifying the first four bodies didn't take long. But there'd been the standard five aboard when they'd dropped off the fire team.

It took her half an hour to find the fifth one; she'd landed seventy-five meters away, close by one of those weird clumps of green that sometimes happened in the middle of the Black. Ten trees, a dozen bushes, and a badly scorched deer that Taz put out of its misery.

The crew member looked as if she was just taking a break—if you ignored the strange bend in her left arm. She lay on her back in a gap between two charcoal-black tree stumps, so undamaged that Taz kept expecting her to get up and ask about the others. Wasn't gonna happen; her impact had planted her so deep in the soil that her chest was several inches below ground level.

"At the helo. All dead," she called to her team's superintendent.

"Roger," his voice crackled over the radio.

He would still be prepping for the fire's onslaught on the far side of the ridge. It was impressive that they could hear each other at all.

"Call it in." At least that's how she interpreted the burst of static.

She double-clicked an acknowledgement, much easier to hear than words, then she dialed to the primary air frequency and reported.

"Roger, hotshot. You were the sole witness, right? We've got a team inbound at first light. Can you hold at the helo for any questions?"

She checked her watch. Less than an hour to sunrise. It

would take her longer than that to rejoin the others. She'd already been on the go for three hours.

"Roger that. Tell them to bring five body bags."

"Jesus! Okay. Ground out."

She'd never understood why the dead made people squeamish. After all, they were dead; they sure as hell didn't care.

Not good at sitting still, Taz looked around.

Deep in the Black, there wasn't much going on. But there were some spot fires and flareups she could work on while she waited. Weirdly, the helo hadn't burned, which was a testament to the crash-proofing of the fuel tanks.

Donning goggles and a face mask, Taz pulled out her Pulaski fire axe and headed for the nearest flareup.

9

Holly tickled Jeremy's feet to wake him from a very comfortable dream. He was still on the couch and it was still dark...outside. A bright side-table lamp was blinding him.

"Hey, cut it out!" He kicked out a foot, but all it did was flap the quilt at her.

He'd been dreaming that Miranda had asked him to be her friend. How strange was that? She was twelve years older and had, like, everything: this island, cool planes, and she was the best crash investigator on the planet. How could she possibly need a friend?

"Get your ass in gear, Little One. Miranda got a launch call. A downed Army Chinook at a wildfire. Breakfast is already up. Departure in five. Nice quilt by the way."

He looked down. The last he'd seen of it, it had been a shadow spread across Miranda's lap. It was a wild piecework pattern of ocean blues, from white-blue of a hazy sky close by his chin, down to the blue-black of a storm-tossed nighttime sea at his feet. Adrift in the middle, a pale-green, two-masted sailboat seemed to be struggling toward the light.

He certainly knew how that felt. He folded it carefully.

On reaching the kitchen, he discovered that he was the last awake. Holly must have delayed waking him, just to screw up his morning even more. It definitely put him at the tail end of the pack and breakfast rush. He managed most of a bowl of granola and honey over Greek yogurt, only because Mike had it prepped for him by the time he got there.

He finished it, without quite wearing it, while riding in the golf cart from the house to the hangar.

Holly then used the cart to chase the deer off the grass runway while Mike and Miranda prepared the plane. That took longer than the flight from Spieden Island to Port Angeles, which had lasted just six minutes in Miranda's Citation jet.

Jeremy wished he was a pilot so that he could fly up front with her instead of Mike. In just the first month she'd whisked them to two incidents in Colorado and another in California. At least they got to arrive together, which was a major improvement on lagging hours behind in the much slower Mooney as had often happened in the past.

As the predawn light revealed the array of firefighting aircraft being prepped at Fairchild Airport in Port Angeles, they shifted from the sleek jet to an old Bell LongRanger. With the retired USAF pilot, who usually went aloft for tourist flights, the six of them and their gear were right up at the load limit. Especially for a mile-high crash site.

But the pilot placed them on site just as the sun cracked over the Cascade Mountains to the east and illuminated the Black in long, stark shadows. The ash coating on the burnt landscape made everything look the same. So much so that the pilot came dangerously close to putting them down in a patch of some unrecognizable tree stumps that would have eaten his helo.

Once clear, just turning their backs on his takeoff wasn't enough. They were blasted with cinders and ash until they all looked as if their backsides had been dipped in ink.

Holly took off her hardhat, which revealed a clean halo at the top. She fluffed her blonde hair to little effect except for smearing some of the ash over the previously clean area.

"Just think of it as temporary dye," Andi offered. Her hair was dyed like fire, red at the tips, gold, and then yellow-to-blue before fading into her natural black hair color.

"Girl who flies like she's on fire is now all smoky," Holly shot back.

Indeed, the colors across the back of her shoulder-length hair were dimmed by the ash bath.

"Just the way I like it. 'Cause I'm smoky hot."

Jeremy could never think of quick comebacks to Holly's verbal attacks. He still hadn't come up with one for her tickling his feet this morning.

At Miranda's request, the LongRanger had dropped them a hundred meters from the downed helo so as not to disturb the site.

As they clambered over the rough ground, Jeremy spotted a wrap of bright orange tape on a tree off to the left. No way would plastic tape have survived the fire.

He called out that he was going to check it out, not that anyone seemed to care.

Nearing the tree—which rose barely over a hundred feet without a single remaining bit of green and only the stubs of branches—he saw why it had been marked.

A body lay spread out on the soil.

Or rather *in* the soil.

He stopped to kick at the detritus lying on the forest floor. Scorched pine needles, bits of tiny branches, possibly meters of organic matter. He'd have to dig a test trench alongside the body. Once he had the thickness and makeup of the various layers, he could estimate the body's velocity on impact.

Because of its prone position, it had most likely struck at a hundred and twenty miles per hour—assuming it had fallen far enough to reach terminal velocity. Reaching terminal velocity typically took five seconds and some five hundred feet. If the calculated velocity at impact was lower, it would let him estimate the body's height of departure from the aircraft.

As he circled around the tree for a closer look, he spotted a woman sitting against the trunk eating breakfast.

Below her smudged hard hat, her brown-black hair was in a ponytail down to the middle of her back. Her yellow Nomex shirt was mostly ash-gray, but the Pulaski axe lying at her side—half-axe and half the sharpened hoe shape of an adze—said she was a hotshot crew member.

"Hi."

"Hello," she answered around a mouthful of the energy bar she'd been eating without looking up from the pack she'd been digging around in. Her voice was little better than a croak with fire smoke.

"Keeping her company?" For the corpse was a woman's.

"Figured you people wouldn't just stumble on her, so I waited to make sure you found her."

"Okay, thanks." Jeremy was never sure how to talk to women. "That's interesting."

"What?"

"The failed safety strap lying beside her. That's one-and-seven-eighths webbing. It has a breaking strength of thirty-six hundred foot-pounds."

"Is that a lot?"

"To a human body? Yes, it's a lot." Jeremy pulled out his camera and moved in to record it.

10

TAZ HAD TROUBLE TURNING TO THE LEFT. A BRANCH HAD fallen, bounced off her helmet, and clipped her shoulder during an incautious moment. Nothing broken, but she couldn't find the damn Tylenol anywhere in her pack.

Then she stopped looking.

That voice...

She *knew* that voice.

Then he stepped into her field of view and unshouldered his big pack.

An NTSB logo was bright across the back of his vest as he squatted to inspect the corpse.

She recognized Jeremy even by how he moved. None of the uncertainty of when they'd made love in the Baja desert on the final day of her former life. No. This was the man in his element, one who had understood the complexities of a Ghostrider's weapon system simply by looking at it—yet had been utterly baffled by how to touch her when they'd made love.

She'd forgotten Jeremy worked for the NTSB. But he was

supposed to be stationed in Washington, DC, not Washington State.

Taz stopped caring about the Tylenol, the half-chewed protein bar for breakfast, or her damned shoulder.

It was unfair.

The United States of America had almost four hundred million people. It had three-point-eight million square miles. Fifty states. God alone knew how many territories.

And Jeremy Trahn was somehow the guy who had arrived to inspect the corpse out in the middle of fucking *nowhere?*

It was a *given* that she'd never see him again.

That she'd never see *anyone* who'd known her before, *ever* again.

Firefighting for the Rogue River Hotshots on the opposite side of the country. How much farther from the Pentagon did she have to get to be safely dead?

Apparently a lot farther.

He reached into his pack without turning to face her.

She didn't think that ignoring her was something he'd do. Unless maybe he hadn't recognized her?

Pulling out a set of shears, he trimmed the last foot off the webbing and tucked it in a plastic evidence bag.

"If she weighed one-forty," he spoke as he wrote a note across the front of the bag before shifting to inspect something else, "she had to hit the end of the webbing with the equivalent of a twenty-six-foot fall to exceed thirty-six hundred foot-pounds—almost five thousand Newton-meters. The standard Monkey Tail restraint harness is only three meters long. This," he flapped the bag before tucking it into his pack, "also would have a safety factor beyond that. It means that within a maximum of ten feet, she was thrown as violently from the helo as hitting the sidewalk after falling off the top of a three-story building."

Jeremy had always liked his words and his details.

Taz held on to her pack and pushed silently to her feet.

Knowing it was a total chickenshit maneuver—but unable to stop herself—she sprinted into the clump of preserved greenery and dove behind the deer carcass.

11

When Jeremy finally turned to pull out his foldable shovel to dig the test trench into the surface detritus and soil, he risked a glance at the woman.

Except she wasn't there.

He looked around, but there was no sign of where she'd gone.

It wasn't likely that he'd imagined her. Granted, he hadn't had more than a few hours of sleep, but...

He circled the tree she'd been leaning against—marked with the orange tape, which was still there—looking for some evidence that she'd been real and he wasn't hallucinating.

He found his proof.

A worn Pulaski fire axe, its wooden handle almost black with months of ground-in soot.

He looked again.

No detectable footprints across the blackened soil, but then his own weren't showing either in the soft organics.

She hadn't climbed the tree. It still towered a hundred

feet above, but only a few frail branches of green remained at the very top. Nowhere to hide up there.

He hefted the axe.

"She was here. She was real."

But she was gone.

"Do they have firefighting fairies who can magically hide from mere mortals?"

He raised his voice and called out, "You forgot your axe!"

There was no response.

12

TAZ DIDN'T MISS THE AXE UNTIL AFTER, WHEN JEREMY'S BACK was turned, she'd hotfooted it out of there.

Jeremy shouted something in the distance, but she couldn't tell what.

Only stubborn self-control, overlaid with some depressing common sense, stopped her from running all the way back to the team.

The loss of a Pulaski wasn't that big a deal, so there was no problem there. She could blame it on a moment's inattention during a flareup. Sometimes they just broke, though you tried to salvage the head.

But if she returned to the hotshot crew, she'd have to admit that she hadn't briefed the NTSB team on the crash. And since that was the whole reason she'd stayed out here...

Why in the hell had she been gawking at Hurricane Ridge like a schoolgirl? If she hadn't, she'd never have seen the crash. Then she'd have done her scouting and returned to the team with no one the wiser.

Conclusion, she had to talk to them.

Well, it was time to woman-up, and hope to hell that Jeremy could keep the secret about her not being dead.

Halfway back to where the corpse lay in the ground, she heard voices off to the right.

The helo.

Slipping through the blackened forest, Taz got close enough that she could see them.

She didn't recognize any of the three women, but she knew both men.

One, it took her a moment to place. She'd made it her business as General Martinez's aide to know everything she could about the people he came in contact with. Under normal circumstances, she wouldn't have recognized Major Jon Swift, but he was the nephew of the Chairman of the Joint Chiefs of Staff Drake Nason.

His Air Force fatigues, and that he was inspecting a crash, fit what she knew about his position on the Accident Investigation Board, confirming his identity. And that she didn't want to go anywhere near him.

He was probably as rule-bound and integrity-worshipping as his powerful uncle. Contact with him was a ticket straight to incarceration at the United States Disciplinary Barracks at Fort Leavenworth.

The other was Mike Munroe, who she'd kidnapped along with Jeremy while on her final mission to destroy the Mexican drug cartels. She was glad to see that he and Jeremy had both survived after she'd put them in parachutes and shoved them off the crashing C-130J Ghostrider gunship. But she wouldn't place any bets on the warmth of his reception —she'd pistol-whipped him into submission *before* she'd saved his ass.

That all felt like a crazy lifetime ago. The things she'd

done for the general... It was a struggle to suppress the shudder.

One of the three women broke off from the group.

Not toward Jeremy.

Instead, toward the rotor blade fragment Taz had orange-tagged off in the trees.

That gave her an idea.

She sprinted back into the woods, circled wide around the helo in the opposite direction from where Jeremy would still be, and arrived at the broken-off blade section just steps behind the NTSB woman.

One steadying breath and she came around a clump of burned brush.

"Hi. You with the NTSB? Like your hair." It seemed like a good line. And the fire motif was pretty. She'd never have considered coloring her own when she was in the military but she could do that now.

"Thanks. Andi Wu. You must be the hotshot we were told to expect." Andi wasn't all that much taller than Taz herself was. Asian to her own Mexican. Her accent was West Coast. Taz had studied carefully to shed any hints of Spanish from her own speech and recognized the tones of California. North. Probably around San Francisco.

"That's me. Ta—Vicki Flores." Taz was far too unusual a nickname. Mike would definitely recognize it when Andi mentioned this meeting.

She should have kept Tanya's name instead of risking the change. She'd been trying to make sure no one looking for Tanya Roberts would find her. Instead, it was her own name that was putting her at risk. Not Vicki Cortez, but perhaps close enough to trigger the memory of her for one of the guys.

"What can you tell us?"

Taz just pointed down at the rotor blade.

Andi sighed, "Kinda tells the whole story, doesn't it?"

Taz nodded, then realized she shouldn't have. What would a hotshot know about the dynamics of a rotor failure on a CH-47D Chinook helo?

"I saw a tree launch, you know." She went for a little touch of Valley speak, softening her consonants as she did so. *Just a gal from LA, fighting wildfires. Pay no attention here.* "They can go up like a Roman candle. Saw this one shoot up at least three, four hundred feet. Pow! I was gonna say they were lucky they didn't land in the fire, but I s'pose that lucky isn't what ya'd call them."

"They never had a chance."

Taz just shook her head. Only the one—who'd possibly survived the equivalent of a twenty-six-foot, five-thousand-Newton-meter fall—might have lived long enough to die after a five-hundred-foot one.

"We were too far away to see much more. The tree went up, then the helicopter came down," she pinched her fingers almost together and held them up against the sky to show how far away and small it had been. "Need anything else from me? My crew will be waiting."

"Just your cell number, in case we need to reach you."

"That was a past life," it had been one of her most useful tools working for the general: the ability to reach out and touch someone—hard. "Can't stand the things now, always buzzing at you. But you can call the Rogue River Hotshots if you need me." She still had Tanya's phone, which hadn't rung once in six months. Not a whole lot of people looking for her; too bad she hadn't kept the name. Taz treated it like an anonymous burner phone.

"Oh. Okay. Thanks for sticking around."

"Andi?"

Taz recognized Jeremy's call through the trees. He was a lot closer than he should be.

"Well, see ya." Taz headed off in the opposite direction before Andi could complain.

Once she heard the two of them talking, she circled back. Jeremy had left her axe by the corpse. By the dirt on the blade, he'd used it to dig the slit trench that now paralleled the body. The hotshot in her gave him only middling marks for technique. It was crazy that she knew that now; it had no relation to her former life.

She knew Jeremy would have some esoteric, long-winded, and yet highly logical reason for cutting it in the first place, but she had no idea what that might be.

She picked up the axe, trying not to be aware of her hands overlapping his on the wood, and headed out at a fast trot. Wouldn't catch her dead or alive in this neck of the woods again—ever.

Once the Rogue River Hotshots broke for the season in the next few days, she'd be gone.

But she couldn't help looking back over her shoulder, long after the dead helo and the NTSB team were out of sight.

13

WITH THE WHOLE TEAM'S HELP, MIRANDA HAD THEM CARRY the heavy section of rotor blade back to the helo. Though her own efforts would add little, she did what she could.

Andi and Holly went back in search of the broken tree mentioned by the hotshot.

The "cause of incident" was already determined, but this was an excellent chance to study the dynamics of a CH-47D Chinook's crash.

"These blades are a mess," Mike set a compass and a ruler on a snapped-off section so that Jeremy would have the orientation of the segment as he photographed it. Then they moved to the next one.

"Rotorcraft never die pretty." Jon was making notes on his Air Force report form as if he already knew what the conclusion was and didn't need the details.

"This is the matching one," Jeremy pointed at a two-foot-long piece sheared off at both ends.

Nearby, a full-length rotor blade—originally thirty feet long, thirty-two inches wide, and three inches thick—had been tied into a knot. Another had been folded neatly like a letter, if only there was an envelope big enough.

Miranda tried to imagine how long it would take to lick a seal. Assume one second to lick a standard Number 10 envelope. With a typical wetted area of approximately three-point-four square inches, a commensurately upscaled envelope would have six-point-eight square feet of wetted area and would require thirty-one minutes to lick. By which time, most of it would have dried. A different solution would be required, such as—

Miranda forced her attention away from the math-and-mechanics puzzle and back to the folded rotor blade.

Then she managed to jump her attention from the blade to the debris field of rotor blade pieces. Many were snapped into sections varying from a few feet to half a blade. They'd been scattered in a wide area around the helo's final resting place.

And finally she shifted her attention back to the primary crash site.

Based on the indentation in the ground, it appeared that the fifty-foot fuselage had landed nose first. This was corroborated by the symmetrical pancaking of the cockpit.

Which was about all that really remained of the aircraft.

Unlike a helicopter with a main and a tail rotor, a twin-rotor Chinook didn't crash from altitude so much as it shattered, then fell. This one was surprisingly intact. The cockpit, lower hull, and cargo deck were still mostly intact. The forward rotary-wing head remained attached, but lay in the middle of the mangled cargo deck. One of the engines and the rear rotor head had broken free, but lay mostly on the deck as well. The second engine had impacted the soil nearby, driving its tail deep into the organics.

The rest of the main fuselage in bits and pieces, as well as two of the other three crew members, were scattered across a hundred meters of charred soils.

There were no objects that would have fallen in such a way that she could calculate how far it had to fall for air friction, at an altitude of five thousand three hundred feet, to orient any remaining piece in a particular orientation.

Miranda double-checked that she had the barometric pressure reading marked in her notebook in order to make an accurate calculation of air density—if she did eventually locate something that she could measure the freefall acceleration of.

"Here we go," Jeremy had finished photographing the matching broken section of the rotor after he and Mike had placed it close beside the longer blade element that Andi had spotted.

"What are we looking at?" Jon knelt down with the rest of them.

Miranda couldn't make sense of Jon's words. Was he asking if it was a rotor blade? No, that was too obvious.

Couldn't he see the common material deformation patterns commensurate with a powerful impact on the underside of the blade? That was equally obvious.

Jeremy began explaining. "See the break patterns in the fiberglass skin? The tearing and spreading of the fibers underneath is more pronounced than on the upper side. Also notice the tearing pattern across the internal Nomex honeycomb—the same material that is used to make a hotshot's fire-resistant shirt. The trailing-edge fairings are a sandwich of wire mesh for lightning strike protection. The fairing was shredded by a lateral force rather than a perpendicular force."

"So, the tree punched through the blade..."

Jon's hesitation lasted so long that Miranda had to finish the sentence for him. She hated the incompletion of a thought.

"It punched through the *forward quarter* of the blade's width," one should be precise in such situations. "But the rotor was still spinning at two hundred and forty rpm. At twenty-one feet from the rotor head, the rotational speed of the blade at the point of impact was three hundred and sixty miles an hour. The rotor ripped forward, and the tree tore out through the back of the blade, including the fairing. We should be able to get an approximate idea of the tree's size once we analyze—"

"Five ruddy inches," Holly and Andi returned, dragging a ten-foot section of tree between them. "Look at the bitch, right there."

And Holly was right.

The top of the tree had been broken off by some storm in the past by the look of the wood. A four-inch blunt tip was what had remained.

Three feet along the shaft of the trunk, where it had expanded to five inches wide, the bark was torn away. Deep scars made in the underlying wood would match the metal deformation of the shredding rotor blade as it swung forward. It had struck far enough behind the tough leading edge of the blade that it had shredded the composite without snapping off.

14

Andi was the first to notice the loud roar coming up the valley.

She supposed that after a dozen years flying rotorcraft, it was built into her bloodstream.

Miranda looked up at her.

Andi tipped her head to the southeast, then Miranda nodded. Not only had she heard it, but she too had identified it. Andi had been on this team for just a month but it kept right on getting better.

Another Chinook. Probably out of Joint Base Lewis-McChord, which lay just eighty miles away. Perhaps come to help with the firefight.

What she hadn't expected was an all black Chinook with a refueling probe sticking forward, low on the fuselage.

The Night Stalkers.

Her old regiment had sent one of their highly modified MH-47Gs. They couldn't be here to fight the fire. And there were no clearings in the burned-over forest big enough to land in, not even for a Night Stalkers pilot. But that wouldn't stop them.

Sure enough, the big helo came to a hover a hundred meters away from the crash. In seconds, they'd kicked out a long Fast rope, and four people slid down its length to the ground.

They strode over with all of the confidence she now lacked. She *hated* that the PTSD meant that she no longer belonged. It sucked almost as badly as if *she'd* been the one impaled by the tree.

But they wouldn't find her wanting.

She saluted them when they approached even if she was no longer in the military. It was too deeply ingrained to be denied.

They returned the salute smartly, though the lead sergeant raised his eyebrows in question.

"Captain Andi Wu, formerly of the 1st battalion of the 160th. Now NTSB. This is Miranda Chase, Investigator-in-Charge. You have five dead. Four here at the helo, one lying seventy-five meters to the northwest."

The sergeant was good. He turned and asked Miranda, "Any reason to delay recovery?"

Miranda looked to Jeremy, who shook his head before she said there wasn't.

Andi didn't know which of them was more impressive. Jeremy was twelve years Miranda's junior, but seemed to know almost everything she did. Andi herself was seven years older than Jeremy, but she still found him a little unnerving to be around. She also had the distinct impression that he didn't like her very much. She'd tried being nicer, with little success.

The sergeant flagged two of his crew toward the woman

who'd been thrown clear. Jeremy scooted ahead to show them the way.

"Extractable?" The sergeant turned back to her. It was strange to be back in the world where minimum-required communication was the norm.

Andi hadn't inspected the bodies, but Holly answered the question.

"Two crew chiefs, yes. Two in the cockpit will take some serious machinery. The entire nose frame was compressed back to, uh, pin them in their seats."

"Roger that." And with no more fuss, he was on his radio.

In under ten minutes, they had the three dead crew members winched up to the hovering helo. The two pilots were left pinned in their Chinook coffin.

Then the hovering Chinook lowered a heavy cable down through the hellhole in the center of the cargo bay's floor. Between the cable and their combined teams, the second engine and cargo ramp were stacked on the CH-47D's open cargo bay. All of the parts of the rotor blades as well. That was all the main pieces, nothing else would need the heavy hoist of a Chinook to move.

"A separate team will be dispatched to gather the rest of the debris," the sergeant announced after a bit of radio work.

When Miranda told them that she would need to further inspect the two adjacent rotor segments where the tree had impacted, they marked them carefully and loaded the section of tree trunk as well.

"It will all be in a hangar at JBLM's Gray Army Airfield."

After they wrapped a net over the whole thing so that it wouldn't shed parts en route, the MH-47G lowered two more heavy cables fore and aft.

Mike and Jeremy gasped in surprise when they saw what

was happening. Even Holly raised her eyebrows.

"Why are they surprised?" Miranda asked from close by her elbow.

"Because most people don't know that a Chinook can lift a Chinook. At least if one of them belongs to the Night Stalkers." A normal Army Chinook couldn't have done this, especially at this altitude, but the Night Stalkers' MH-47G Block II wasn't just some average heavy-lift helicopter.

"But it's just simple math."

Andi glanced over, but Miranda looked serious. "Are there any aircraft that you don't know all of the operational specifications of?"

Miranda grimaced. "I know very little about aircraft that predate my Sabrejet, which was one of the last built in 1958."

Andi watched the Night Stalkers attach the cargo hooks onto on the downed Chinook. Then they were calling instructions on the radio to take up the slack in each line.

"Which means you still know more than most people, all the way back to the Wright Flyer."

"Well, that wasn't really the beginning, if that's the reference you were making. Before they flew the Wright Flyer in 1903 using Charlie Taylor's engine, there was the 1899 Kite and the three Gliders between those. And they—"

Andi giggled.

"What?" Miranda turned from watching them ease the Chinook into the air. It might be the first time Miranda had looked her in the face. It hadn't taken long to figure out that was something Miranda just didn't do.

There was a cloud of black ash as the downdraft from the hovering MH-47G blew across the area previously covered by the Chinook's shattered frame.

"I'm sorry to laugh, Miranda. But someday you're just

going to have to accept that when it comes to aircraft, you're smarter than absolutely everyone around you."

"Oh."

She was silent for as long as it took the Night Stalkers crew chiefs to double-check the security of the cargo hook attachment points.

Then the crew were winched aloft one by one on a lightweight rescue hoist.

Finally, the crew chief sent her a sharp salute. "Captain."

She saluted him back. "Sergeant."

And he too was gone aloft.

It felt good, even for that moment, to once again be acknowledged as a Night Stalker. As if she still belonged. As if she could still fly, which she didn't dare try.

Miranda maintained her silence as the MH-47G eased upward.

There was a pause for the final balancing of the cables, then the deep roar of the big Lycoming T55 engines filled the sky as it eased the broken Chinook aloft.

Everyone remained still and watched the spectacle of one Chinook carrying the other southward and away. Fading until they were two dots, then gone.

The silence that was left seemed to echo.

The fire had crossed the ridge to the east and the planes dropping water on it circled nowhere near their position.

There was an uncertain bird call from high on one of the burned trees, perhaps asking after its favorite perch.

"If I'm so smart," Miranda whispered, "how is it that I don't know how we're getting off this mountain?"

Andi bumped her shoulder against Miranda's. "Because being wicked smart about aircraft doesn't mean that you get to know everything."

15

By the time a helo could be freed to return them from Hurricane Ridge to Port Angeles, it was late afternoon and Jeremy's stomach was beyond growling. A hurried bowl of granola before sunrise was long gone. An energy bar for lunch simply didn't fix that.

Thankfully, the helo pilot was the same local who'd delivered them to the crash site.

"Best fancy or best burger?" he'd asked at Jeremy's question about places to eat.

Jeremy didn't even poll the others before saying they wanted the latter.

So the pilot sent them to The Rail. It was just a mile or so from the airport, close by the Port Angeles waterfront.

The building had the gambrel roofline of an old Dairy Queen.

Inside, the ice cream parlor had been converted into pure pub: wooden walls, a long bar well stocked with microbrew taps, and a kitchen in the back pumping out awesome smells. It was quiet in the late afternoon, and they took a round table in the corner on the side opposite the bar.

He went for the Porter: mushroom, red onion, a rich porter beer sauce, and topped with swiss. A pile of Buffalo-style wings and fried onion rings in the middle of the table as appetizers, and he was in heaven.

The silence of a good meal descended for a moment.

"Good to be off that damn little hillock," Holly set aside her already half-eaten double Bacon Cheese Burger and was the first to break the silence. "'Minds me of this time me and my mates were out in the Simpson. That be a little dry spot up to Queensland way."

"Meaning it's deep desert," Mike laughed at her.

Holly gave a happy shrug and was about to continue when a crowd burst in through the door.

Even before he saw them, Jeremy could smell them. The sharp bite of fire smoke.

"We done killed that sum-bitch blaze."

"Hell of a weenie thing to end a season on."

"Yeah, it saw us coming and just put its little ashes up in the air and we drove all the way in." There was a round of happy laughter and high fives at that.

The hotshots were still dressed in their boots and Nomex. The former position of their hardhats marked by moderately cleaner spots atop their heads.

"Round on the house for the hotshots and their awesome job saving the visitor center," the barkeep called out to a roar of approval.

Jeremy took another bite, wondering if his disappearing magic-fairy hotshot was somewhere in this crowd.

He glanced over his shoulder and spotted one woman, but her ponytail would be blonde if not for all the soot.

Then he saw her.

She stood out because she was half the size of everyone else. Under five feet, slender, with a dark ponytail half down her back.

Her arm was around a big guy's waist who was holding her close.

If he didn't know she was dead, he'd say that—

Andi called out loudly enough to be heard over the noise. "Hey, Mike. You said you wanted to talk to that hotshot yourself. She's right over there."

Then the hotshot tipped back her head to laugh, far enough for Jeremy to see her profile.

Jeremy spun back to the table and coughed up his bite of hamburger onto his plate.

He grabbed the table and tried not to barf the rest of it all over everyone's lunch.

"Hey, Jeremy," Holly grabbed his shoulder. "You look kinda green." She shook him, and it almost released his iron hold on his jaw.

"Oh fuck," Mike's voice was little more than a whisper.

It was just enough to confirm Jeremy's worst fear.

"What?" Holly asked.

Colonel Vicki Cortez hadn't died in the Ghostrider's crash.

"That's Taz."

Who hadn't come to find him.

In fact, she'd *run* away when he'd almost found her at the crash site.

"Taz who?" Andi's voice sounded from somewhere far away.

"Taz is dead." Jon.

Jeremy had spent the last six months wishing that they'd had even one more day together.

And now, there she was.

Laughing.

In someone else's arms.

Holly pushed away and left him...

Alone.

16

TAZ HAD JUST ENOUGH TIME TO SEE THE INCOMING BLONDE from the NTSB team before her hair was yanked back so sharply it felt as if her scalp was coming off.

Taz flicked her arm to drop her knife from her wrist holster into her palm.

The blonde grabbed her wrist before it had even released, then gave her an "Oh, come on!" sideways look.

"Hey, you can't do that." Max made a grab for the blonde, but stopped when she snapped open Taz's Benchmade Phaeton and held it half an inch from Max's nose. Slim, black-anodized steel, it was a vicious-looking blade. Which was kind of the point.

His eyes crossed trying to focus on it.

"Think again, bozo. Back the fuck off if you want to survive the next two seconds."

Jeff came up behind her, not understanding how fast the blonde was—nobody out drew Taz in a knife fight. At least not before now.

For his trouble, Jeff got a hard, downward kick to his

shins that the blonde didn't even turn to deliver. He screamed before dropping to the floor.

Clare looked like she might try a move when Andi, the NTSB woman Taz had spoken to so briefly, stepped in front of her. In her hand was a Cold Steel Recon Tanto blade, also anodized black. Another vicious-looking knife.

"I wouldn't do anything unexpected at the moment." Her voice, which had been friendly San Franciscan up at the crash site, was military sharp.

Taz recognized the fighter's poise. "I—"

The blonde jerked her hair hard enough that Taz swore she could feel each individual follicle screaming.

"I didn't give you permission to speak." She hadn't looked away from Max. "You still haven't backed the fuck off, mate."

"It's okay, Max," Taz managed, though the pain was tunneling her vision badly. It was all over now anyway. Her new identity was blown.

Thankfully, Max slowly raised both hands and shifted back a step. That was good. It was obvious that no one here, not even herself, had the skills to take on the blonde.

"Let's you and me go for a walk." The blonde yanked her toward the door using Taz's hair.

"Will you cut that out?"

"Nope!" The blonde flicked Taz's knife closed before dragging her out through the door.

"Are you going to kill me?"

"I thought you were already dead."

Taz gave up struggling, and almost choked before she managed to whisper, "I thought so, too."

17

"Keep them all inside. Especially Jeremy." Holly snapped it out.

After Andi had checked on the guy with the barked shins, not much blood, and signaled Mike to keep Jeremy in place, she followed Holly out the door.

Holly marched Vicki around the corner of the building, then slammed her against the wood of the bar's side wall so hard that it almost knocked the air out of Andi's own chest. A life-sized black-iron flat sculpture, of which she'd seen several in town, loomed over Vicki. This one, a man with a raised railroad spike hammer appropriate for outside The Rail tavern, looked as if he was going to crash it down on Vicki's head.

Andi doubled back and stepped once more into the pub. It had all happened so fast that no one had even started to move toward the door.

She knew how to handle this.

"I'm US Army Captain Andrea Wu of the 160th Special Operations." From an aviation regiment that had nothing to do with security, but she'd hope that it sufficed for the moment. "I'm sorry, but I have to ask that no one leave, we may have questions for you. Feel free to return to your meals."

The big hotshot started to move forward, but his friends pulled him back.

Jeremy was still faced away, his head hung down like he'd been beaten.

Andi had no idea what was going on, but she never again wanted to see someone looking the way Jeremy did.

She went out to rejoin Holly just as police sirens sounded nearby. The barkeep, at least, had kept his head.

It looked as if neither Holly nor Vicki...Taz...whatever her name was, had moved an inch while she'd stepped inside.

Holly came over. With a quick slap of her palm against Andi's, she transferred three knives—the one she'd taken from Taz and two others that were equally high-end and lethal.

Andi tucked them away and Holly returned to facing Taz just before the police car rounded the corner and screeched to a halt. They rushed over.

"Everyone please keep your hands in the open."

They all turned their palms out.

"We had a call of an altercation involving knives."

"Just having a word with a friend I haven't seen in a long time." Holly smiled so pleasantly that Andi couldn't equate her with the seething Spec Ops operator of moments before.

She turned to Taz.

"How long has it been? Since the funeral?"

Taz just grimaced.

"Are you armed?" The lead officer approached as his

backup remained near the car, hand on his weapon. They were ignoring Andi standing so far off to the side. Small town cops wouldn't think to suspect the little gawker woman of having four military-grade knives stashed about her person, so she did her best to look like that's all she was.

In answer, Holly just raised her arms and turned slowly. "Care to check me out, mate?" She even offered him a wink.

It was hard to imagine the tall, beautiful blonde as being anything but innocent. Or that she was actually madder than a kicked snake.

"Are you okay, ma'am?" He turned to face Taz.

"No. Yes. Yes, I'm fine. Old friend. Like she said." Taz didn't put much oomph behind it.

This Taz was also smart enough to read the officer's uncertainty. It didn't take a genius to know that keeping the police involved wasn't going to help things.

"Seriously, officer. We did a lot of martial arts together as kids," she held up a tight-held knife hand worthy of any Bruce Lee movie. "It's part of how we greet each other. Maybe we got a little rough for others." She stepped away from the wall until she was closer to the officer than either Holly or Andi herself, proving her freedom of movement.

"Okay. If you're sure, ma'am. We're glad to give you a ride wherever you want to go."

"I'm good here, thanks. We've got some catching up to do."

Once the officers were gone, she crashed back against the wall as if Holly had again thrown her there.

Holly held out a hand toward Andi and snapped her fingers to get her knives back.

Andi shook her head. "Look at her, Holly. If she looked any more miserable, she'd look like Jeremy."

Holly turned back to inspect Taz.

Her hair had been ripped out of its ponytail by Holly's rough handling, and was now a bedraggled mess. Smoke soot still smeared her forehead and one cheek. Rather than glaring defiantly at Holly as she had been in the bar, she was staring at the ground as if she hoped it would swallow her whole.

Andi knew the "graveyard" look. How many hours had she spent looking in the mirror, wishing it was her in the grave rather than her copilot and best friend?

This last month spent working with Miranda's NTSB team had made her glad, for the first time in half a year, to *not* be the one in the grave. But it had been a long road that she didn't fool herself was even half over.

"Aw, shit." Holly reached the same conclusion.

"I just," Taz didn't look up. "I just can't face him."

18

"WHY NOT?"

Taz looked up at Jeremy's words. He stood there, close behind Andi.

"Why can't you face me?"

"Shit, Andi," Holly sighed. "I said to keep him inside."

"My bad," Mike raised his hand from Jeremy's shoulder.

"Mike!" Holly's voice was more pissed-off woman than angry warrior. Mike had better be careful.

"No, Holly. This is their thing first. We'll deal with the undead issues later. Come on. Let's go inside. Miranda's kinda freaking, and Jon isn't helping."

Taz didn't move as Holly ground her teeth together.

Then Holly leaned in close so suddenly that Taz banged the back of her head on the wall.

"You hurt him one tiny bit more, and I will dedicate my life to shredding your zombie ass. We clear?"

Taz nodded. "I never meant to in the first place."

Holly snorted, "Well, that's something." Then she strode

off and disappeared around the corner. She swept up Mike as she went.

Taz wished Mike had stayed. Even if he might have more reason to hate her than Holly. Talking to Jeremy alone...

Andi watched the two of them quietly for a moment, but her expression made no sense.

Had Jeremy regaled his team with stories of screwing the dreaded Colonel Cortez before a life-threatening mission? Had he—

No. That was other people. Some part of her knew that wasn't Jeremy.

Andi's look finally made sense.

It was pain. Empathy for Jeremy, because he truly did look miserable.

Then Andi was gone and it was just the two of them.

19

A HAND RESTED ON HER SHOULDER.

Miranda would recognize Holly's grip anywhere. It was always firm. Always friendly. Reliably safe.

It helped her to ease her breathing.

To regain her focus.

They were in a restaurant.

Seated at a table.

A half-eaten meal.

Everyone here...except Jeremy.

"Where's Jeremy? Is he okay?" She tried to push to her feet, but Holly kept her pinned in place.

"He's fine. He's just having a little chat with his old friend Taz."

"Taz?" Jon leaned in from her other side. "That really was *the* Taser? I thought Colonel Vicki Cortez was dead."

"We all did, mate."

Jon yanked out his phone.

Holly jerked it from his fingers and dumped it in his beer glass.

"Hey!"

"Major Jon Swift..." Holly's voice sounded nasty.

Miranda didn't need to check her emotions list to know that Holly was angry. Or in dead earnest. Or... Maybe she did need to check her notebook, but her fingers couldn't seem to close on it when she attempted to draw it out of her pocket.

"...do *not* be a dunce!"

"She's a criminal. A traitor." He pulled his phone out of his beer, gave it a brief shake like a wet...phone, and began wiping it down with a napkin. "It's waterproof."

"Unless you're suddenly a judge and jury, you don't know that about her."

"She needs to be arrested and—" he began to dial his phone.

Holly grabbed it again, dropped it on the floor, then hopped her chair quickly away and back. There was a loud crunch. She then picked it up and dropped it back into his beer. The screen had been shattered by a chair leg punch that had struck in the center of it. It now leaked air bubbles in the beer.

Miranda wasn't wearing her tools vest or she'd have pulled out a ruler to check. It was easily within a millimeter of the *exact* center.

"Grab a damned clue, mate, and shut the fuck up."

Miranda looked at the floor over the side of her chair. If she wanted to do that, could she have planted the chair leg so accurately on the screen? She latched her hands on either side of the seat and tried to aim for a specific spot on the floor. Even by her third try, she was nowhere close.

Yes, Holly was the team member with exceptional physical skills. Like Andi had said, Miranda might know airplanes but, despite her best efforts, she couldn't know everything. If that turned out to be true, it would be a great relief. One, or perhaps many less things to worry about.

One of the hotshots came over. He stopped a step behind Jeremy's empty chair and shuffled from foot to foot.

Uncertainty. Also nervous.

Miranda knew that one. It was very distinct from moving lightly and quickly on one's feet. That was preparing for a fight—sometimes. Or dance. Then there were variations that—

"Excuse me. Is Taz coming back?"

"Worried about your fuck-buddy, mate?" Holly's tone hadn't got any friendlier.

"We never actually... Haven't..." He sighed.

"Well, that too is something." Holly finally sounded more like herself.

"You smell of smoke." It was tickling Miranda's nose, making it hard not to sneeze.

"Something that happens when you fight a wildfire, ma'am." The hotshot looked down at his soiled clothes.

"Oh. Yes. That makes sense. I'm sorry. Did I interrupt?"

Holly's pat on her arm was reassuring before she addressed the big man. "What she does is up to the woman, but her past just caught back up with her."

"Yeah, she was always a bit squirrely on that."

"Well, she's having a tough time of it now. And probably for a while to come. So I wouldn't be placing any bets. Is that going to be a problem for your crew?"

"What are you talking about?" Jon practically shouted. "She's—"

Miranda felt Holly's foot pass within millimeters of her own shins.

Jon yelped, swore, and knocked over his beer glass and the shattered phone before grabbing for his shins.

Miranda knew what to do when there was a spill at the dinner table. She began gathering everyone's napkins to mop up what she could, and build little dams where there was too much.

Mike went to get a bar towel. Good. That was the next appropriate action.

The hotshot took a step back and raised his hands palm out, just as he had when Holly had threatened him with a knife.

"Look. The season's over. They just kicked us loose until the next fire season—nice bonus, too. So she's free to go. Never talked about what she was going to do next. I have a gig up at a lumber camp in British Columbia. Got a lot of pine-beetle-killed trees to drop before they rot. I'd asked if she wanted to go with—its good money—but she said some funny thing about not having a *new* passport yet."

"So, no loss, right?" Andi had been sitting quietly, leaving everything up to Holly until now.

The man looked sad at Andi's question.

"I guess. She's a damn fine hotshot. Not a lot of naturals, but she's one of them."

"As Holly said, the future's up to the woman," Andi confirmed.

And everyone turned to look at the blank sidewall of the pub.

Miranda wasn't sure why. There were some pictures of old Port Angeles there, when the railroad had still run lumber down to the waterfront here. But she'd already looked at those and didn't understand everyone's sudden interest.

Mike came back with the towel, so she started the next appropriate action for a spill at the table—lifting and replacing plates as he mopped the surface.

20

On the other side of the wall, when Taz still didn't speak, Jeremy repeated his question.

"Why couldn't you face me?"

"You're looking good, Jeremy."

"You look...unbelievable." Her hair was longer, thick, and lovely without all the twists of being constantly bound up in a tight, Air Force bun.

She'd been strong before, but now he could see the clear muscle definition along her forearms where her sleeves were rolled up. Her hands, which he remembered had been so soft when they touched him, were now rough with calluses.

"When you laughed... I almost didn't recognize you."

"*I* didn't recognize me. Haven't had a lot of reasons to laugh in my life."

Jeremy closed his eyes for a moment at the pain. "But now you've found someone who makes you laugh. That man in there."

Taz glanced at the wall for a second with squinted eyes. "What? Oh, Max?"

"Is that his name?"

"Yes, Jeremy, that's his name. And don't make it sound so shitty. It was a good day. We beat the last fire of the season, got paid nicely, and they asked me back next year. Do you have any idea how good that felt?" She held one hand in the other and rubbed at the calluses.

"Sorry." Everything he said to her seemed to come out wrong.

"You? *You're* sorry?" Taz thumped the back of her head against the wall a few times. "I kidnapped you and Mike. Forced you to do something so much against your nature that I still can't believe you did it. Then almost got you killed."

"You gave me a parachute. Though I definitely need practice. I broke my arm when I landed," he rubbed at the memory. The break hadn't hurt once the bone had been reset, but the entirety of his forearm that had been covered by the cast still itched in memory sometimes.

"Great. Add that to the list. I'm sorry for a thousand things. You'd be so much better off if you'd never met me."

"No! That's not true!" He knew he was shouting at her. Which wasn't nice but she was so wrong.

If there was one thing that had come clear to him over the last six months, it was how much better he was now for having been with her. However briefly.

"I still have nightmares about the explosions and the deaths." They'd torn up four drug cartel headquarters with the Ghostrider gunship before it crashed.

"Great. Anything else to beat me down with?"

"No! It's not like that." He reached out to touch her but thought better of it.

Taz watched the gesture, but didn't say anything in turn.

"That was the wrong thing to say. God, I wish I was Mike. He always knows what to say to beautiful women."

Taz turned enough to rest a shoulder and the wall and face him directly.

"Jeremy, we knew each other for one day."

"Twenty-eight hours and nineteen minutes. Crumbs! I'm doing it again."

"What again?"

"Mr. Over-specificity. Mr. Anal Exactitude." How many times had he been told not to do that? Thousands? Less than tens of thousands? Most likely...so...thousands of times—

And...he was doing it again. *Crumbs!*

Taz rolled her eyes. "It's you, Jeremy. Don't try to change that. Okay, twenty-eight hours and nineteen minutes. It can't have been that important."

21

And yet it was.

Even as Taz denied it, she knew it was true.

"Jeremy," but she didn't know what to say next. She took a deep breath and closed her eyes.

She'd spent the hotshot summer lying about who she was. During her nineteen years in the Air Force, she'd lied about who she'd been. Every day since crossing the border at eleven—and suddenly becoming fourteen because of a new identity—had been a lie. Even before that, while they'd still lived in Mexico City. Some of her first memories were being taught not to mention that her father was an enforcer for a drug cartel.

She'd never *not* lied about who she was.

"Oh shit, Jeremy. I'm such a screwed-up mess. Why are you even talking to me?"

"Because you are...were...*are* important."

"To absolutely no one who matters."

"To me."

And how the hell was she supposed to argue with that?

Taz held no illusions about her importance to Max beyond a mutual good time.

"So, what? We both morph into people we've never been, run into each other's arms, and live some fucked-up version of a fairy tale?"

"Well," Jeremy actually smiled. In the middle of all this mess, he actually smiled at her. "I did spend part of the day wondering just that. For a while I thought you'd been a magical fairy the way you evaporated at the crash site. If you hadn't left your fire axe, I might have decided that I'd completely hallucinated you. Oh no! Your fire axe! I left it up there."

"How can you worry about that— Never mind. It's you. Of course you would. Well, don't. I got it."

"Oh good. I'd have felt bad about that."

And he would have.

She could see that he was different than he had been, though at the core he remained himself. When she'd first met him on the Ghostrider, he'd been just "oh so excited!" to tell anyone willing to listen about the cool technology used to guide the HEL-A laser weapon.

Even when they'd made love, he'd had to talk about every aspect of how great and wonderful it was, as if it was his words that made it real.

Then she'd made him help her kill.

Taz hid her face. It was the worst thing she'd ever done in any of her lives.

"I can't believe that I made you help me kill. I don't regret their deaths, but I hate that I did that to you."

Jeremy was staring at something so hard over her head that she turned to look. There was just the hammering man.

"I..." he hesitated even longer before looking back down

at her. "I don't regret doing that. I could never kill someone. But they were such awful people that I can understand why you would want to."

"But...it changed you."

"Yeah," he leaned a shoulder against the same wall as hers. "You made me think more about the world around me than just the physical characteristics of the latest plane crash. Miranda at least tries to think about people. I never really did that before you."

Then, of all the most ridiculous and stupid things—the man she'd probably hurt the most in her entire life—slid his arms around her and pulled her against his chest.

He stroked her hair and whispered in her ear.

"It'll be okay."

"How?"

Again that soft Jeremy half-laugh, "I have no idea."

22

Out of more words—even Jeremy—Taz followed him back into the bar.

The first person she saw was Max. He sat at the barstool closest to the door, facing away from the others, just watching the door and waiting.

"I'll be over in a minute," she whispered to Jeremy, then turned to face the music. It wasn't going to be some sweet song.

The other hotshots sounded like they were most of the way back to normal, celebrating a fire season. The party atmosphere dampened a little as she came over to them, but the hotshots were suddenly trying to pretend it hadn't by calling loudly for another round and more platters of fries. Their sudden laughter sounded false, brittle.

This sucked!

She'd enjoyed her new life. Her "hotshot summer." And now they were treating her like an outsider; only Max actually looked at her directly.

Fair enough, she was an outsider now. Didn't mean she had to like it.

She stopped in front of Max.

"They got something bad on you, Taz?"

"It's not blackmail, but it's sure not good."

Max harrumphed, "You're pint-sized enough. I could always smuggle you across the border in my pack, and we could work that BC lumber camp together."

Taz liked the sound of that. "Tempting..."

"But...no," Max sighed.

"But no," she agreed.

"See you next season?"

That was too much. It was the first time in her life where she'd just been herself. And liked herself—a wholly new concept.

She stepped between his knees and hugged him where he sat on the stool.

"God, that sounds so good." She wasn't going to cry, but it did sound amazing.

"But not gonna happen," he whispered into her hair.

She could only shrug. Six months from now, at the start of the next fire season, would she be incarcerated in Leavenworth? On the run again? Dead? For *real* this time? None of those would be a surprise. No way to guess. Six months was all that *this* life had lasted.

Taz stepped back and patted his chest, "Keep an eye over your shoulder for me. Besides, you still owe me some sawyer lessons."

"You show up, you'll get 'em."

They shook on it.

"That your past over there?" Max sobered, then nodded toward the table where the NTSB team still sat.

"Only a little slice. But they're the ones who get to decide my future."

"Shit, woman. No pressure. Need a friend in that circle?"

"Not afraid of the blonde's knife up your nose?"

"Maybe a little." His attempt to shrug it off didn't look too convincing.

"No. Thanks, but no. I'll take whatever's coming. About time I did."

"Go get 'em, hotshot."

"Yessir."

As she crossed to the table, she searched for her old take-no-prisoners confidence from Colonel Vicki Cortez.

No luck.

Instead, she found it in Taz Flores, the hotshot who'd earned her place.

23

Even after an hour, Miranda was still a little startled to see Taz mixing with her team.

She'd come over to the table, taken the open seat that Holly had placed between her and Mike, and asked Andi for her knife back as if she'd always been there.

For the rest of the meal, she'd told them about how she'd survived the crash and spent the summer hotshotting.

When they'd left for the airport, it had seemed only natural that she'd said goodbye to the hotshots, grabbed her personal bag from her team's buggy on the street, and joined them.

Mike and Holly were waiting until Jeremey and Taz had talked about something, though Miranda wasn't sure what.

Jon had tried convincing her that *she* needed to report to someone that Taz was alive; though Miranda didn't understand that either, especially why it was up to her.

She had few opinions about that herself.

Taz had been General Martinez's aide, and *not* a significant factor in the three related crashes of a Spectre gunship and two Ghostriders. So why would it be up to her to report Taz's survival?

Besides, this team hadn't investigated the final Ghostrider crash. Someone else had missed that Taz's corpse hadn't been among the wreckage.

Then she remembered the signature on the report and looked at Jon chatting with one of the air tanker pilots. How *had* he missed that? He'd headed up the final AIB investigation. That wasn't good. Yet in all his protests about reporting Taz, Jon hadn't said a thing about that failure.

Miranda still didn't understand why it would be bad to call in and correct the inaccurate final report of the crash, but Mike insisted that it would.

Mike knew about such things, so she'd listen to him rather than Jon, who missed counting dead people.

Andi was right. It was better to not have to worry about everything herself.

For the moment, she'd worry about the preflight of her airplane.

"Nice jet," Taz had done a quick scrub and changed in the hangar's bathroom, so her presence no longer made Miranda want to sneeze like the other hotshot had. That was a relief.

"Thank you. Textron Cessna gave it to me last month. I'm testing the safety protocols and instrumentation for their next series of Citation jets."

"Oh. Learn anything interesting?"

"Yes. I don't like change. I already knew that, but this jet only emphasizes that. The convenience of transporting my team all at once is offset by all of the innovation. I prefer my F-86 Sabrejet."

"Now *that's* old school. By the time I joined the force in

the spring of 2001, the last of the Sabrejet pilots were hitting mandatory retirement."

Miranda liked that connection. "I missed them. I was given my Sabrejet in 2003 by a general whose father had flown it."

"People seem to like giving you planes."

"I only have one other. A Mooney."

"Who gave you that one?"

"It was my father's. Well, before I crashed it and replaced it, it was his." She'd actually replaced it again with a newer model thirteen years after that but she guessed that might not be relevant to the current conversation.

"How did he feel about that?"

"He'd already been dead for seven years when I crashed it. I believe...no, he *would* have been glad that I survived. Though he'd certainly have missed his plane."

Taz cricked her neck. "I think my father would have been surprised that I survived this long at all."

"*Would* have. Then he's dead, too." Miranda wondered what else they had in common. "When did he die?"

"I was eleven."

"I was thirteen."

Close, but not exact. "Was it in a plane crash?"

"No. He stole money from a drug cartel, and they executed him for it in the middle of the street outside our living room window."

Apparently that wasn't a common connection between them either. Though her own father had been in the CIA without her knowing, no illegal or even secret activity had been related to his death.

One of those silences happened where she'd noted that

others grew uncomfortable because they didn't know what to say next. Miranda *never* knew; she was fine with silence.

Taz eventually spoke, "I, uh, actually meant, when I asked if you'd learned anything interesting, was about you testing the jet."

Miranda glanced over at her. Taz was five inches shorter than she was, which created a difficulty. At five-four, most people were taller than Miranda was so that she could just focus on their collarbone or shoulder and not have to look at their face.

Andi was slightly shorter than Miranda herself, but she'd kept the vivid colors in her hair, which made those easy to focus on.

When she looked downward while facing Taz, Miranda saw her face. Her thick dark hair framed her features, forcing her attention again to the face. Then Miranda found the solution: Taz's hair was so thick that it didn't seem to have a part. That was interesting. She, Holly, and Andi all had distinct parts.

She also liked that Taz had returned to her original intent in the conversation rather than dropping it. Someone else who appreciated the comfort inherent in completeness of thought.

"You meant to ask if I learned anything about the jet? Mike has told me to answer questions like that with a question: would you like the short answer or the long one?"

Taz laughed, but there was an odd tone to it. A small gasp for air right in the middle of it.

"Maybe we should just stamp this conversation for later. I'm all nerves right now; I barely know what I'm saying."

"There's no reason to be nervous. The Cessna Citation

M2 is an exceptionally reliable jet. I'm a fully qualified pilot, and Mike is learning quickly."

"I'm nervous about what the future holds."

"Oh, we're just going to finish our inspection of the crashed Chinook CH-47D in a more conducive environment. Though it's late enough that I think we'll put that off until tomorrow morning."

"And you want me to come with you?"

"Want? I don't think I have much of an opinion on the subject. You're certainly welcome to."

Taz looked around.

Miranda saw that Holly was watching them carefully. Just out of earshot, leaning on the M2's hull with her arms folded as if she was bored, but not looking away when she and Taz glanced over at her. Mike too appeared to be hovering. Jeremy and Andi were already aboard.

"I don't think I have a lot of choice," Taz turned back to her.

"You always have choices."

"Do I?" Taz shook her head. "I'm not so sure. I think that's a luxury that passed me by when I could still count my age on my fingers." She held up just one hand with the fingers spread, not two.

Without saying anything else, she too climbed up the M2's few stairs.

Through the windows, Miranda could see that Taz had the advantage of only having to duck two inches to walk the length of the jet's low interior. Close behind her, Holly had to practically scuttle down the aisle.

Miranda had often considered the disadvantages of being only five-foot-four rather than taller. She'd never considered the implications of not being even shorter. She pulled out her personal notebook and made a reminder to speak further with Taz about that.

Jon also climbed aboard.

"Everything okay?" Mike, the last of the team on the ground other than herself, strolled over.

"Well, I haven't gotten very far on the preflight."

"Okay. Why don't you read them off and then you can check my technique as I do the tasks."

Miranda began reading.

But a part of her wondered what it would be like to have no choices.

It just didn't make any sense.

24

"So, I'm a prisoner. Or is this where someone shoots me and you lose my body?"

Jeremy looked at Taz, but couldn't make sense of her question, "What are you talking about?"

Taz waved a hand around them.

Jeremy looked. The sun was setting over Vancouver Island, filling the skies above Miranda's island with dark reds rather than the usual soft summer golds. The red was probably due to the lingering smoke and airborne ash from the smoldering remnants of the wildfire just a handful of miles to the southwest. He shrugged, still not understanding what she meant.

"Okay, it's not a desert island and there's no sand to bury me under, but it might as well be. It's an island, surrounded by freezing water with wicked currents."

Jeremy had never thought of it as a trap. Instead, it was where things came together. This is where he got to be near Miranda, even more than all of the hours they spent together at the office or inspecting aircraft debris.

Jon, Miranda, Mike, and Holly had filled the golf cart. Andi was perched on the rear-facing seat.

"I'll come back for you." Mike was at the wheel.

"We can walk." Jeremy propped his big crash-site pack on the seat beside Andi. That left him and Taz with just their small personal gear bags. He waved Mike off.

Mike gave him an encouraging smile as he rolled down the grass runway toward the main house. That was nice. Just being around Taz, he was as nervous as...a sika deer during a Citation M2 jet landing. They were only now peeking back out through the forest along the edge of the runway.

From the departing cart, Holly twisted around to face them. Jeremy didn't know how to interpret whatever her sharp look was meant to communicate.

He turned his attention back to Taz as they strolled toward the house no faster than the family of deer now grazing along the far side of the runway.

"You could leave whenever you want to."

"I don't know how to fly."

"I thought everyone in the Air Force could fly."

Taz just shook her head. "It's called being an administrative assistant. I spent a lot of time on planes as a passenger. I spent even more time talking about them—nineteen years' worth. But I never learned to fly."

"Well, if you need to leave, I'm sure Mike would be glad to fly you."

"I bet not."

Jeremy didn't get why, but she seemed pretty certain of that.

"Well, there's a boathouse down at that end of Miranda's island," he pointed past the main house just as the interior lights came on. "Not that I've ever been inside, but there must be something there. Knowing Miranda, it's probably pretty nice."

He gazed in that direction, but he knew less about boats than almost anything. Mike or Holly would know, of course. They were the sort of people who knew things like that. And Miranda, of course, because she knew about everything.

"I'd be glad to fly you, if I could fly." *If you wanted to leave.* He kept the last thought to himself because it hurt too much to think she might want to.

"What? Mr. Super Geek doesn't fly?"

"No. I might be able to fake it, I used to be good at several of the flying sim games but..." He looked more closely at her face. "You're teasing me?"

Taz burst out laughing. "I'm sorry. There's a name for what you are. It's a Navy term rather than Air Force, so two apologies, but you're a total gudgeon."

"A..."

"It's a small fish that will swallow almost anything with a hook through it."

"Oh." He could feel the heat on his cheeks. Why was she even wasting time talking to him if he was as useless as a small fish?

Taz sobered. "Sorry, I've never had many dealings with civilians. Air Force personnel and defense contractors were all I ever met before six months ago."

"What changed?"

Taz just looked up at him. He'd forgotten how dark her wide eyes were. If there was an answer to his question, it was hidden in depths he didn't begin to understand.

Finally she looked away. "Let's talk about something else."

"Okay, like what?"

"Like why you're here and not in DC."

"Why would I be in DC? I was there for the NTSB Academy. I went to college at MIT and Princeton. But I haven't been back there much."

"Then what were you doing on the Ghostrider at Andrews Air Force Base that day?"

Jeremy wondered how different his life would be if he hadn't been there. Would he still be the naively excitable geek? The mascot kid of the team?

In the last six months, it felt as if he was a different person. He understood…he wasn't sure what. But he understood whatever "it" was now, which old Jeremy wouldn't have.

"We were trying to stop you from getting that plane."

"Oh, how did that work out for you?" This time he was sure it was a tease.

"Pretty well, actually."

"How's that?"

He liked surprising her.

"I met you."

Taz groaned as they circled around the garden.

"Jeremy, didn't we already discuss that was probably the worst thing that could ever happen to you?"

"I'm sorry," Jeremy held open the door for her.

"For what?" She stopped on the threshold and the evening shadows made her face even more mysterious.

"I'm still going to think that, other than working for Miranda, you're the very best thing that ever happened to me."

Taz stared at him with those fathomless eyes for another long moment.

Then she hung her head enough that her long hair covered her face and turned to step inside.

Why?

What had he said wrong this time?

"You okay, buddy? Or are you just gonna stand there all night holding open the door?"

Jeremy looked up at Mike. He had a wooden bowl full of produce fresh-picked from Miranda's garden.

"The second one, I think."

"Aw shit." Mike looped an arm over his shoulders and led him inside.

The door shut solidly behind him.

Why did Taz see everything as a trap?

25

ZHANG RU ALWAYS MARVELED AT US AIRPORTS.

Not the security, that made him want to laugh, but the airports themselves.

Like all of the others, SeaTac was spotlessly clean. The technology might be a couple generations behind China's major airports, but the frequency and clarity of the information they posted for anyone to see was very impressive. Even *finding* the proper flight in all but the largest Chinese airports required the services of a Buddhist witch doctor and mystic charm amulets. The military bases were *beyond* arcane. No one trusted anyone, especially not the State.

"So few security cameras compared to home," Chen Mei-Li whispered at his elbow.

"Yes, no one to notice that they just allowed a senior member of the Central Military Commission through Seattle customs." Of course, his passport was under a completely different and scrupulously maintained name. A lowly Army sergeant, who looked enough like him to pass, traveled several times a year to give the identity a well-heeled tourist record in the world's security systems.

Mei-Li, who never misplayed a role, slipped her hand about his elbow but she trailed behind by just a quarter-step as would be proper for a favored niece being led by her favorite uncle. The light touch evoked the memory of her lithe former-gymnast's body. It gave him an arousal despite the two armed airport security who'd just walked by with M4 rifles.

But they continued on their way. By other people's reactions, this was an unusual sight, causing many to flinch in surprise. The *lack* of an armed guard in easy sight would be unusual in China.

He looked at Mei-Li's bright fresh face. Maybe he'd better refer to her as *grand*niece.

Ru hated getting old. He was careful to spend less time looking in the mirror than he once had. Though his new wife, Daiyu, just twelve years Mei-Li's senior, did a fine job servicing him in ways that made him feel very youthful. She never fired his blood the way an artist like Mei-Li had, but that was a gate he was no longer allowed to plunder.

Without saying a word out of place, Mei-Li had made that one of the prices of aiding his advancement onto the CMC—a price he'd gladly have paid a thousand times. That didn't mean he didn't still fantasize about her whenever Daiyu was performing her duties.

His former mistress had soon made it clear that her own choices were going to be quite different—and surprising.

He'd considered having a video made of Mei-Li and her lover—the girls were both great beauties—but he didn't dare cross Chang Mui's grandfather. Ru knew that his every move was only at the sufferance of the CMC's vice-chairmen. Li

Zuocheng had placed him on the CMC and could sweep him aside any time he chose...for now.

But the thought of the two girls together...

He sighed. One day it would be their world, but not until he was done having his piece of it.

Sometimes it seemed that the power would never be his to wield. Of course, even the all-powerful President had to keep the seven members of the CMC happy—*all* power had a price. But, oh, what a seat to possess. It made him hard all over again just thinking about that.

This trip should bring it one step closer to that.

"To walk through an American airport, unnoted, that is a power, too."

Mei-Li often read his thoughts. It was one of her gifts.

"As will be attending an American university," she continued with an easy confidence that *no* woman would have had in his youth.

Yes, Mei-Li and her lover Mui had plans of their own. As long as they didn't conflict with his, he'd allow them. Not that he knew what they were this time. That's why he'd insisted on escorting her to the beginning of school himself, to see what he could uncover.

Of course, visiting the University of Washington was only one of his own many purposes for this trip.

26

"Am I good? Or am I good?"

Actually Drake was entirely too pleased with himself to be the four-star general Chairman of the Joint Chiefs of Staff. Though he was *amazingly* good, but it wasn't the sort of thing she'd be silly enough to admit to her already full-of-himself husband.

"Just look at it all!" he waved a hand toward the operations floor of the largest building in the world. This was where Boeing was building the last of the 747s, as well as the 767, 777, and the 787 Dreamliner—all under a single roof.

The largest building in the world was...breathtaking.

For their delayed honeymoon, he hadn't taken her to some tropical beach and tried to convince her to wear a bikini. Which was so completely not her.

Instead, he'd led them on a whirlwind flight-tour of the country. They strolled through aviation museums, visited launch sites at Canaveral and Vandenberg (both of which she knew well but Drake didn't), and visited Houston, JPL, and others. Along the way they'd visited the Big Five—the major satellite manufacturers of the nation—as well as several of the newer, edgier ones.

As she was the Director of the National Reconnaissance Office, and having come up through the launch side of NRO operations (rather than the analytic or political divisions), he couldn't have picked a better itinerary.

Their two-week tour was ending but it wasn't over yet.

"Let's never stop."

And Drake just grinned. "Works for me. I'm already past mandatory retirement if the President hadn't extended my appointment." Of course he knew he'd gotten her from the first day, no matter how she'd tried to pretend otherwise.

"My, you *are* old."

"No, I just started young and—"

"Never grew up. I know, dear." He'd completed his thirty-five years maximum service, then been extended as the chief of staff of the Army under one President, and as Chairman of the Joint Chiefs under President Roy Cole.

"There's no way you can be blasé about this," he was doing a much better job than she was ignoring the Boeing staffers who were hovering nearby. It had happened at every site they visited, and she still wasn't used to it.

"You forget, I flew combat jets long before I joined the NRO. Now my job is space. These civilian things? Feh." Not that she'd have given up a single second of the day. They'd first played civilian and done the public tour. Drake had also lined up the plant manager for the personal tour afterward, letting them actually walk each manufacturing line.

The last handful of 747s to ever be built were massive rivet projects. A million holes, literally, were drilled in aluminum, every tiny curl vacuumed up, and then a rivet slipped in and set. It began its life as little more than preformed panels and frames, thousands of components, and bundles built of mile upon mile of wire.

The building sprawled so wide that four complete jets could be lined up nose-to-tail. Doors on one side allowed the arrival of parts and subassemblies. At the far side, hangar-sized doors rolled aside, and newly manufactured jets rolled out ready for a paint job and their acceptance flight.

In the middle bays of the building, the 757s and 777s swept through with a studied ease—sliding along the assembly line as if it was the most natural thing in the world for three million parts to achieve final assembly in a matter of days.

At the far end of the massive operation, the silence was startling.

The 787 was the pinnacle of composite manufacturing. Large, pre-built sections arrived from all over the world. Inside the building, they were temperature equalized before liquid-cooled drills slipped almost silently through the overlaps of the fresh-joined sections. Bolts threaded cockpit, fuselage, tail, and wings securely into a single plane. It also had thirty percent fewer parts than the smaller 767 and a third as many as a 747.

The wiring harness was a single, massive snake that could be installed in two days.

Lizzy's favorite aspect was that that the whole operation was constantly moving, just under two inches per minute. It moved a quarter of a plane length every eight hours along the assembly line. Everything moved in synchronized harmony. Not just the assemblies, but the machines to connect them, the walkways to enter the planes, even toolkits trundled along with the plane. Engineers sat at workstations to either side of the moving line to answer questions and carry out inspections on their phase of the operation.

An efficient and implacable pace that was amazing to see and produced a finished jet liner in the time it took to travel just four lengths across the width of the building.

Looking down from the high walkway, she could almost picture a more efficient methodology for procuring, launching, and controlling satellites. But she was too happy to focus on that right now.

"So, what are your master plans after this?"

He scooped her against him. He was only rarely demonstrative around DC, but she could get to like this freer, more relaxed version of Drake very much.

"We're going to take a dinner cruise along the Seattle waterfront, then I'm going to take you to a lovely historic hotel and make wild passionate love to you."

"I like that part of your agenda. And tomorrow?"

"And tomorrow?" He held a finger to his lips. "Secret. I've got a special treat for you."

27

TAZ DIDN'T KNOW WHETHER TO LAUGH, CRY, OR SCREAM.

Nothing was making sense.

Mike, who she'd battered to the Ghostrider's deck, then threatened to kill in order to force Jeremy's hand, should be one of the most guarded about her. Instead, when he'd found out about her love of food, he'd recruited her as his sous-chef.

Taz had been peripherally aware of the others throughout the dinner prep.

Holly's eyes were tracking her every time she looked up. The woman wore a serious case of pissed like a shearling coat on a hot summer's day, ready to shed it all over Taz if she even breathed wrong around Jeremy.

Jeremy was sitting beside Miranda as they worked over details of the Chinook's crash on a computer screen.

Andi and Jon appeared to be on the verge of battle about Army versus Air Force. Then she finally heard Black Knights and Falcons, and it began to make sense. They were arguing football. Army was finally beating Navy, but the

Falcons were still a league above, even if Andi wouldn't admit it.

That was aside from the bias instilled in every single Air Force officer, competing to be the most "up" on their service's team. There would never be a major military operation scheduled by the Pentagon that would conflict with watching a Falcons game.

An Army-Air Force game was just an invitation for an enemy attack, because no one at the Pentagon would be paying attention to anything else.

And this year? She didn't even know how the lineup had changed, never mind the preseason results. That was very strange.

Miranda and Jeremy were hunched over a computer the entire time.

When she went around, pouring what Mike called "a very respectable Oregon Pinot Noir," they'd still been working on modeling the poor Chinook's final flight. As she delivered plates of her contribution of bacon-wrapped Jalapeño poppers stuffed with smoked salmon cream cheese, they were working equally intensely on some card game.

But Mike was the master of the meal, and he chatted happily with her about favorite places to eat as they cooked.

He grilled a great slab of salmon in a butter-hazelnut-rosemary sauce. Enhanced that with fresh-dug new potatoes dressed with a simple sun-dried tomato pesto and an Asian cucumber-shallot salad. She threw together a peach-mint gelato and got it into the freezer in time to be ready for dessert.

The ingredients were so fresh—only the salmon had been frozen—that the flavors needed little additional work. She was in food heaven.

So, apparently, was everyone else by the amount they consumed around the big dinner table. It was late by the time they finished the meal.

But they didn't all just drift off to bed.

Instead, they lingered long after the herbal teas and second helpings of gelato were consumed.

Jeremy pulled out a deck of cards and tossed it to Mike, "Let's try these."

Mike dropped it faceup on the table and did a very neat spread with a simple flick of his wrist.

Aircraft.

The suits were easy to spot. Spades were combat aircraft, clubs were transport planes, and diamonds as rotorcraft made sense due to their pointed rotor blades as viewed from above. The hearts bothered her for a moment until she realized they were all historical, and some of the coolest planes of all.

"What in the world is the Spruce Goose doing in here?" She plucked the card from the pack and held it up. "It's one-and-only flight was just seven times longer than the Wright Flyer's fourth flight. Super sad!" She spun it off into the fireplace. That it wasn't lit on this warm summer evening took away some of the drama of the gesture.

"But it's the largest plane of its era. It's wingspan wasn't superseded until the Stratolaunch in 2019. That's six decades later!" Jeremy retrieved the card and dusted off a bit of ash.

"By wingspan, sure. But the Convair B-36 bomber is older, could carry more, and they built almost four hundred of those, not one."

"But I always liked this plane. You know it's in a museum just south of here in the middle of an Oregon hayfield."

Jeremy sighed, then tucked it carefully into his pocket rather than returning it to the pack.

Holly's glare couldn't be darker if she'd shot Jeremy's dog. The woman was starting to seriously piss her off.

"I don't see how any of these could compete with modern aircraft if this deck is meant to be even a partially realistic game. The F-86 Sabrejet? It ruled the Korean War, but the MiG-17s wiped them off the board at the beginning of Vietnam." She might not be able to fly planes, but any Air Force officer knew their outfit's airborne history.

Mike was smiling at her.

Taz sighed. "Alright, whose toes did I step on this time?"

Mike pointed at Miranda, who had pushed back enough from the table to look at her toes while Jon rolled his eyes. It looked as if she was making sure no one was stepping on them. It had to be a joke, except no one was laughing. Jon just rolled his eyes and sighed.

Taz turned back to Mike and raised her eyebrows in question.

"Hers is parked at our Tacoma office hangar."

Taz studied the card for a moment, then turned it to face Miranda. "You fly one of these? Oh, wait, you mentioned that at Port Angeles. Sorry."

Miranda nodded.

"How many of these are still airworthy?"

"That's uncertain. My best estimate is twenty-eight of the original nine thousand eight hundred and sixty are still flyable."

"Globally?"

"Globally, though several are in uncertain states being restored in museums." Miranda didn't appear upset; she just answered the questions.

Taz tucked the card carefully back into the deck and decided it was time to put her mouth firmly in storage.

Mike swept up the deck and began shuffling.

Then he began spinning out cards one at a time, faceup in front of each person at the table without looking at them again. She made a mental note to never play poker with him.

Miranda received her F-86 Sabrejet.

Then, going clockwise away from Jon, Andi got the S-97 Raider Rotorcraft.

At Taz's—silent—question, she explained. "Former Night Stalker. I did a lot of the testing on this aircraft," she tapped her finger on it. Her grimace said there was a dark story there.

Mike dealt himself a Mooney M20V, the little four-passenger prop plane that Miranda had said she owned.

"I fly that a lot for the team, though less since Cessna gave Miranda the Citation M2 jet. It's also down at our Tacoma hangar. It's a quick, friendly plane, and not overly complicated."

Taz wondered if he was underselling himself. And why?

He dropped a Russian Mi-28 Havoc helicopter in front of Holly, and Taz couldn't stop the laugh.

Holly's grimace was even darker than Andi's. "Former SASR, the Australian chaps. Twelve years in. Mostly in the business of *creating* havoc."

That sobered Taz right up. No wonder Holly had been so damned fast in the knife fight. Over too quickly to even be called a fight.

Mike studied Taz herself for a long moment, shuffled the deck, and spun out a card facedown.

She scooted it up as carefully as the hole cards in a game of Texas Hold 'em.

Holly tried to lean in, but Taz kept it shielded.

An F-35 Lightning II.

She tossed it to the table faceup in disgust. "Are you kidding me? These things are ridiculous!"

Mike's smile was easy. "Stealthy. New generation. High flying. Powerful. Fighters that are lethal as hell when they're working, which they will eventually."

"Stupidly expensive." She ignored his implications that she was a malfunctioning aircraft, too overdesigned to do anything properly. The rest of it was uncomfortably accurate, at least in relation to her past self. She'd much rather be something sweet and reliable like the F-14 Tomcat —even if it hadn't been all that great a design.

"Sure, they might be a little high cost to run alongside," he was still talking about her, of course. He slid across another card facedown. "Would you prefer this one?"

An F-22 Raptor. America's other fifth-gen stealth fighter jet.

An alpha predator of the sky.

Without cares for anyone else. Even forcing Jeremy to help her kill.

She placed the card firmly back on the table, facedown, and slid it back to him.

"I'm good with this one," she rapped a knuckle on the F-35. As if she had a choice.

"What's he?" she hooked a thumb at Jeremy.

Mike took the top card and spun it across the table to land in front of Jeremy. When he'd shuffled the cards, Mike had stacked the deck: two cards for her and then Jeremy's.

She looked at the card.

"The Chinook? Because he just investigated the crash of one?"

"Solid. Fastest in its class. Genius design. Insanely reliable. Can lift huge loads off Miranda's shoulders when she needs him to."

"Finally, a metaphor that I fully understand," Miranda sounded quite pleased.

"But all I do is—" Jeremy's protest was cut short by Miranda's hand on his arm. For some reason that gesture surprised several of the people at the table.

She glanced at Mike, who whispered, "Miranda is a high-functioning autistic. She rarely touches others. And never touch her lightly—it screws her up something fierce."

Taz should have recognized the patterns. She'd worked with any number of engineers who were definitely on the spectrum, but were particularly good at what they did. Seeking them out on the more messed-up aircraft development projects provided a lot of useful answers because they were crap at lying. Unlike all of their politically savvy bosses seeking to protect the cash flow of their Air Force contracts.

"The metaphor is completely accurate, Jeremy," Miranda assured Jeremy as she patted his arm.

Again, Taz had to readjust her thinking.

Out of this intensely competent crew, *Jeremy* was the one Miranda relied on the most? No mere genius cyber-geek could earn that, especially as Jeremy had not an ounce of guile in his blood.

He really was something special. In ways that she *herself* didn't understand. Or maybe some crucial gap in her upbringing and personality *couldn't* understand.

Maybe the F-35 Lightning wasn't such a bad fit after all. What ways was she herself malfunctioning beyond the ones that she could see?

Mike waited until the others were explaining some of the nuances of the various card metaphors to Miranda before he turned back face Taz. All of his easy-going manner since the moment they'd met at The Rail in Port Angeles, and all through dinner, was gone.

"He's *one hundred percent* reliable," his voice was soft and his expression was dead serious, "unless someone breaks one of his rotor blades."

Holly might threaten her with physical destruction.

Taz understood that.

Was ready and willing to take a physical challenge.

But unlike Holly, who threatened to confront her with force, Mike had confronted her with Taz's own past actions of how she'd hurt Jeremy by manipulating him.

A slap more painful than when she'd smashed Mike to the Ghostrider's deck by slamming her sidearm against his face.

Mike wasn't some friendly little Mooney. He hadn't been underselling himself. She'd been right about his attempt at misdirection by laying down the M20V Mooney card.

Once she'd recovered her breath, Taz took his deck, spread it until she spotted the card she wanted, and tossed it down in front of him.

The A-10C Thunderbolt II, the Warthog, the close air support specialist. It was the master of the ground attack—flying low, often below the radar, and protecting the troops like no other.

He glanced down at the card—then smiled.

But he didn't deny the change.

28

"No! No! No! No!" Taz shoved back deeper into her seat. "No one said anything about landing at an Air Force base."

Like a damned idiot, she'd climbed aboard Miranda's jet after a long, sleepless night, resigned to take whatever else was coming to her. No matter what she thought of in a locked bedroom last night, she couldn't figure out how to undo what she'd done to Jeremy six months ago before she'd died.

The flight had been so short that she was able to pretend the view out the window was too interesting to allow for conversation. It *was* beautiful. Puget Sound was a land of water, islands, mountains, and the extended metropolis of Seattle.

And she remembered none of it.

That was before they came in to land, and she saw the neatly arranged lines of black-painted Chinook and Black Hawk helicopters parked on the tarmac. The Army's 160th Night Stalkers were located at only three bases in the country, and Joint Base Lewis-McChord was the only one west of Kentucky.

Her seat in the group of four faced backward, so she hadn't even seen it coming.

"Technically, we're landing at Gray Army Airfield in Fort Lewis. The Air Force base is three miles that way," Jeremy sat knee-to-knee with her and pointed off to the right.

"They'll know me here!"

The tiny Citation M2 jet compressed around her until she felt it crushing her.

"Good!" Major Jon Swift called from the last seat on the plane. Somehow it was him, not her who was relegated to sit in the worst spot of all.

Mike flew up front with Miranda. Holly, Andi, and Jeremy completed the four-seat group. The only open spot left was the fold-down cushion atop the lavatory behind a half-partition at the rear. Somehow, Miranda's boyfriend was more ostracized by the team than she herself was—which was definitely saying something. Something she'd wager that Miranda didn't understand at all and Jon understood only too well.

Holly twisted around enough to glare back at Jon. "Shut yer yap, Jon! Stop being a bloody *yobbo* or I'll be making you a seat back in the cargo compartment. Might have to fold you up some to get you in there."

"*Yobbo?*" Taz hadn't heard that one before.

"Tosser. Fuck knuckle." Holly was on a roll.

Taz wondered how many words Strine had for calling someone an idiot.

"Five coldies short of a six pack, you wanker." Apparently quite a few.

Even when she herself had been facing down the very

worst of the Pentagon elite for General Martinez, she'd never have considered going to a base insult. Yet Holly seemed to make them work for her.

"He's going to report me soon, you know that?"

A bright squeal of tires on the runway was the only thing that announced they were down; it was a remarkably smooth landing. Come to think of it, last night's on the island's grass runway had been equally effortless. For a moment, Taz wondered what someone like Miranda Chase considered to be a "fully qualified" pilot. She'd ridden a lot of C-21A Learjets with the general, piloted by USAF pilots, who only rarely made such a perfect landing.

Holly sent another scowl toward the rear. "If he's dumb enough to, V— What the hell should I call you, anyway?"

"My chosen name is Tasia Vicki Flores." Not that it would matter for long. "I'll answer to any of them."

"Okay, Taz it is," Holly's grin was in happily evil mode.

Taz shrugged. She'd answer to that too. Holly's little games didn't faze her in the slightest.

"So, *Taz,* if Jon is," she raised her voice much louder than the reversing engines, "*actually that stupid,* then we'll deal with it then."

"Why aren't *you* turning me in?"

In answer, Holly fired a punch sideways across the aisle without bothering to look. It caught Jeremy hard on the arm as Miranda turned the jet onto one of the taxiways.

"Ow! Hey! What was that for?"

Taz didn't need to ask.

Holly had actually meant what she'd said yesterday. She was withholding judgement, and possible execution, until Taz somehow made things square with Jeremy.

Since every idea she'd come up with last night had been

even dumber than telling Major Jon Swift to make his phone call, that was going to be a long hold. Except Holly didn't strike her as the patient sort.

She definitely needed a subject change.

Taz looked at Andi and waved a hand toward the helicopters they were taxiing past.

"So you're going to be right at home here. Night Stalker city."

"So not!" Andi shuddered.

Taz almost laughed, assuming she was fooling around. Then she noticed Andi's clenched jaw and her tight-fisted hands resting in her lap. Couldn't she say anything without alienating her jailkeepers?

"Besides," Holly broadened her accent, "unlike Jon, my jurisdiction is a little thin on the ground here in your United States of Nonsense. Even we Aussies, with our penal colony heritage, do a better job of getting along than you lot." She pointed a finger at Jeremy again, who raised a fist defensively.

Holly must have great peripheral vision as she grinned wickedly. Or perhaps she simply knew how Jeremy would react.

"I'm no more interested in playing stool pigeon than to be inspecting an emu's arsehole. I *am* interested in helping out my little buddy here—though he's way taller than Andi and you, but he's still my young Padawan." Then the Strine went away. "If Jeremy needs to talk to you, I want to make sure he has a chance."

"Well, that's decent of you."

"And if my wee pal..." her accent snapped back into place, "...needs a body to have a *real* funeral, I've a mate with a lovely float of salties living out back of his cattle station.

That's crocodiles to you."

"I know what salties are, thanks so very much."

When the jet stopped, Taz rose and left the cabin first.

No question but this day was only going to keep getting worse; time to see just how far down it could go.

"Nice landing," she called into the small cockpit. Miranda at least had seemed to be on her side.

"Um, okay." Miranda was reading down a checklist and barely seemed to hear her.

Or not.

29

JEREMY HAD SLEPT ON THE COUCH OF MIRANDA'S SECOND-floor library again.

He'd half-hoped that Miranda would join him once more; half-feared that Taz would.

Neither had.

All he wanted today was to lose himself in the crash investigation. There really was no need to pursue the CH-47D's demise further, but Miranda had said it would be a good opportunity for them all to brush up their rotorcraft skills. She'd arranged for talks from the Army mechanics who'd been responsible for the ground maintenance of the Chinook helicopter. He loved that Miranda always went right to the primary source.

But when he entered the hangar at Gray Army Airfield on the south side of the sprawling JBLM base, all he could see was the crumpled helicopter flopped onto the immaculate concrete.

As the rest of the team, even Taz, moved in to inspect some detail or other, all he could see was the shattered helo.

That and the playing card Mike had dealt him last night.

He *was* the crashed Chinook.

None of his systems were functioning correctly.

It was a given that he wasn't smooth around women, but he hadn't even said "Good morning" to Taz. Not that she'd tried to talk to him last night or this morning either. The brief moment that he'd held her outside The Rail pub had consoled neither of them. It just reminded him of the past, and she'd probably been thinking about that big firefighter she'd hugged in the bar.

He wished he'd never seen her again. Life would be so much simpler if she was still dead. Or if he believed she was.

Instead, he was a crashed helicopter, and she was the finest jet that modern technology could build. Sleek, powerful, and in a whole different class than fifty-year-old rotorcraft designs—no matter how good they were at their jobs.

Andi got to be the new stealth S-97 Raider, and he was a Chinook—like the salmon they'd eaten last night. Thoroughly dead.

The pair of crew chiefs who arrived to lead them through the Chinook's systems looked as if they wanted to barf.

Right. This had been their aircraft. They'd probably been friends with the crew.

He felt a little better that someone was having a worse day than he was.

Then he felt awful for feeling better because of that.

30

"YOU *WEREN'T* KIDDING!"

"I think this is where I say, I told you so!" Drake only had to watch Lizzy's face to know she was in heaven.

She dragged him down into a kiss that confirmed the assessment.

They were at JBLM AWE. The Joint Base Lewis-McChord Airshow and Warrior's Expo was one of the finest military airshows he'd ever been to. No vendors hounding his heels to talk about the last strategic and tactical innovations, or Block III upgrades to existing aircraft, or "special" projects that just needed a few billion dollars in funding to make them happen.

AWE was about the men, women, and machines that made the military tick.

A hundred thousand civilians and servicepeople would come through here in the next two days, and, for today at least, it was all he and Lizzy were going to be—two civilians on the last day of their honeymoon.

JBLM was the fourth largest military base in the US, and

also in the world. Located in the Pacific Northwest, it was a major base for reaching the entire Pacific Rim. Most of it was hidden from view: massive training areas buried in the thick Douglas fir forests. But McChord Field itself was still a standout. When they put on a show, it wasn't some neat little collection of jets.

Within the roped-off area, so that people could get up close and personal with them, were the big three transporters: a C-130 Hercules, a C-17 Globemaster III, and the monster of them all, a C-5 Galaxy. Drake was amused. Just to make everyone feel small, himself included, an additional pair of C-17s and another monstrous C-5 sat just beyond the rope line as if they had nothing better to do at the moment than look imposing.

There was a line of rotorcraft, rescue vehicles, a B-1B bomber—he always forgot how damn big those things were—and numerous smaller displays spread across the parking area.

Up at the fence line along the runway were VIP sitting areas, lots of standing room to view the field, and a food court that was already smelling pretty good despite the breakfast in bed they'd shared just a few hours ago.

Over McChord's two-mile-long runway was a rotating aerial display. There would be massive cargo drops, the Air Force Thunderbirds show, search-and-rescue demos... It was more than could be seen in two days, never mind the one they could spare before they finally had to return to DC. Their attempts to stopgap their honeymoon with an hour teleconference here and there wasn't going to cut it any longer. The mountain of work that awaited him back in DC was—

Lizzy slipped an arm around his waist, breaking the downward spiral of that train of thought.

He kissed her on top of her head and vowed to focus only here for the rest of the day. "I've jumped out of a lot of these planes, but they aren't really in my blood like they are for you." Drake watched the Army's Golden Knights elite jump team descending over the airfield with elaborate parachute antics and streaming smoke that they wove into elaborate red, white, and blue knots. He'd been a good jumper, US Rangers had to be, but never as good as these guys.

"Look again. I flew single-seat F-16 fighter jets. JBLM is all about transport and rotorcraft. That's why this is so amazing; I have no experience with these aircraft. Let's go sit in the C-5 Galaxy's pilot seats."

They headed over to the biggest transport jet of them all. The rear clamshell doors were open and the lower ramp down. The nose was also raised, turning the plane into a giant tube for easy loading and unloading. They joined the queue walking ten abreast up the ramp and into the cavernous interior.

He saluted the flight crew hanging out at the head of the ramp. They returned the salutes cheerily enough even though he and Lizzy were in civilian clothes.

"So what can you fit in here?" Drake asked. It was fun playing tourist.

A chief warrant grinned, "What do you want to carry?"

Drake almost suggested the fuselage of a KC-135 Stratotanker, but that had been a top-secret mission that Miranda Chase's team had pulled off for them last year.

"How about some helos?" Lizzy joined the game.

"Three Chinooks, six Black Hawks, or a dozen Apaches.

And those last two we can carry after just folding their rotor blades. They come back together so fast that the first ones can be flying before the last ones are unloaded."

"A pair of Abrams Main Battle Tanks," a tech sergeant chimed in.

"Two of these can carry the entire Presidential motorcade of over thirty vehicles, including the three Beast limousines, along with all of their support staff." The last one, a senior airman not to be outdone by his superiors, pointed up at the rear stairs presently raised up to the ceiling. "Plus, there's a whole aircraft worth of seating tucked in the curve of the hull up there."

"Nice," and Lizzy offered them one of her lovely smiles.

Drake wanted to ask why *they* thought the airplane had only a sixty-percent mission-capable rate. He'd heard the excuses from all the generals, but these were the guys who lived with the planes. The fact that few of the military's aircraft were over seventy-percent mission capable at any one time, and several were consistently in the forties and fifties, was an endemic problem. One that no one had yet figured out how to fix.

Lizzy distracted him by taking his arm, thanking them, then effusing, "Let's go, Drake. I still want to go sit in the captain's seat."

One of the men looked at him, then startled in surprised recognition.

Drake sighed; his wasn't a common name.

The senior airman whispered to his buddies, who all snapped to attention and saluted sharply.

Lizzy returned the salute when he did, which surprised them again. He didn't know whether to be pleased or pissed that everyone underestimated General Elizabeth Gray. The bias about her gender should be long gone but, alternately, he liked that she was a little bit stealth.

Lizzy held a finger up to her lips to silence the flight crew, "Shh. We're just being civilians today."

"Glad to have you aboard, sir, ma'am. Under any circumstances."

They escaped and had made it to the base of the ladder that went up to the cockpit when his phone beeped with a message.

"Shit! I told them not to bother me unless it was a major emergency." Drake stepped them out of line and checked his phone, but there was no message.

Then he pulled out his personal phone and hoped that there was nothing wrong with either of his boys. Both were overseas at the moment, and a call didn't bode well.

Except it wasn't one of them. Nor his daughter, who—God help him—had followed in her murdered mother's footsteps into Doctors Without Borders. Thankfully, she had accepted his once-in-a-lifetime parental veto and had promised not to go to Southwest Asia, where al-Qaeda had killed Patty for vaccinating children. Besides, she was in DC at the moment for meetings. Maybe she'd shift over to administration. He could always hope.

It wasn't any of them.

It was a blocked number.

And the message was short: *JBLM AWE – Chinook.*

31

"Ah, Drake, my old friend." Zhang Ru could feel him arrive just by the tidal wave of fury Drake exuded, scattering the crowd to either side.

Chen Mei-Li had long ago insisted that he work hard on his English if he wished to climb any higher in his career. He'd never thought about it easing his way speaking with Drake, but now it would be very useful.

He and Mei-Li had watched many American movies together to help. At first with Mandarin subtitles, but she'd eventually switched them to English subtitles, which had been an entirely different challenge. He could read American military documents now without having to look at imperfect translations very often, as long as he didn't have to write any words down himself.

He kept his attention on the old US Army Chinook helicopter, parked last in the row of rotorcraft, like a lonely cousin. A long line of people streamed into the rear loading ramp, like cattle overeager to board it and sit in the cockpit seats.

He was content to admire its proud military squat from in front of the broad windshield, though he'd sent Mei-Li into the fray. He wanted to greet Drake alone.

"Ru! What the fuck are you doing on our soil?"

Ru ignored him. "I think we miss important thing when we do not copy this helicopter. Instead my counterparts in rotorcraft insist that bigger was better. 'We must have the size of the Russians' Mil Mi-26 Halo.' Sadly, our AVIC Advanced Heavy Lifter is gigantic machine but has lower capacity than your CH-53 Sea Stallion. And all the problems. Though it is new program, we have losed...lost even more of those than you have of Sea Stallions, without the wars of Southwest Asia as excuse—that information is just as embarrassing as it is highly classified, of course."

Finally he turned to Drake. The man's jaw actually twitched with how tightly it was clenched. Good. Ru turned to the woman by his side.

"You must be his lovely wife that he told me not about. A niceness to meet you, General Gray." Drake managed to look even angrier, but she didn't blink.

He shook her hand and noted her fine fingers. The slender Eurasian, at least half Japanese, had aged well; her slender body splendidly nice and tight. *You chose well, my friend, even if she is a* xiao riben guizi*—a little Jap devil.*

"Ru!" Now Drake's teeth were audibly grinding.

"His is not good moodiness to introduce an old friend." He kept hold of Gray's fine hand just because he knew it would irritate Drake all the more. "You call me Ru. I traveling under another name, but—"

"General Zhang Ru of the Chinese Central Military Commission." She kept a tight hold on his hand, as if she was the one in control. There was a reason he didn't like these American women. “The one... Ah. The one who lost a Shenyang J-31 Gyrfalcon over Chengdu Province.”

He yanked his hand free.

“I had your word,” he hissed to Drake. That unfortunate incident was supposed to be strictly between them.

“Underestimating my wife is not a mistake I *ever* make. Even when I don’t tell her something,” Drake’s smile was dangerous. “Now answer the damned question.”

“I actually escorting my grandniece,” yes, that *was* best, “to her first day at your American University of Washington. We see there is airshow, and she very eager to see it.” He waved to indicate where she had just sat in the cockpit of the Chinook. Yes, his timing was most fortunate.

“And you just happened to know I was here and texted me. Cut the bullshit.”

“Is he always so coarse?” Ru turned to General Gray.

“He was only a US Ranger. I’ve tried to teach him, but...” she shrugged easily.

Patience. Yes. It was not a virtue he’d ever enjoyed either. Ru took a deep breath and let it out slowly as he watched Mei-Li chatting with the helicopter’s pilot. Her smile could open any door. Right this instant, the pilot would fall upon her in sight of everyone at the least invitation.

Yes, he must keep calm if any of this was to work.

“My friend, Drake, we—”

“You can cut the bullshit, Ru. I haven’t seen you face-to-face in twenty years; not since we were both mere attachés in at the meeting in Geneva. Why now?”

“My friend, Drake,” he at least could be civil, “we have mutual problem. One that I could not trust to a phone, no matter how careful encryptionated. A problem neither of our country can solve alone.”

That shut him up.

32

MEI-LI'S HANDS ITCHED TO ACT.

Ru stood directly in front of the helicopter's nose.

But when she asked, Captain Simeon informed her that the Chinook had no missiles to fire at him, no machine guns accessible from the pilot's control.

Nothing with which to blow Uncle Ru off the face of the Earth.

But she dreamed of so much more than merely destroying Zhang Ru, so he must be allowed to live —for now.

"We're a cargo helicopter, ma'am; the very best. However, our defense is three machine guns aft, but mostly the gunships we fly with." He was patient and cheerful, though she was perhaps the hundredth person this morning to sit here and ask naive questions.

His patience allowed her to extend their conversation about his helicopter and his career. It also allowed her to observe the interaction on the other side of the windshield.

Ru had made sure that she had access to the full Internet, not merely the Chinese government's preferred slice.

She had studied every aspect she could of the American's military hierarchy; it was impressive how much was available even on Wikipedia in the West. Every photograph and article about their military was something they called public domain—free. Paid for by their tax dollars, so it therefore belonged to the people.

The Chinese military was hidebound and reclusive from the public eye. The CMC itself was shrouded in mystery, and she was probably one of a very few who had actually met all seven members of the commission without being one of them. And she knew more than just names and faces; she knew details.

For Zhang Ru, she had researched each member in depth, uncovering every aspect of their past and present that could be used to leverage their support as needed.

For herself, she had done even deeper research about Zhang Ru and his benefactor Li Zuocheng, one of the commission's two vice-chairmen. Her lover Mui was his granddaughter. Zuocheng might be just as ruthless as Ru, but he lacked the cruelty and avarice of his protégé. She hadn't even found any affairs—Zuocheng was still married to the match arranged in his childhood.

Her "uncle," however, was even dirtier than she'd thought.

It had taken much maneuvering to discover her supposed-uncle's closest held secrets. She had no doubts that if he knew how much she had learned, her life would be over.

So many backs you have trodden on, Uncle. It is good that

you are useful, or I would give your past to someone who would not understand the power of patience.

Instead, she had watched for the little signs.

The next clue came when he'd turned her attention to the Americans. As she fed him précis after précis of the top tiers of their military, he'd shown no interest in the most powerful one of all, their four-star general, Chairman of the Joint Chiefs of Staff General Drake Nason.

And yet, when she'd happened to mention that he'd recently married, Zhang Ru had demanded every detail about her.

That meant that Uncle Ru *knew* General Nason. Knew him well enough to not need the details of his past, but not well enough to know about his marriage.

It hadn't been hard to find General Nason's itinerary—in America as in China, men at that level did not move unpredictably. And feeding that information to Uncle Ru had brought them together.

They had talked long enough to cover old times. She saw suspicion give way to surprise on General Drake Nason's face.

Now, it was time.

She thanked Captain Simeon.

Then she eased out of the cockpit to move everything to the next step.

33

Staff Sergeant Bob Wang.

He stared at his own signature but didn't recognize it.

Over the years he had signed Form 1352, "Aircraft Inventory, Status and Flying Time", before thousands of flights. Like his trainer before him and those he now trained himself, he'd tried to instill that it was more than a scrawl at the end of a standard report.

No, this form, one that they completed many times every day, was their promise to the flight crew that a particular aircraft was mission-ready to the very best of the ground crew's abilities.

His initials in Column E, FMC (Fully Mission Capable) was a point of honor—his guarantee that this aircraft was functioning at a hundred percent.

Except this time it was a lie.

A promise broken.

In exchange for a promise kept.

Damn the old man to hell!

Bob hadn't cleared base until late last night due to a

balky hydraulic system flush. The trivial twenty-minute job had taken three hours. After that, all he'd been looking forward to was a cold beer and a quiet hour with a nuked burrito and a Seahawks football game.

Instead, he hadn't even made it to the shower when there'd been a knock on the door.

An old Chinese man had stepped in as soon as he'd opened the door. A young woman of impossible beauty had seemed to float along in his wake.

"Your parents visiting in China," the old man had begun without introduction. His accent was thick, and his English awkward, but it was better than his own Mandarin. "It is two in the afternoon in the village of Yehou in Anhui Province. They walk on the Chao Lake beach with your grandparents."

"I don't—"

The woman held out a phone so that he could see the picture.

The video.

The *surveillance* video.

Two couples walking along the beach.

Instantly familiar, he had walked it many times himself. They were just past the turn that hid the small family home from view.

Grandfather's stiff gait, distinctive from arthritis in his right hip. Grandmother stooped just so with age, her favorite shawl resting easy on her shoulders—one he'd bought for her while on a training mission to Hawaii. Covered in great bursts of vibrant tropical flowers like she'd never seen, there was no mistaking it. Mother and Father—

The girl turned off the phone but remained silent.

"You have a choice, Wang Bob."

He almost laughed. Even his grandparents didn't invert

his American name like that. One look at the old man's face and Bob lost even that brief sense of the ridiculous.

This couldn't be happening.

But it was.

One side of the equation was obvious without further words.

The State would charge two generations of his family with something—anti-state rhetoric? It didn't matter. They'd live out the rest of their short lives in terror and pain.

The other option?

The old man explained...such a small thing.

A thing that would turn Bob's signature into a lie.

Ruining everything he'd spent a decade building. Something that had given so much pride to his immigrant parents.

He should turn the old man in...but to who? He didn't even have a name. Some untouchable Chinese security spook. And if he did...again, that answer was known.

Turn himself in?

That wouldn't save his family either. Perhaps save them from a slow death with a fast one, but no more than that.

He forced his gaze up from his lie of a signature as Captain Debbie Smithey came up to him.

"We good to fly, Bob?"

Unable to speak, he turned his clipboard to face her.

She didn't even glance at it as she signed her name in the bottom right corner.

"So, Bob Wang. When are you going to proposition me for real?"

It was a joke she made before every flight.

He managed to deliver the next line...almost normally.

"Soon as you go Navy."

"Never gonna happen!" She had the greatest laugh. The spark was absolutely there. But they were sergeant to captain in the same Night Stalkers battalion, so it wasn't going to happen. Though he was in the Aviation Company rather than her Heavy Assault Company...

She waved her crew aboard.

Now, it definitely wasn't going to happen.

As soon as they were clear of the hangar, he'd set down his clipboard and tool belt.

"Need five," he called out to his crew as they moved on to the next bird. He headed out the hangar's side door.

He couldn't bear to look as he strolled past the hangar where the crashed Army National Guard Chinook still lay. Debbie had looked grim after retrieving that one from the wildfire yesterday.

Joint Base Lewis-McChord was far more than the Air Force's McChord Field and Gray Army Airfield. Even with the two hundred thousand active personnel here, plenty of the base's four hundred square kilometers were undeveloped forest for realistic maneuver-warfare training.

It could be months, or even years before they found his body.

34

"THE CHIEF WARRANT SAID THAT THE BEST FOOD TODAY IS over at the airshow at McChord."

Miranda had to admit that there wasn't much more they were going to learn from the crashed CH-47D. And she was *quite* hungry despite a minimum of physical activity. Yet the morning had been highly educational.

She made a note in her personal notebook to research the amount of energy burned in learning new information compared to various physical activities.

Jon requisitioned a van, and the whole team piled aboard.

Jeremy was reading from his tablet computer about all of the aircraft they could tour after lunch at the Airshow and Warrior Expo.

"Oh my God! They have a B-1B Lancer bomber on display."

"And this is a good thing why?" Taz and he had at least calmed down a little around each other through the morning.

Miranda hadn't been sure what it was, but Mike had pointed it out to her, so that must be what had changed.

"Because I keep drawing that stupid card every time we play the game. It's like that thing has it in for me."

Miranda nodded. "Jeremy does seem to have a particular affinity for that card, over thirty-nine percent beyond statistical norms."

"Being bombed by a bummer of a bomber. I like it." Taz's tone was upbeat and she was smiling.

Miranda would interpret that as...pleased.

"*They* have a Chinook, a Black Hawk, and an Apache," Jeremy continued.

"No MH-6 Little Birds?" Andi asked so softly, it was hard to hear her.

"Not listed."

"Well, that's a relief."

Taz asked why they made her so jumpy.

When Andi didn't answer, Mike offered her story for the remainder of the quick three-mile drive between the airfields.

Miranda already knew the details.

Andi's years flying MH-6s for the Night Stalkers were cut short when her copilot was killed while seated close beside her—blown up by a fired grenade that had entered the armhole of his vest and become lodged there during flight. To make the hit, it was almost certainly an UBGL—an under-barrel grenade launcher. No throw would have been sufficient.

It had given Andi a brutal case of PTSD that still dropped her at the most unexpected times. Miranda understood very well that need to sometimes shut out the outside world.

But there was something curious about the end result.

The inside of an MH-6 was significantly smaller than the two front seats of the van they were presently riding in. So she had to imagine that she was a little cramped, and that Jon's shoulder would be almost touching hers from the driver's seat.

If Miranda herself had been shot by a grenade that became trapped against her chest...

She turned to face the side door as Andi said her copilot had done to protect her.

The force factors were uncertain, but—

"Andi, what armor were you and Ken wearing?"

"Miranda!" Mike shouted. Mike never shouted at her.

"What?"

"You can't just—"

"It's okay," Andi's voice sounded from behind her. "We both wore the newest vests from FirstSpear, the ABAV—Aviation Body Armor Vest. We both also wore a low-profile Gold Flex Kevlar vest underneath it."

"Ah, that explains why you survived. The Russian VOG-25P would have had an immediate *initial* explosion designed to bounce it back into the air before detonation of the primary charge. So we may surmise that it was the standard VOG-25 grenade."

"What's your point?"

"I'm saying that if your copilot only wore the ABAV, the explosion wouldn't have been so well contained, and you were seated so close that you probably wouldn't have survived. A confined and compressed explosion trapped between the body and the armor would have exceeded the ABAV's armor on its own. But if the grenade was trapped between the armor and the under vest, that helped contain the explosion."

"Perfect. Now I owe Ken even more of my life—he's the one who suggested buying those ourselves. Can I find a way to feel more miserable about surviving?"

"Yes, I assume you can. But I don't understand why that upsets you." Miranda climbed out of the van and waited until Andi joined her.

Because they were an official vehicle, they were able to park close by the airshow field, rather than out in the remote lots that the tourists had to use.

Ahead of them, Jon showed his ID, received salutes, and escorted them through.

Taz was hovering close by Andi's other side.

This close, they had to wait for the roar of the passing C-17 Globemaster III as it eased by just three hundred feet over the field. It rolled a dozen parachuted pallets off the stern ramp, which scattered their loads over the grass on the far side of the runway.

The crowd cheered loudly when the last pallet dropped a Humvee. It would have been more impressive if they'd dropped one of the new Joint Light Tactical Vehicles, but it was still prettily done, with a stars and stripes parachute. And she saw that there was a JLTV for viewing: a Category C ambulance with four litters. She'd have to look at that more carefully after lunch.

"It upsets me," Andi shouted a bit over the jet's departing roar, "because Ken died saving my life. If he hadn't turned his back on me at the last instant, the force of the explosion that ripped off his arm from the inside would have ripped off my head, rather than smearing the windshield with his blood."

"But would you have done any less to save him?"
Andi didn't seem to have an answer to that.

35

UNTIL THIS MOMENT, TAZ HADN'T ONCE THOUGHT ABOUT THE two men who had died beside her in the rear of the crashing Ghostrider. Without question, she'd be dead if they hadn't been there as buffers.

But there'd been nothing noble in what any of the three of them had done.

They'd hidden and cowered. She'd lived, they'd died. Simple, done.

What Mike hadn't said was as clear as what he had. Night Stalkers didn't quit; it just wasn't in their makeup. Yet Andi had. Loss of confidence? Unlikely. But the alternative would explain her reaction to the arrayed Night Stalkers helos and her cautious question about MH-6M Little Birds being at the airshow—PTSD.

Yes, that fit Andi as clearly as the ASD fit Miranda. Again, she should have seen it sooner. Then she'd have been more careful about what she said. Based on her success rate in the last fifteen hours, maybe not.

Did she have PTSD or some kind of shock reaction herself?

She hadn't spent years flying beside either of the men who had died beside her. She'd never even met them until that mission. General Martinez had given her their names, she'd called, and they'd come.

The Order of the Coin.

Unlike many commanders who distributed their personal or unit challenge coins far and wide, General Martinez's were rare. They were given to only the most trusted. Every single person involved in that final operation, all dead now, had been part of the General's Order of the Coin. For all she knew, she might be the sole surviving possessor of one of his coins. She could feel it in the watch pocket of her jeans.

Though Taz had followed General Martinez for so many years, she wasn't sure that she'd ever felt close to him. He was there and she was at his side. She'd...belonged. The coin was a tangible symbol of trust. But no more than that.

These people *cared* about each other. Deeply. Deeply enough that Mike was kind to her and Holly had both threatened to kill her for Jeremy's sake and had *not* actually done it for the same reason.

Cared enough for Mike to actually yell at Miranda for Andi's sake.

Yet Miranda was still trying, in her odd way, to help Andi with her pain.

"Is that what friends do?" The question slipped out because Taz actually didn't know.

"What?" Miranda inquired as Andi seemed presently past speaking.

"Help each other? Try to protect them?"

"I don't know," Miranda nodded at the rest of the team leading the way through the crowd toward the food booths.

Taz kept a careful eye on Andi to make sure she stayed with them.

"Prior to this team, I only ever had one friend. And she was my therapist and my governess for years before that. She and I only found friendship recently."

"Aren't these people your friends?"

Miranda shrugged uncertainly.

"Yes!" Andi shook off her own thoughts and declared emphatically, "Oh my God, yes! Miranda, don't you dare doubt that. I've been with your team for over a month and Holly still doesn't trust me around you."

"She threatened to kill me." And Taz wasn't so sure that she'd been kidding.

"She does that sometimes," Andi's wince at some memory made Taz feel a little closer to her.

The C-17 roared into a landing.

Then it performed one of its neater, and louder, tricks. Once it was fully stopped, it reversed its engines and the pilots backed the massive plane along the runway, off onto a taxiway, and over to its hangar. She'd always liked watching them do that.

During the jet-enforced silence, Taz considered the others.

No need to ask about Jeremy, he worshipped Miranda and would probably give his life for her without even thinking about what that meant. Taz certainly hadn't for all those years she'd given to the general.

"And Mike?" Taz had to know.

"Mike's great!" The two women said almost in unison.

That would teach her to ask.

Mike's threat over the card table last night had made Holly's look inconsequential.

Taz understood force and knew how to confront it. Holly and Andi going for their knives was exactly what she'd tried to do at The Rail pub in Port Angeles.

Mike, in the quiet of Miranda's spectacular home, sitting at a crowded table, had managed to threaten her entire future without anyone catching on.

It reminded her of her own techniques as an Air Force colonel. Finding a weakness—exploiting it. She'd forgotten that in six months of being a hotshot.

Though she doubted that she'd *ever* been as smooth as Mike had. She'd have blasted her way through, embarrassing her target in front of everyone, especially his superiors. To use Mike's card metaphor, her F-35 would have dropped a B61 nuke on her target—often had.

Mike had slipped in under the radar and cut her heart out without her even noticing until after it was done.

Thankfully, her stomach found a distraction.

It only took a moment to zero in on the best booth in the airshow's food court. The burger guy had the longest line, and the burrito guy was a close second. But off to the side was a domed steel wood-fired pizza oven on a trailer. His signage was poor and his line short, but she could see by his face that all he cared about was the pizza.

She pulled Miranda and Andi with her when they started for the Asian noodle booth, clearly the worst of the lot by the scent of their scorched sesame oil. Though their signage did make it all look good.

Holly veered over to follow. The three men went for a burger and a beer.

Once they got close enough, the quality of the ingredients was obvious. The tomato sauce wasn't some thin red slime, but looked darkly rich, thickly speckled with spices, and the perfect scorching of diced fire-roasted tomatoes. The mushrooms were fresh sliced, and the basil was still on its stems, with the ends in a water bath until he plucked them moments before baking.

"Ah," Holly breathed in deeply. "The woman has a good nose on her. Okay, Taz, I'll put off killing you for at least a little while."

"Gee, thanks."

"No worries." Holly ordered three slices of double pepperoni. Which was a little startling as the slices were very generous—six per full pie instead of the more typical twelve.

Andi and Miranda went for a slice each of the mushroom.

She herself ordered the garlic chicken in a white sauce, and the chorizo with caramelized onions and goat cheese on that chunky, fire-roasted tomato sauce.

While they waited, a helicopter demo began overhead.

A trio of MH-6M Little Birds came racing in over the eastern tree line. Once clear, they dropped to five feet so fast that she was afraid they'd crash. But they were Night Stalkers, so of course they didn't.

At the edge of the field, they came to land. No, they came to stop, and not even quite that. They pulled nose high to kill their speed, then appeared to roll their skids on the ground, aft-to-front.

On either side, bench seats were folded down and six Army Rangers sat three to a side aboard each helicopter.

As the rear of the skid contacted the ground, the Rangers popped their belts and stepped off. They dropped into crouches with their weapons raised. The Little Birds continued their roll and were all racing back for the trees within seconds. That fast, eighteen soldiers were on the ground, armed and ready.

As the Little Birds climbed to clear the towering Douglas firs, a trio of MH-60M Black Hawks burst into view.

Instead of diving for the ground like their little cousins, they raced to a halt a hundred feet above the crouching first wave. Fast ropes were tossed out either side. In moments, pairs of Rangers were sliding down from each helo. The second pair were on the ropes before the first ones were clear. The initial eighteen soldiers were joined by another thirty in well under a minute. They were now at platoon strength.

She turned to shout how impressive it was, but Andi wasn't watching the display. She was staring at the departing Little Birds with a look between envy and agony.

Shit!

Andi had asked if there were any Little Birds on display. And Mr. Literal Jeremy had only looked at the display aircraft, not the aerial demonstration teams.

"Crap bunch of pilots," she shouted to Andi as the Black Hawks roared off. "Bet our Air Force combat search-and-rescue guys from the 38th could kick their asses."

"Are you nuts?" Andi spun to look at her. "Those are Night Stalkers." Her flailing arm, indicating the field now behind her, almost smacked Miranda in the nose.

Taz just grinned back. She'd forced Andi to get out of her head, apparently not a good place to be in at the moment.

"Oh, right. You *were* one of them. Forgot for a moment. Still..." Taz could see over her shoulder that more Little

Birds were coming into view, the heavily weaponized AH-6M versions.

Definitely better if Andi didn't look that way.

"Yeah, I'll put our CSAR teams up against you guys any day. Air Force rules! Just like the Falcons in football. Here. I'll prove it." She thumped down her elbow on the pizza guy's counter. "Arm wrestle you!"

Andi went for it.

She was no weak fish, but she hadn't been hotshotting all summer. Taz let it be a battle—until the Little Birds were gone—then put her down.

"Shit!" Andi glared at her arm. "I'm so out of shape."

As Taz turned to pick up her pizza order, she caught Holly looking at her. "What?"

"Not a thing, Air Force. Not a thing." But it sounded like a compliment. Former SASR, Holly hadn't missed what Taz was doing, even if Andi had. Which had been the whole point.

They snagged a fold-up table for four close by the fence line just as it cleared. It offered a sweeping view of the airfield: a wide grass verge, taxiway, the short and long parallel runways, and more field beyond. A great seat to watch the show. A quick scrounge and they had enough chairs crowded around for the guys as well.

Holly flicked a finger against Taz's paper plate. "Okay, in the future, Taz orders first. Because, damn girl, those look amazing."

"You snooze, you lose. Because you can't have any of mine."

"Stingy," Holly took a huge bite of her double pepperoni, then sucked in air against the heat. "Ow! Damn but that's good."

She took a more careful bite of her own.

Taz didn't fool herself that there was any future for her, but it would be nice if her demise waited until she'd finished these. Because Holly was right, the pizza was damn good. Her two slices would make a fine final meal.

36

"I HAVE VERY MUCH WANT OF A BEER," RU LED THEM BETWEEN two of the massive transport jets and toward the food stalls that bordered the runway. The two American generals following as if they had no choice.

Mei-Li had never learned how to stop Zhang Ru's power. He plowed through any objection until he utterly dominated everyone near him. He always made her feel so helpless, but inch by inch she'd been clawing her way out of his grip. She hadn't succeeded yet, but perhaps soon—if she could find the right help.

The crowd they strolled through were talking excitedly about this jet or that helicopter. Mei-Li had only learned about the one helicopter Ru had her research.

And she hadn't known why until last night. Whatever change Ru had insisted that mechanic Bob Wang make, it couldn't be good. Mei-Li didn't understand enough about these machines to know if it was a small bad or a big one.

Once again she was docilely caught up in Ru's wake.

She'd seen the three little helicopters arrive and unload their people. Then the three bigger ones.

Now the six of them were performing an aerial display as if there was a real attack occurring. One of them shot a missile, except it was bright yellow and had no rocket flames. It flew less than fifty feet, then floated down to bounce on the ground. It was made of foam.

Five more followed.

The crowd roared in approval.

Perhaps foam missiles were an American thing. She considered broaching the subject as an opening to conversing with one of the generals, but neither one seemed to be the right choice for what she needed.

General Nason was too angry.

And General Gray, while looking a little more approachable, was kept busy being the buffer between him and Ru. There would be no feasible way to speak with her that Ru wouldn't overhear as they reached a small table and she was sent for four beers.

Ru waved expansively at the clean-up of the battle scenario. The troops loading back onto their helicopters, waving the foam missiles about like banners. Machines of war and yellow toys. It was a very strange combination. In China, they would have fired real rounds and destroyed massive targets, just to prove the military's dominance over everyone, including the Chinese populace.

Under cover of all the rotor noise, she almost missed what Ru said to the generals as she served out the four beers.

"All of these little helicopters. They not solve our problem, old friend."

"And what problem is that?" General Nason's face was again

growing red with anger at Ru's constant evasions. One of his many tactics for manipulating others. That she could see what he did never diminished her inability to escape his tactics.

This time, he turned it around, and increased the force of his words by stating them simply.

"Now that we control Hong Kong? Taiwan." Ru turned to watch the departing helicopters.

Mei-Li watched the American generals, and saw the skin of both of them turn a bloodless white. Fury replaced by fear; by the threat of an imminent war.

Ru's timing was almost as perfect as a gymnast's.

37

Captain Debbie Smithey brought her MH-47G Chinook *Princess Jennie* in low over the end of the McChord field runway. It was almost too big.

Her typical landing area was two hundred and twenty feet, her hundred-foot baby plus a rotor's diameter of safety margin. In combat, she'd occasionally squeezed that sixty-foot margin down to six.

Gray Army Airfield on the other side of JBLM was sixty-one hundred feet long, but McChord was another four thousand, with a three-thousand-foot parallel strip. It was so expansive that it made her feel like a pinprick. For the show, they'd cleared most of the aircraft off the north parking apron and replaced them with hordes of people.

The Air Force show runners had been chapping her ass all through practice this week, as if they knew what her little Army baby could do better than she did.

"Who the fuck do they think they are, Night Stalkers?" Velma, her copilot, summed up her own feelings with her usual aplomb as they prepared to make their run. A high speed pass. Vertical climb. A series of dramatic stalls, then spin the top—a twin-rotor Chinook twisting on its midship's center of gravity was much stranger looking that a Black Hawk spinning its tail around its rotor axis. After that would come the groundwork.

"Screw 'em!"

Debbie selected the command frequency rather than the show frequency where her radio calls would be broadcast over the show's speaker system for the crowd. As if. The whole point of being a Night Stalker was that they were invisible. And, like most of their customers (mainly Delta Force, Rangers, and SEAL Team 6), they were silent.

"McChord Tower, Chinook *Princess Jennie.* We'll be running the script exactly backward. *Princess Jennie* out." She always used her helo's full name to honor the very last full-blooded Clatsop Native American, a tribe of the Chinook.

Before they could start sputtering, she dove for the runway. Good luck to the announcer keeping up with her.

Velma warned the crew of the flight plan change. It wouldn't even make them blink; they were Night Stalkers after all—the absolute best.

She raced along at her full two hundred miles an hour until she was just at the centerline of airshow, lined up on the middle of the runway.

A hard pull, and Princess Jennie practically stood on her tail. Her rear rotor would be less than ten feet off the pavement as she went almost vertical to kill her speed. It would look like less. She could *feel* the crowd gasp.

As she approached zero speed, Debbie eased the nose down. When she was at a thirty-degree angle, she let the rear wheels settle to the runway and kiss the surface.

"Dare a Black Hawk to do this trick." Velma chortled between calling out rear rotor-to-ground distances.

They couldn't even come close.

Debbie taxied a hundred meters down the runway, balancing the twenty tons of helo perfectly on just the rear wheels. They sat in their seats twenty-two feet up in the air and tipped back like they were about to launch aloft in a rocket.

Then she brought the helo to a stop and lowered the nose so slowly it would look as if it wasn't even happening until it was done. As the nose descended, the crew chiefs were also lowering the rear ramp. Few would notice that. Instead it would just look like a black shadow they'd left lying on the runway.

At least until the moment a JLTV—Joint Light Terrain Vehicle, the Humvee replacement—shot out the back, towing a 105 mm M119 howitzer.

While they were pulling onto the grass behind her helo, setting up to fire a blank training round, Debbie re-raised the Jennie's nose.

Once the ramp was up and she again sat high in the air, she began the same balancing act, but rolling backward this time. *Princess Jennie* was acting like a curtain unveiling the now-rigged howitzer.

"They're eating it up," Velma called in the middle of reporting angle-of-attack.

Just as she cleared the line of view from crowd to artillery piece, she heard the hard thump of the howitzer.

But it was twenty seconds earlier than scheduled.

She glanced out her side window.

There was no smoke from the gun. Instead, the Ranger team was all turning to look at her.

Another thump.

This one she felt despite the heavy padding of her seat.

It was—

“Blade strike!” Velma shouted.

Debbie slammed down on the left-hand thrust control and rammed the cyclic joystick between her knees all the way forward to level and fully land the bird.

How could they have hit their blade on the pavement? Their deck angle was precisely on program.

Perhaps it wasn’t—

38

JEREMY WAS THE FIRST ONE IN THE ENTIRE CROWD TO HIS FEET.

That first bang was too high a frequency for the howitzer. A round from the big gun should have hit him in the gut with a bass note.

It didn't.

It spiked into his ears as his eyes caught what was happening.

A single thirty-foot blade on the Chinook's rotor had drooped suddenly.

First it impacted the top of the fuselage, gouging a deep scar across the metal skin, but it didn't break.

Instead, it was deflected upward, bouncing high enough to spin around cleanly for several revolutions.

Then it dipped again.

The Chinook was dropping its nose toward the runway, but it wasn't fast enough.

This time, when the blade hit the fuselage, it broke, but it didn't separate.

Instead it swung around until it slammed into the

cockpit, shearing off the nose cone radar dome and the windshield close in front of both of the pilots. It would have sliced far deeper if not for the long refueling probe that stuck out low on the right side. It's hard shaft forced the blade to flex upward. Probably all that saved the pilots' lives.

Then it all came apart.

Jeremy threw himself at Miranda and Taz. Taking them both down to the ground, he rolled all three of them under the table.

Looking beneath the empty seats and through the low boundary fence, he saw chunks of rotor blade flying off. Several of them raining down in their direction, though few reached this far.

The Chinook began an obscene bouncing twist as if it was trying to spin, roll over, and climb aloft all at once.

Another blade bent and crashed so solidly into the middle of the fuselage that he was surprised it didn't cut the helo in two.

Then it rolled all the way over before landing back on its wheels. Not even the blade stumps had survived that. Free of the weight and resistance of the big rotors, the engines began to scream.

The nose ended up facing him.

He could see the pilots, still sitting in their seats, but with no controls in front of them.

One reached up for the fire extinguisher T-handles, but the overhead console was lying twenty meters away on the runway.

The other reached down and cut the fuel selector valves.

The high whine of the engines slowly began to wind down.

When the engines finally died, there was a silence so deep that it echoed.

Then the members of the crowd started to scream. Some ran away, some ran forward. Kids who'd been bored to tears moments before were now crying for real.

"Everyone okay?" Holly was the first of their group to break the silence.

Jeremy looked around. She lay across Mike. Andi had Jon pinned to the ground.

They eased out from under the table and determined that the only damage was a star-cracked section of the windshield—perhaps the pilot's side window—that had skidded across the table and shattered Taz's chair to splinters.

They looked at each other for a second, but he couldn't tell what she was thinking.

Then the whole team turned, jumped through the hole in the fence, and sprinted for the field.

39

The forest was so quiet.

Bob Wang's ears rang with it. His own passage silenced any bird song.

There was a distant buzz, too minor to be noticed if he hadn't heard it a thousand times. The helicopters at the airshow. He was too far away to hear the Little Birds at all. The Black Hawks were no more than an occasional thudding sound at this distance.

Finally, the bass note hammer—more felt than heard—that was a part of his blood. So low, it barely carried through the dense pine trees.

It wavered along the edge of hearing as he dug himself a pit in the forest detritus. The sharp scent of pine needles and loam filled the shadowed cloister.

The sound built briefly as he lay down and swept the brush and branches over himself. Here, beneath a snarl of blackberry surrounded by scrub alder, he might never be found.

That would be best for everyone.

He should have left a note for his parents not to worry, but it was too late for that.

The low thudding of the Chinook's big rotors was silenced.

He hadn't heard the crash, though at this distance that wasn't a real surprise.

No hard thump of an explosion either.

If the helo hadn't exploded on impact, maybe someone survived. Then he recalled that, in order to extract the pilot's remains from the CH-47D that had gone down in the forest fire, they'd had to cut off the entire nose of the aircraft. If anyone survived the crash of this Night Stalkers Chinook, it wouldn't be the pilots.

Then he heard it.

The few birds who'd returned to their song were all silenced at once.

In the sudden stillness, the high thin whine of sirens sliced through the trees.

Bob couldn't even bear to think her name. He'd killed her, her crew, and the helicopter he'd sworn to maintain.

Slipping his sidearm up under his chin, he did the same for himself.

No one heard the single shot or the harsh cries of alarm from the jays flitting away through the Douglas firs.

40

The first thing Drake heard was the shouts of surprise from the crowd. That quickly turned to screams.

He leapt to his feet and followed the direction they were scattering away from.

It created an opening that let him see the last thrashing of a Chinook helo as it flopped hard onto its side. Chunks of rotor and helicopter were flying through the air. Most of it landing back on the field.

Directly in front of him, there was hole in the fence and a small group of people trying to push onto the field.

A senior airman with the Security Forces SF badge on his sleeve was shouting at them to get back just as they were shouting to be let through.

He only needed to see one face to know who they were.

"Miranda. Thank God! Airman, let these people through." He held out his ID. To his credit, the man checked his face twice against the badge.

"No disrespect, sir," the airman stood his ground, "who are these people?"

"The top crash team for the NTSB," though he'd thought there were only four of them, not seven. Then he spotted Jon. "Oh, and Major Jon Swift of the US Air Force Accident Investigation Board. You have a crash, now let them through. No one else except emergency services, by my order."

"Yes sir!"

Then he turned to face Miranda's team. "Hi, Miranda. What are you doing here?"

"Eating lunch."

"You...what?"

"I had a slice of mushroom pizza, as did Andi. Holly had pepperoni. Taz had a slice of garlic chicken and... I'm sorry. I don't remember the other one."

He couldn't have heard that right.

He rested a hand on Miranda's arm.

"Could you repeat that?"

Miranda didn't say anything. Instead, she was staring at his hand.

"Miranda?"

Nothing. She was just looking down, her breathing fast and blinking hard.

"What the—"

Holly slapped his hand hard enough to hurt like hell.

He yanked it back.

"Don't do that to her, you idiot!" Then she raced toward the helicopter, accompanied by a Chinese woman he didn't recognize.

As he nursed his hand, he replayed Miranda's words, *Taz had...*

He turned very slowly.

Close beside Jeremy stood...

"Aren't you dead?"

41

TAZ WONDERED IF IT WOULD BE BETTER IF SHE WAS.

It was bad enough running into Jeremy in the wilderness atop Hurricane Ridge. Running into General Drake Nason and—

"Hello, Colonel Cortez. How have you been?" —General Elizabeth Gray. Their last meeting had not gone well. Taz had been trying to extract classified information from the NRO's director, and hadn't been…subtle.

"Good, General Gray. Yourself?"

"Very good. Except you're dead, aren't you?"

"I was. Until yesterday." Taz scowled at Jeremy's back as he headed over to the wreck, leaving her alone with no protection. "I—"

"General Nason," Jon cut her off. "I tried to report that we found this criminal, but was unable to do so."

"Who stopped you?"

"Holly Harper," Jon pointed an accusing finger toward the wreck.

"She has her reasons, sir," Mike stepped up from behind her.

Taz wasn't sure if she should feel better because "friendly" Mike-the-Mooney M20V-passenger-plane had arrived. Or was she about to catch hell because he was in A-10 Thunderbolt II-ground-attack mode? She didn't know how to tell.

The general looked down at Miranda, started to reach for her, then flexed his hand and apparently thought better of it.

"Miranda, do you have anything to add to that?"

Miranda shook her head. "No, Drake. She's only been a member of my team for nineteen hours and eleven minutes. In that time, I haven't been given any cause to second guess Holly's and Mike's suggestions that it would be better for Taz to remain with us and keep a low profile."

"I don't have time for this. For now, as long as I don't have to deal with her, she stays with you," he faced Taz for just a moment, then turned back to the wreck. "What the hell happened here?"

"Until we have done our investigation, Drake, how are we supposed to know?" Miranda said it without any of the demeaning "you idiot" subtext Taz would have used.

For a moment Taz could only blink.

At their very last moment together on the crashing Ghostrider, before she'd pushed Jeremy to safety, he'd made the ridiculous claim that he knew the Chairman of the Joint Chiefs and the President. Through them, he'd offered to get her a full pardon. As if.

Apparently the first part of the statement was true.

But General Nason had made it sound as if Miranda's word was all he needed to not court-martial her ass out of existence on the spot.

Miranda—on a first name basis with the chairman, and fully trusted.

Did she somehow call the President of the United States by his first name, too?

Who the hell *was* this woman?

The general turned back to a table where an older Chinese man and four beers were waiting for him.

Miranda walked toward the wreck, but Taz couldn't move.

General Gray spoke softly, "A low profile includes coming to JBLM AWE?" Her smile might have even been an actual smile, not a threat.

"Out of my control, ma'am. Miranda was studying another Chinook crash over at Gray Army Airfield, and the team came here for lunch." Taz had shifted to stand at attention without realizing, but now that she had, she couldn't undo it.

"Another?"

"In a forest fire yesterday, ma'am. Tree exploded and speared the helicopter. Not related to whatever this is." She was even speaking in addressing-superior-officer clipped sentences.

"Oh, okay."

When she, too, turned to follow General Nason, Taz just had to say something.

"General?"

"Yes?" General Gray turned to her once more.

"I'm sorry for..." so many things, "...for before. Going behind your back. Getting... Doing..." Oh God. "I guess for almost everything I did before the moment I died. Supposedly died. Very nearly did die."

The general studied her for a long moment. "Good. That

means you learned something by dying. Don't stop." Then she returned to her companions.

What the hell did that mean? Nothing was making any sense. In fact, the only one who did was Major Jon Swift, and his desperate need to report her to somebody.

"Colonel Vicki Taser Cortez," a voice whispered by her elbow.

Who had recognized her now? A female MP with a shotgun?

Taz turned, and blinked in surprise.

The woman standing quietly behind her was beyond elegant in designer clothes, straight hair almost down to her waist, and a face from some ancient Chinese myth of artistic perfection. Women like her didn't occur outside the movies, nor even inside them.

Taz wore her backup jeans, fire boots, and a red t-shirt that declared, "I rang the bell on the Echo Mountain Fire Complex." It was from a nasty wildfire her hotshot team had helped fight into the ground just a few hundred meters before it wiped out an Oregon Coast resort town.

"That's not a name I use anymore. Nor a rank I deserve." Which hurt less than she'd expected.

"But it is you."

Taz sighed. It was.

42

MEI-LI CONSIDERED.

The two generals were again seated to either side of Zhang Ru at their table. Observing or talking—for her purposes, it didn't matter. She'd hesitated at the wrong moment, allowing General Gray to walk away. She wouldn't be getting either one aside again easily.

Or perhaps that she'd missed the chance, meant that *not* speaking was "right action" at the moment. Ru would grow very suspicious if she spoke at length with General Gray. Would he even notice that she spoke to this tiny woman in civilian clothes?

Was it wise for her to do so herself?

Mei-Li had briefly considered approaching Jon, the angry Air Force major. But he was cut from a military cloth she was entirely too familiar with. She didn't need a man of rules.

But Colonel Cortez...

Among so many others, Mei-Li had profiled Lieutenant General JJ Martinez along with all of the other three- and four-star generals for Ru shortly before the general's death. And she'd become curious about the tiny woman who'd appeared close by his side in so many photographs. No mention of marriage, and only a rare reference to her at all —his aide. Invisible in most media.

Yet the more she'd searched, the more prominent the woman became.

A stealthy enforcer? Ru might discount both herself and this woman for their size, but it was a mistake Mei-Li knew not to make.

The Colonel's apology to General Gray implied that she'd done things the hard way, yet still remained in the military until her supposed death.

"I wonder if we might speak, Colonel Cortez?"

"Only if you stop calling me that. Taz or Vicki."

"Taz," it was a strange word, "are you needed at the crash?"

The woman snorted out a laugh. "I don't know crap about helos. Jeremy will take care of it."

She was...astonishing. Everything Mei-Li wasn't.

Even at the pinnacle of her own gymnast's strength when she'd taken silver at the Olympics, she had always been very slight.

Taz's shoulders *looked* strong, and she was so...brashly American.

"Is there somewhere private we can talk?"

"Doesn't get any better than this," Taz waved a hand as if she owned the airfield. But she had a point.

At the crash fifty meters away, emergency teams were helping the crew members into ambulances. There was one pilot still in a flightsuit and helmet who refused their help.

Instead, she too stood like an American, glaring at the helicopter with her fists on her hips.

The people Taz had arrived with were beginning their own inspection of the wreck. Taz's Jeremy, they'd stood as close as only a couple would, was gesturing sharply at the front rotor.

The three generals drinking beer together were nearly obscured by the return of the crowd, which had surged up to the fence—smartphone cameras to the fore.

A line of heavily armed soldiers had manned the fence. Unlike such an event in China, their weapons were slung over shoulders, not clasped in fisted hands.

And the craziest part of all was the announcer apologizing for the delay in the airshow. Then he went on to announce that other than a broken arm and a number of bruises, the crew was going to be fine.

By some miracle, no one in the crowd had been killed by the flying debris. Medics were moving through the crowd, dealing with cuts and bruises.

And the two of them stood alone on the fresh-mown grass a few meters past the security line. They were the only ones.

"You do a lot of thinking for someone who said she wants to talk. The old man is your uncle? Granduncle?"

"He is my owner."

Taz's face went dark.

"He is immensely powerful. When the Chinese Olympic Committee dismissed me for being too old and only winning silver," she rubbed her cheek where her coach's fist had smashed her to the floor for that failure, "he took over my care from the State."

"He didn't..."

Mei-Li was almost amused. American's had such a high opinion of their rights. Didn't they look at their own statistics? One in five hundred women in America were sex trafficked. Up to fifty thousand immigrants were sent into the trade in their "free" country every year.

"Shit!" Taz glared toward Ru's place back in the crowd. "Are you asking me to help you seek asylum? I should warn you that I'm technically dead and probably will be jailed soon enough. Or to kill him?"

"No. Not either of those. I have blackmailed him into stopping that. And I am already coming to your country; I and my girlfriend start at the University of Washington next week. But I am hoping that a woman who has dodged death and who can make your General Nason shudder, can help me with what I need to do."

"What's that?"

"I have all the evidence I need to destroy Zhang Ru."

"So do it! Do it before he figures that out and kills you."

"He doesn't dare. He knows that my death will release everything to ruin him."

"Ru knows about your girlfriend?" Taz made it sound as if she didn't think much of Mei-Li's intelligence.

"Mui is not the holder of this information. It is a member of your government. I do not trust her, but she knows I can ruin her too if she acts prematurely." CIA Director Clarissa Reese was almost as avaricious as Uncle Ru, but she was no more invincible than Zhang Ru was—just extremely dangerous.

"Great, so Ru goes after your girlfriend to control you."

"Again, I know he won't. He still needs the support of her grandfather. He is one of the vice-chairmen of the CMC."

Taz whistled in what Mei-Li took to be a Western sound

of surprise. "You are crazy connected, girl. Why in the world would you need my help? Sounds as if you have it wired."

"I am also very close to having the information to ruin the entire Chinese Military Commission, but I cannot do this myself. That is the help I need."

Then Colonel Vicki Cortez did the strangest thing; she laughed. "Is that all?"

"Yes. Can you help me?"

She sobered, then looked away. Her gaze sought upward until she was looking at Jeremy, standing atop the battered helicopter. He was photographing something there.

"What is he looking at?" Mei-Li knew so little about helicopters.

"The rotor head. Maybe the pins that hold the rotor blade root to the head."

Mei-Li knew she must trust someone. Her entire reason for manipulating Ru to being here at this moment was because Mei-Li knew she needed someone in the US military to help with her plans.

Taz was still gazing at the helicopter.

"Would there be something there called the centrifugal droop stop or a pitch link?"

"Could be. Weird question. Why?"

Mei-Li just shook her head. They were words Ru had used last night in speaking to the helicopter mechanic. Now she understood both what had happened to crash the helicopter, and that it was being uncovered.

Mei-Li watched Taz watching the man on top of the helicopter. As strange as this American was, Mei-Li might never have another opportunity as good. There were times to gamble. Her last play had freed her from Ru's servitude. Now...

"I might have information on those for you."

Taz turned back to face her very slowly. "What information?"

"Only after you help me."

Taz's face had become unreadable.

Mei-Li felt nervousness surge into her stomach worse than the moment before she'd stepped onto the gymnastics floor at the Olympics. But she didn't blink or look away. Not even when she'd stood on the podium to accept her medal had anyone been able to read the fury building inside her.

No one except Clarissa Reese, who had witnessed her coach's blow. Then arranged for the man who had beaten and raped her since she was nine to die most painfully.

Only now that she'd offered Ru's secret did she realize that if she gave that last piece of information to destroy Zhang Ru, she would destroy herself as well. She'd been witness to a sabotage of a US helicopter of war. Had taken part in the blackmail of an American military personnel.

Taz could ruin her entire year of work preparing for a moment like this. The moment Ru was destroyed, all of her own protections would disappear as well. And all of her power as well.

No!

She wouldn't give up that detail until the CMC itself was destroyed. Not until her country lay in smoldering ruins would she give up that secret of Ru's sabotage.

Mei-Li took a careful breath.

She resented that the last was beyond her reach, but the seven old men of the CMC would suffer horribly for taking General Zhang Ru into their bosom.

Also, if she herself was exposed, Chang Mui would be exposed as well. Her sweet lover and co-conspirator wouldn't survive the purge of the CMC unless they all went down together. And that is why the two of them were coming to America, to have the best chance of survival.

But she couldn't think how to take it all back.

Before her thoughts were ordered at all, before—

Taz turned and pointed at a tall blonde at the wreck. For some reason, the woman noticed her immediately. Taz then sliced a hand at an equally tall man, before making a "come here" gesture. The blonde grabbed the man roughly by the arm, then hurried over.

"What the hell trouble be you causing now, corpse?" The woman addressed Taz with an Australian accent so thick that Mei-Li could barely understand it. Taz's fast, soft American had been difficult enough.

"Holly, Mike, this is Chen Mei-Li. Mei-Li, tell them what you told me."

This was too many people. She needed a scalpel, not a hammer.

Taz, rather than encouraging her, said, "You tell 'em or I do. Your call."

Was she trapped, or was this her best chance? She had decided to trust Taz, and now she must. Mei-Li repeated what she'd said, leaving out any reference to the crashed helicopter.

43

"You said something about Taiwan." Drake wished he was at the crash, but he could hear what practical Lizzy would say, *What do you know about helicopter crashes?*

Not a damned thing.

He'd never actually seen Miranda's team work in the field before, but all the wishing that he could even observe now wasn't going to make Ru go away.

His duty and his problem was sitting across from him.

Their table was encapsulated in a strange, living bubble of privacy as the first wave of people drifted away from the fence line and a second wave pushed forward, all flowing around them in a constantly moving stream.

"With Hong Kong managed—" Ru forced Drake's attention away from the crash.

"Repressed and trapped behind your abusive national security laws that fully violate the 'one country, two systems' principle that was agreed to—"

"By men now dead," Ru put in.

"Because your present leaders permanently and aggressively retired them all."

"Deng himself was old and died of Parkinson's. Others?" Ru shrugged and laughed. "I like you, Drake. I always like you."

"For fuck's sake, why?"

"For that. You and Ru," he tapped his own chest. "We both patriots. Both fighters. Damn diplomacy! Bring out the guns!" He thumped a fist on the table that threatened to topple their beers. Ru had finished his own and swept up Mei-Li's untouched one.

If Drake had a gun at the moment, he'd...start an international crisis by murdering a member of the CMC on American soil. He knew that Ru was playing some game, but he'd be damned if he was going to play along.

"Focus. Taiwan." Drake was unsure which of them he was lecturing.

"Yes. We own Taiwan. Everyone agrees."

"Except for twenty-four million Taiwanese."

"Even they do not dare deny our unity openly."

"Only by staging the kind of protests that you people are experts at suppressing everywhere else."

Lizzy placed a hand on his arm, as lightly as he'd touched Miranda—before Holly slapped him for it. Whatever Miranda's strange reaction had been, Drake found the touch calming. Lizzy's touch was always soothing, and it seemed to sap enough of his anger that he could think clearly.

He was the Chairman of the Joint Chiefs. Losing his temper wasn't an option. Yet there was something about Ru that burrowed under his skin every time. Miranda's team and the US Air Force were dealing with the crash. Which meant it was left to him to deal with Ru.

"So, let us two warriors make world peace. But don't hurry too much. I enjoy much staring at your lovely general. She is much better for looking at than you. Or me." Ru laughed aloud at his own joke.

Drake could see by the set of Lizzy's jaw that he himself wasn't the only one Ru pissed off.

Maybe he should step out of the way, and see what happened when Lizzy went off the leash on the cocky bastard.

44

"What the hell is going on up there?"

Jeremy looked up. A team of ten parachutists had deployed Air Force blue-and-white chutes and were presently creating interlocking spirals of red, white, and blue smoke in the sky.

He looked down toward whoever had shouted up at him.

Mike had suggested the rescue team park the line of emergency vehicles between the shattered helicopter and the crowd, mostly blocking their view as the injured were tended. The officer in charge had liked the idea.

From Jeremy's vantage atop the fuselage, he was the only one who could see over the tops of the Oshkosh 3000 Striker fire trucks. Service trucks were also pulled up close because, while the Chinook's landing gear had survived the hard use, all three of the left-side tires had blown. A team was already replacing them, then the chassis could be towed out of sight.

He could see Miranda rushing around with the others below, attempting to photograph and catalog everything before it was removed.

It took him a moment to spot the woman glaring up at him from the crowd below. She wore a flightsuit and had captain's bars.

"I think they're doing a parachute show," he pointed up at them soaring above the field.

"I know they're doing a goddamn parachute show. What are *you* doing?"

Oh, right. Mr. Literal strikes again. "I'm trying to understand how your helicopter was sabotaged."

"How it was—*what?*"

In moments, the woman had ascended the kick-in steps just forward of the rear-mounted engines and hurried along the length of the fuselage's battered top to him. She crowded so close that he almost stepped backward off the narrow, flat inspection spot.

She grabbed his arm until she was sure he was stable. He glanced at her name badge. Captain Smithey.

Thankfully, Miranda had overheard and come up as well.

"We haven't even defined the debris perimeter yet," she protested as soon as she arrived.

He knew that Miranda liked to approach her investigations in stepwise fashion from the outside in but—

"I saw it, Miranda. While we were eating. I saw the rotor blade drop abruptly, then slam into the fuselage. Because of centrifugal stiffening, that shouldn't have happened. The only thing I could think of was that the pitch link had failed."

"That would allow the blade to free float."

"Precisely. And since the helicopter was backing up at the time—"

"There would be just enough impetus to down-pitch the

blade. And because it was spinning, the droop stops would have been retracted."

"And from there, the result was inevitable. It does fit with the—"

"—forces necessary to induce the roll without destroying the—"

"Wait. Stop!" The captain held out her hands palm up. "You two sound like the same person debating with each other."

"No," Jeremy glanced at the name stitched on the pilots flightsuit. "No, Captain Smithey. I'm male. She's female."

"Right," Miranda agreed.

"Oh my God! Look..." the captain took a deep breath and let it out slowly "...why did *you*—" she pointed at Jeremy's own chest "—say sabotage?"

Jeremy pointed at the pitch link. It was still attached—at least half of it was—atop the waist-high turret of the forward rotor.

"What am I looking at?"

"The pitch link. It's basically a glorified turnbuckle that allows the swash plate to shift the rotor blade's angle of attack. That in turn—"

"I know what a goddamn pitch link does."

Of course she would.

Miranda hadn't been wearing her vest, it was back in the van along with all the tools in his field pack. But she still reached into her slacks pocket and pulled out a small jeweler's loop magnifying glass.

Jeremy definitely had to do that himself in the future—a few critical tools that were never off his person. Maybe cargo pants...or a hip pouch.

Miranda inspected the stub of the pitch link carefully through the magnifying glass, then nodded.

"Let me see that." The captain took the magnifier from Miranda and did her own inspection.

When she didn't say anything, Jeremy wondered if she had the training to interpret what she was seeing. Maybe it would be better if he helped her out.

"Do you see how most of the break is completely smooth? Only a small portion of the metal shows brittle breakage. That's a cut, with a very sharp saw."

"Thirty-two teeth per inch," Miranda agreed. "You can see the last line of scarification."

Still without speaking, Captain Smithey stood up slowly, returned the magnifier to Miranda, then stared up at the sky.

Jeremy looked up, but the last of the parachutists was down. For the moment, the sky was clear.

"I was supposed to start my routine with a zoom climb to fifteen hundred feet, hammerhead stall, and after three of those, I'd do a spiral descent."

"If you had, you'd be dead right now." Seeing the dead woman in the dirt atop Hurricane Ridge yesterday made the image uncomfortably real.

"Yes, I would."

"That would be a bad thing. I had a friend who was dead recently—at least for a while. It was a *very* bad thing."

Captain Smithey looked at him strangely, but his own words had reminded him of Taz for the first time since he'd tackled her and rolled her under the table for safety during the Chinook's crash.

He looked around, fearing she might have disappeared again.

But then he saw her by the gap in the fence with Mike,

Holly, and a young Chinese woman not much taller than she was. Good. He really didn't want her to be dead again.

When he waved, she hesitated, but then waved back.

Captain Smithey pulled out her phone.

Whoever she was dialing didn't answer.

"Bob, Debbie here. Call me the instant you get this."

She dialed again.

"Velma, medics clear you?...Good! That's great. Now find Bob Wang. He—...What do you mean, he just walked out of the hangar and disappeared? Find him now! Crash priority. I don't care whose toes you step on. He's not answering. Start with tracing his phone. If anyone knows who attacked the *Princess Jennie,* he'll be the one on top of it....Yeah, attacked. Someone on his team is a saboteur."

45

A SHRILL RINGING DRAGGED HIM BACK FROM SOMEWHERE.

Another ring.

Not church bells. They wouldn't have church bells in Hell, would they? Definitely where he was bound.

A phone.

He was so tired. So cold.

It stopped ringing.

Only slowly did he decide that he wasn't dead.

But he was wet. Around his neck, down his cheek.

In his hand, on his chest, lay the hard, warm metal of a gun.

Right.

He'd shot himself.

Shot himself and somehow missed. Trying to move his jaw sent a slash of pain across the whole right side of his face. He didn't have the energy to scream. The shot had gone in under the chin. Must have exited out through the cheek.

Cold.

Except for the slow, warm streams of blood leaking out of him.

The phone chimed that he had a message. Good luck with that.

He'd bleed out soon.

Fine with him.

He wasn't sure he could find the energy or motivation to shoot himself again.

Maybe he could.

But it was a relief that he wouldn't have to.

46

THE CROWD DISPERSED TO THE FOOD BOOTHS—SUDDENLY thirsty from seeing the crash.

Drake could see that they had towed the battered Chinook out of view and cleared most of the emergency vehicles. All that remained were a small crane, a dump truck, and a field of debris.

Miranda's team had assembled into a line and were slowly sweeping back and forth across the accident area. Ru's grandniece along with Taz—didn't know what to think about her sudden return from the dead—stood to one side watching the others as they moved along with all the deft precision of a parade ground review.

Three steps, stop, survey both forward and behind them, then three more. Each area they covered, the cleanup crew followed close behind. The Chinook's remains were rapidly disappearing from the field.

If only Ru would do the same. Instead, he remained stubbornly real. Drake flagged the airman who'd been guarding the gap over and pointed to the star-cracked slab of windshield that had flattened one of the chairs a few tables away. "Let the cleanup team know this is here, too."

He saluted and took care of it.

"Taiwan." Drake turned back to Ru and cut him off in mid-rhapsody to Lizzy about the flavors of Chinese stout beers versus the weak showing of American beers.

"He always cares not but business," Ru tried to engage Lizzy again. By her pleasant smile and narrowed eyes, Drake estimated Ru was under ten seconds from engaging a fist to his chin.

"Taiwan, Ru."

He had the decency to look uncomfortable.

"Someday we will take Taiwan. Why do you struggle against it? You Americans barely care about it anymore."

Which was both true and false. The US had agreed that there was only one China and cut diplomatic ties with Taiwan, including having them no longer recognized as a separate country by most of the world, including the UN. However, the US sold billions of dollars of arms to Taiwan under the hand-waving of "in better defense of China's outer island chain." The fact that all of that weaponry was pointed toward the mainland was Taiwan's choice, not the United States'—technically.

"We have *not* forgotten about Taiwan, but don't *you* forget about the Japanese."

Ru's glance toward Lizzy was fast and angry, but he covered it quickly. "Well, this lovely Japanese may have conquered you, Drake, but China is another matter."

Drake wondered how much self restraint it took Lizzy to not kick Ru in the balls.

And they all knew that China couldn't ignore them, especially not over the Taiwan issue.

Japan's Navy could turn from defense to offense in a matter of minutes. He'd once witnessed just how fast. So quickly that he'd barely kept North Korea from being wiped off the face of the Earth last year. Couldn't have even done *that* without Miranda's help.

And Japan could become the world's tenth nuclear power within hours—everything poised at the ready except for some final assembly...if his reports were accurate. Otherwise, they already had a secret stockpile.

"There's still the Taiwanese. They dropped thirteen billion into the military last year. That places them in the top thirty militaries worldwide."

"Is there that," Ru admitted, and sipped his beer as if China didn't care about so trivial a number. Against China's quarter of a trillion, he did have a point.

The airshow burst back to life as the Air Force Thunderbirds screamed by low overhead with no warning. One moment not there, the next everyone covering their ears in surprise.

He was amused that no one in Miranda's team so much as looked up.

Lizzy, however, had a look of longing on her face like he'd rarely seen. He reached out and took her hand, which she squeezed hard but didn't look away.

During a brief silence, or at least a less deafening moment, he asked, "Did you ever try out?"

She shook her head and followed the diamond formation doing a twisting vertical climb that he didn't know the name of.

"Chicken?"

She shook her head. "I wasn't good enough."

"Are you kidding me? You've got serious medals; I've seen them in your office. You were the leader of an entire flight."

She looked down from the aircraft, and he felt like a heel for breaking in on her enjoyment of the moment.

"Look at them."

He looked around, but during his moment of inattention, they'd disappeared again.

"Not the Thunderbirds. Look at Miranda and her people."

They were all huddled around something on the ground.

"They're all very skilled. Even your nephew Jon."

"Okay." He'd had proof that Jon was more than skilled, Miranda had accepted him as the Air Force liaison on a number of incidents—high praise indeed.

"And then there's Miranda."

"Oh." He got it now.

"These pilots are past the level where mere excellence becomes art. I was very, very skilled in the air, but I was never an artist."

She turned her attention upward once more.

Less than a second later, two jets came screaming in from either end of the runway. Closing fast, they were headed straight for each other. At the last instant, so close it seemed impossible they wouldn't collide, they each rotated sideways so that they were belly-to-belly for just an instant in a knife-edge pass, then they were racing past each other and gone.

"How close did they just come?" He had to shout over the thundering roar that slapped in a second after their passage.

"Under twenty feet. About half of their wingspan. At a closing rate of a thousand miles an hour."

Numbers like that just made him dizzy. Drake left Lizzy to her airshow, turning to Ru and the Taiwan problem.

But Ru also was gazing aloft with a look of longing not all that unlike Lizzy's. Right. He'd been a pilot forty years ago during the Sino-Vietnamese War.

Drake had read hundreds of reports on the "Taiwan Problem" over the years. It wasn't an issue of ownership...mostly.

It *was* a matter of defense and commerce. The outer island chain of Japan, South Korea (cut off from the mainland by North Korea effectively made it an island), Taiwan, and the Philippines controlled much of China's access to global commerce. All sides were well aware of the balance of power, and what it would mean if the connecting pin of Taiwan actually disappeared back into the PRC's control.

Was Ru warning him of an imminent move against Taiwan?

Maybe if Drake retired tomorrow, he wouldn't have to face another war as Chairman. Not that he'd trust anyone else to avoid it.

The law legally stated that there was One Country, Two Systems. But no one other than the PRC actually wanted the one country. And, as they'd just proven with Hong Kong, the PRC didn't view the two-systems concept as a worthwhile long-term scenario.

"If our President were holy man," Ru looked down at Drake, then waved his beer like a Catholic priest scattering holy water over a crowd, "he might say he had divine right to rule the One Country, *One* System. He made himself President-for-life but he feels his age. Before he dies, he feels must do this. Must break the outer island chain and take Taiwan in his fist."

Drake was eight years younger than China's President,

and he *himself* was feeling his age. Not that he had any aspirations to conquer the occasional country; though there were a few governments he wouldn't mind stamping out of existence. Ten fewer suppressive, authoritarian regimes and eighty percent of his stress would be gone.

And if China was one of those, he wouldn't be sorry.

Ru leaned in close as Lizzy's jets roared by close overhead.

"We can *not* let him be doing this."

Drake could only stare at Zhang Ru in surprise. He couldn't have heard that correctly.

Ru smiled brightly, leaned back comfortably in his plastic chair, then he toasted his beer toward the field.

The jets so loud a moment before had once again raced away.

The only thing on the field was Miranda's team. Except for a single piece of hardware that Jeremy was carrying over his shoulder like a club, all of the debris had been cleared.

He looked back at Ru.

What the *hell* was he being so happy about?

47

Taz watched the approaching team. The team that she wasn't a member of, even if Miranda had told Drake Nason that she was.

Besides, she knew nothing of crash investigations. The only crashes she knew about in any detail were the three she'd been a part of. And she didn't know much about those except that she'd survived two of them when the odds said she shouldn't have.

Mei-Li had only had time to tell Mike and Holly the barest bones of Zhang Ru's and the CMC's vulnerability. Before they had a chance to confer, Jeremy had found something at the forward rotor head, and everyone went running.

Except her, because she still didn't know any more about site investigations than she had ten minutes ago.

Mei-Li had begged for their silence until she could tell them more.

Taz was actually impressed that Holly hadn't hunted down Ru right away and beat the shit out of him for what he'd done to Mei-Li herself. That was completely aside from the brutal political manipulations she'd managed to verify.

The fact that Drake had taken him away into the crowd was probably all that saved his life.

Holly and Mike returned to them while Miranda, Andi, and Jeremy continued on to the fence line with the piece they were carrying. Major Jon Swift had followed the broken Chinook as it was towed away.

All six Thunderbirds raced over the runway in a delta group. Now that the clean-up crews were off the field, they passed by just a hundred feet up with an ear-splitting roar. Only after they'd passed did she realize they were all upside down as they did it.

Holly yelled at Mei-Li as soon as she arrived. "You're saying that Zhang Ru did all of that? Why I can't kill him right now?"

Mei-Li's voice was drowned out by the Lead Solo pilot breaking from the formation and returning to fly a continuous twisting roll down the entire length of the runway.

"Try that again," Holly was up on her toes, poised for action.

"If you kill him, then we do not get to destroy the Central Military Commission," Mei-Li's voice was as small and delicate as she was, and shouting out the whole sentence left her breathless.

Holly didn't ease back.

Mike rested a hand on her shoulder.

Holly slammed him to the grass so hard he could only grunt. Taz didn't even have time to jump back despite him landing on her toes; Holly was just that fast.

With her feet trapped by Mike's weight, Taz fell to her butt on the grass.

"Oh, shit, Mike," Holly knelt down beside him. "I thought you knew not touch me when I'm like that. I'm so... sorry." The last word appeared to pain her.

48

"Sabotage," Jeremy thumped the pitch-varying housing down on the plastic table. Maybe he did it a little hard because the table groaned as if in pain. He could definitely sympathize. Why was it always Holly who got to be with Taz?

Instead, it had somehow become his job to show off the sabotage just because he'd uncovered it.

Drake was staring at the metal housing as if it might attack him. Maybe because it was upside-down. That's the orientation Jeremy had found it in, rammed into the dirt where the helicopter had rolled over on its back and snapped it off.

He flipped it right-side up.

Still nothing. Oh right. General Drake Nason had been an Army Ranger, not a helo pilot.

Jeremy spoke quickly, before Andi (who *had* been a helo pilot) could take that away from him as well.

"Okay. The rotor blade attaches here and the other end is anchored to the rotor head."

Then he lifted and lowered the pitch arm a few times. "See, as this raises and lowers, it changes the pitch angle on the rotor blade by rolling it up or down. The amount of change is controlled by a fitting called a pitch link. It's this little rod that's dangling here. Except that's only half of it."

He patted his pockets until he felt Andi pull it out of his back pants pocket. She handed it to him, rather than using it as an opportunity to jump in. He could only look at her in surprise.

She mouthed, "What?"

Maybe he was making assumptions about her trying to take his place. Maybe he should try just talking to her...but not until after he'd talked to Taz.

He turned back to Drake, Lizzy, and the old Chinese man.

"This," he held it up, "is the other half of the lifter, the part that was still attached to the swash plate that controls the angle of all three rotor blades. Except it was no longer one piece. As Captain Smithey applied back control on the cyclic to taxi backward, it caused two of the blades to twist—angle the leading edge upward—into a stronger lift mode. The third one, with the broken lifter link, didn't. Instead, it remained neutral and the helicopter backed into it. The catastrophic failure was assured from that moment."

"Who the hell would do something like that?"

Jeremy looked at Drake, "Debbie, Captain Smithey, said she knew who would know."

"Where is she?"

He looked around but didn't see her anywhere.

49

At Velma's call, Captain Debbie Smithey raced to the nearest hangar. The first vehicle she reached was a Striker airport fire engine.

She climbed up the short ladder into the passenger side of the monster eight-wheeled vehicle.

"Hey, you can't be in here," the driver, a senior airman—*Christ but they got younger every day*—was filling out a logbook.

"Drive!"

"Where? I'd need to check with the sergeant, he—"

"See these?" she tapped her captain's bars.

"Yes…"

"Now fucking drive before I shoot your ass."

When he didn't, she yanked her sidearm.

She didn't have to point it at him, he started moving plenty fast.

The cockpit could seat five: driver, engineer, fire control, and two observers. The Striker had a bumper sprayer and a boom arm with a nozzle folded up on top of the vehicle.

Forty-five feet long and carrying twenty tons of water and foam, it was lacking the one thing she needed most—speed.

"South. Step on it." She holstered her sidearm and yanked out her phone. Velma had sent her the locator information on Bob Wang's phone, and it was hell-and-gone from anywhere it should have been. Deep in the woods of the Army's practice ranges.

"It tops out at seventy-five and I'm not yet trained to exceed—"

"Just do it!" She directed him off the end of the runway access road. A left along a rugged dirt one-lane, then a right onto a track that had probably been here since the goddamn Lewis and Clark Expedition.

The Striker's big tires rolled over it all easily.

"Down."

The driver eased over the edge into a narrow valley with all the verve of a doddering geriatric.

"Cross the river."

The truck made far easier work of it than the driver.

"What the hell *are* they teaching you kids these days? How to run up a paved runway? Trust me, you get out in the field and it's way the hell worse than this. Why do you think they made these things to climb sixty-percent grades, and be stable side-crossing a thirty-degree slope? Crashes don't always happen on pretty runways. Now drive like someone's life depends on it." The moment she said it, she felt a cold chill slide up her spine.

The airman drove a little better after that, just enough better to keep her from screaming in frustration.

The last track they were on was more like a rabbit trail than a path. The steel plate under the sloped nose battered a path into the trees.

"Here. Stop here."

Unable to force open her door jammed against the forest's branches, she pushed out through the top escape hatch. Sliding down the sloped windshield, Debbie landed on her feet in the middle of the trail.

Nothing.

She checked her phone again. According to the locator, she should be practically standing on Bob's phone.

Debbie signaled the airmen to cut the Striker's engine, and the big diesel thudded into silence. Not a sound. Not even birdsong.

A Thunderbird shattered the silence, sweeping wide on one of its turns.

Nothing remained that she could hear.

But then she smelled it.

There was just enough of a breeze to clear away the lingering remnants of the Striker's exhaust, and she could smell the iron tang of nightmares.

"Oh, shit!"

She scouted for the smell's origin.

Blood on the air.

Lots of it.

Bob Wang was well hidden, but she finally located him by almost stepping on his face.

What was left of it.

His pulse was so weak that she had trouble finding it.

Debbie called Velma to mobilize the battalion's CSAR bird.

"No! There's no time for the hassle of aborting the Thunderbirds airshow. We're the goddamn Night Stalkers. I don't care if they scrape off all the paint by sliding through the treetops. Get their asses here now! We'll worry about violating TFRs some other day." Temporary Flight Restrictions for a stupid airshow be damned.

And, being Night Stalkers, they'd gotten it done.

She did what she could with the Striker's first aid kit and her limited knowledge. It *seemed* like it was enough. That thready beat was still there at his throat by the time a medic had winched down through the trees from the Black Hawk —it was more than she'd expected to achieve with how much blood there was.

They all winched up together: her, the medic, and Bob Wang in the wire litter.

"What the hell am I supposed to do now?" the Striker's airman called after her.

Like she gave a shit.

The medic went to work on him right away as the pilots turned them for the short race to Madigan Army Medical Center.

Bob slowly regained consciousness, though the medic was shaking his head.

"What?" She kept her voice to a whisper.

"Too much blood loss. I'm pumping more into him, but his organs have pretty much shut down." His grimace said just how terminal a diagnosis that was, even if she didn't know how to read the screen he was pointing at.

"Debbie?" Bob's voice was vague and wandering. Her name would be incomprehensible through his shattered jaw if it hadn't been her own.

"Right here, Bob." She rested her hand on his shoulder and ignored the amount of blood that squeezed out of his uniform as she did so.

"You...okay?"

"Yes, Bob."

"Good," with a terribly long U sound and hardly any D at all.

The next thing she heard was the high, steady tone of the alarm on his heart monitor.

She rocked back on her heels to get clear as the medic tried jumpstarting his heart with the shock paddles.

No question about who had sabotaged her helo, though for the life of her she couldn't imagine why.

For an answer, all she had was the alarm tone of a flatline.

50

The American Thunderbirds did some final noisy aerobatics, then swooped in to land. Finally, they would have peace to speak until the next segment of the airshow began. Though Ru would miss watching the longing in General Gray's face.

They shared that combat pilot's pain, watching others fly. It made him like her more than he'd have thought possible of a *xiao riben guizi.*

Drake shooed everyone except his wife and the Chase woman off to a nearby table. He could hear them talking about the crash, as if that's what was important. Taking her to Wang Bob's last night had been a fine test of Mei-Li's loyalty. No, not her loyalty, her level of fear.

It was important that after declaring her new independence by coming to America, she witnessed the power he could still wield over her—even if she was in America. Good! If she dared reveal him, he had another move to protect himself. It was good that he didn't need it this time.

Ru eyed the new arrival carefully.

This Miranda Chase looked about as exciting as a mouse. Small, disheveled brown hair, no standout features at all.

"To avoid more surprises," Drake was unreadably calm, which was far more dangerous than when he was snarling like a wild dog. "Ms. Chase is the one who solved your Gyrfalcon problem. She's our absolute best crash investigator."

Ru looked at her again. Still a mouse—a highly intelligent one. And perhaps a useful one?

No time to find that out now. The report some minion had made to Drake that they'd found the helicopter mechanic meant he was fast running out of time. He'd rather hoped that the man had the good sense to become permanently lost.

"The Gyrfalcon?" That bit of insight had launched him onto the CMC. "If that is true, Ms. Chase, I give you present." He picked up his phone, swept the character *Zǒu* and pressed send. "I have telled a friend to 'Go'—maybe not a friend, but he will go if he cares about wife and daughter. You now go also."

She didn't ask where. He couldn't even be sure if she was paying attention. Instead she was staring so hard at his left shoulder that he brushed at it to make sure nothing was there.

Not an intelligent mouse. A blank-faced one. This was an American best? That seemed unlikely.

"She's not moving without my instruction. Where is she supposed to go?" Drake was toying with his empty beer glass as if he couldn't care.

"Drake, my friend, are you now simple in head? What do

we speak of all this time? To Taiwan! There will be a crash there. Very pretty Chinese plane. *Mighty Dragon.* You call the J-20 a *Black Eagle,* yes? Though I not know why; *Mighty Dragon* is very good name. Very lucky. I give this information as good will. Good will? Yes? To prove niceness to you. You have twelve hours."

He could see the avarice on Drake's face. Yes, the Americans would like to see that very much. Even just the scraps from a crash. The only thing they would like more was the new J-31 *Gyrfalcon,* but that they would not be seeing.

"Twelve hours?" Drake just shook his head. "We couldn't get her team there that quickly even if we wanted to."

Ru pointed at the big cargo planes parked along the left side of the show area. "You put her and people in plane. And you fly."

"Do you think I'm stupid, Ru? If I fly a US Air Force C-17A Globemaster III cargo jet into Taipei International, you're going to turn right around and make a media spectacle out of the US interfering in Chinese politics."

Ru made a show of looking at his watch. "It will crash with or with not your peoples there. If they are not, the Taiwanese will take it. Then one of our people tell our agents in Taiwan quickly to destroy any evidence."

"You're a cold-blooded bastard, Ru."

"Yes." And Drake had best remember that.

Drake opened his mouth but, before he could say anything, the mouse woman spoke for the first time.

"A 767-300ERF, the Extended Range Freighter, is what's needed. It is six thousand and seventy-four miles, that's nautical miles (eleven thousand two hundred and forty-nine kilometers), from SeaTac to Taipei Songshan Airport. It has the advantage over Taipei Taoyuan Airport in that it also services their Air Force if we need any specialized equipment. Such a distance is safely within the range limit of a Boeing 767-300ERF if it travels below a sixty percent load. It would be lower profile than flying a military or even a special commercial flight. It would also allow us to retrieve key components up to three-point-four by four-point-three meters without any specialized transport. Assuming an unlikely hundred percent recovery of the crashed aircraft, an unfueled Chengdu J-20 weighs approximately six thousand kilograms less than the 767's maximum load capacity. Therefore, there is no limitation there either."

Ru hadn't seen the woman consult her phone or anything else.

Then she turned to face him. "You should be ashamed of yourself, General Zhang. Ordering a crash."

What simple world did this woman live in?

Drake didn't look surprised, though perhaps puzzled. "The US Air Force doesn't have any unmarked Boeing 767 freighters."

Drake's Jap, who'd already been smiling during the mouse's recitation, began laughing quietly to herself like the devil she probably was.

"What?" Ru's words echoed Drake's. At least he wasn't the only one who didn't understand what was so funny.

Gray opened her mouth, but again this Miranda mouse spoke over her as if she was the one who was in charge.

"We need a helicopter. Right now." She stood up and signaled her team, waiting at the other table. In a heartbeat they were all on their feet and moving. "We'll get our packs from the van. Drake, please go and speak with the pilots. We'll be ready in two minutes. They will need at least three."

"The pilots? The pilots of what?"

Miranda Chase simply pointed at the Black Hawk that was on display in the middle of the crowd.

"Wait!" Drake rose to his feet, but his wife stopped him with a hand on his arm.

"Miranda is perfectly correct. And it's an ideal cover." She pulled out her phone, looked up a number, and began dialing.

"What is?"

"Go," she made shooing motions at Drake toward the Black Hawk helicopter. Like he was *her* servant.

Ru would never let a woman treat him that way.

Then someone answered her phone call.

"Hello, FedEx? Do you have one of your 767 freighters parked at SeaTac airport at the moment? You do? Excellent. This is General Elizabeth Drake of the National Reconnaissance Office. ...No, I don't need a satellite moved at this time. ...No, nor a launch vehicle. What I do need is the plane fully fueled in fifteen minutes. I want to move a small team across the Pacific overnight. And they'll be returning with a highly classified cargo within twenty-four hours. Yes, I'll hold."

Drake slapped his forehead, then hustled toward the Black Hawk.

Ru decided that all Americans were completely insane. But he liked this *xiao riben guizi* more with each passing minute.

51

Mei-Li had been abandoned at the table with no warning.

One moment, they were questioning her closely about the types of information she had on Ru and the CMC. The next, the little woman at Ru and Drake's table had merely risen to her feet and raised a hand. Taz had squeezed her shoulder briefly, and an instant later Mei-Li sat alone.

They moved with an undeniable eagerness to follow her.

People followed General Zhang Ru from fear.

But the brown-haired woman wielded *true* power.

Ru came from the other table, leaving the lone woman on the phone. He then led her from the airshow back to the parking lot. They went against the general flow of the crowds watching old planes—so old they might have been from World War II—buzz by loudly overhead.

Over her shoulder, she saw a security team clearing a wide circle around the helicopter next to the one she'd sat in earlier. Its rotors slowly turned to life. Only Holly—who had the most aggressive questions—was visible by her gold hair as the team hurried over to it. Mei-Li lost sight of them in the crowd.

"It is good that we have an understanding, Mei-Li."

Ru's pleasure worried her. She needed to know what he'd said to the Chairman of the Joint Chiefs, but had been unable to leave the table under the barrage of questions.

"You and Chang Mui may have your fun at the American university. I will let you know when I need something done here in America. Yes. That is good. Very good."

"Yes, Uncle. We have a good understanding."

When questioned, she had withheld many things about Ru, including his responsibility for the sabotage of the Chinook helicopter. By keeping them focused on the destruction of the Central Military Commission, they had worked together on ideas about how to destroy them.

It was a long way from possible—yet.

But now she had more hope than she'd felt since her gymnastics coach had selected her at nine years old to also receive his personalized "training."

"Yes, Uncle. A very good understanding."

52

"Where's Jon?"

Miranda looked around but didn't see him.

In moments everyone was looking, which wasn't terribly constructive. There was not very much to see.

Then she recalled that he hadn't been on the Black Hawk for the short jaunt from JBLM to SeaTac's FedEx terminal either.

Still everyone was looking around.

The inside of the FedEx Boeing 767-300ERF was cavernous. Stripped to the hull, only a steel deck divided the long tube of the airfreighter's fuselage into upper and lower cargo storage. The upper two-thirds of the hull made a very empty tube.

The hull's interior was finished with white-painted aluminum. The eighteen hundred square feet of cargo deck was interrupted only by the tracks of the automated cargo handling system that could safely transport twenty-four containers. Holly could park her Corvette eight times from nose-to-tail down the length of the plane, and eight more beside those.

For this flight, there was only a simple pallet that had been attached at the very front of the bay, close behind the cockpit's rear wall. On it were eight chairs in two facing rows of four, a small cooler of drinks and snacks, and a headset system so that they could talk among themselves—sound insulation was not a priority in the 767's cargo bay. A tiny toilet was available in the cockpit.

But only six of the seats were occupied: herself and Andi, Mike and Holly, and Jeremy across from Taz. The other two seats were empty.

The noise level increased sharply as they accelerated to takeoff from SeaTac. The CF6-80C2 engines, the second-most powerful in the class, practically hurled the empty aircraft down the runway. It was impressive what a difference it made not having the normal forty-seven tons of payload aboard.

Holly finally barked out a laugh. "Jon said he was going to do the paperwork on the crashed Chinook at the airshow. Got his ass left behind."

Miranda was unsure what Holly found funny about the situation.

"Perhaps it's just as well," Mike tipped his chair back now that they were airborne. "Having an Air Force major along might have caused problems at Taiwan security."

Holly laughed again. "How about a dead colonel? Thoughts, Colonel Cortez?" she saluted Taz sharply with a palm-out, Australian Army gesture.

Taz didn't return the salute. Miranda thought officers always did. Maybe because they'd been in different services, Taz didn't feel it was necessary? Perhaps, being still technically dead and no longer Colonel Cortez, she didn't feel the need to. Or—

"Oh my God! She's right. I can't be here. We've got to turn around. I'll jeopardize the whole mission. I don't have a passport that says I'm a civilian."

Miranda knew how to manage that.

She pulled out the phone that she'd already synced to the onboard wireless system.

53

CLARISSA REESE'S PHONE RANG SHARPLY IN THE HOTEL ROOM. If she ever unleashed a magic genie from its lamp, her first wish would be to turn the damn thing off. But, as the Director of the CIA, it wasn't an option for her to ever be fully out of touch.

Her assistant knew to block all calls for a few hours. Either the world was coming apart or it was from one of the few who had her direct number.

She dug for her phone; it had better not be Clark. He never understood that just because he was Vice President and she'd married him, it didn't mean he could interrupt her whenever he was feeling bored.

This was the last Friday of the month, time for her very low profile monthly dinner meeting in the Presidential Suite at the Kimpton George by the Capitol Building. Originally the night that Senator Ramson, the Chairman of the Senate Armed Services Committee, reserved the suite to spend the night fucking his wife, it now began with a strategy meeting over dinner for the three of them.

Rose Ramson, a former Miss Utah, might be the body beside the man, but Clarissa had learned that for four decades Rose had also been the brains behind his success. She knew exactly how to lead the senator where they both needed him to go—by his dick.

These meetings were sometimes just a pleasant dinner and friendly gossip about the Washington, DC, elite. Other nights were very...useful. It was still unclear which way tonight's conversations might fall.

She'd adopted Rose's idea for Clark. They stayed in their home, because nothing compared with the Vice President's Victorian home...except the White House, of course. But she made the first Friday of each month an occasion with "naked chef" dinners, though the food was all catered of course, and an entire night of sex. It had become a cornerstone of their rather active sex life. For an older man, his stamina was very pleasantly impressive.

However, when Clarissa saw who was calling, she excused herself from the dinner table.

She could feel the senator eyeing her, but Miranda Chase of the NTSB was a true wild card in a world that ran best on predictability. Clarissa preferred that neither of the Ramsons overheard until she knew what this was.

Clarissa knew one thing as she locked herself in the suite's bathroom, checked herself in the mirror, and answered the phone.

"Where's the crash this time, Miranda?"

"There isn't one."

"Are you stealing another plane?" That was still a major embarrassment. Clarissa had offered only minimal support to a mission led by Miranda's team last year. Against all odds, they proceeded to pull off one of the greatest intelligence coups in recent years, and the CIA had gotten absolutely no part of it. Everything they'd captured had been compartmentalized inside the NRO. The Director of National Intelligence had backed them up—and Clarissa got nothing.

"Not exactly. Further information is classified."

Crap! Experience had taught her that Miranda was a true stalwart, and gave away absolutely nothing under such conditions.

"I need a passport."

"You don't have a passport?"

"Of course, I have a passport. I never know where a crash is going to be, or where the NTSB will need me."

Clarissa closed her eyes for a moment. Talking to Miranda was like walking into a goddamn minefield. How many different ways could Miranda call her an idiot without ever changing her tone?

She knew about Miranda's absurdly logical autism, which meant that none of what she said was passive-aggressive. It only felt that way—every damn time.

"You need a passport," Clarissa approached the topic carefully.

"Yes." Miranda didn't say anything else. Wouldn't think to.

"Not for you."

"We already established that."

Clarissa sighed. "Then for whom?"

"I need it in the name of Tasia Flores. We need it to be delivered to the FedEx terminal at Taipei Songshan Airport in eleven hours and forty-three minutes." She then read out a social security number.

"An actual US citizen? That shouldn't be a problem."

Damn! She didn't have any useful agents in Taiwan at the moment. Clarissa tried to think of who she could get there fast enough to find out what was going on—and came up blank.

Her chief of station at the American Institute in Taiwan, the only semi-official diplomatic channel the US had there, was an institution. He'd been there forever, was completely reliable, and had all the subtlety of a rock. How in the hell he'd survived so long in the CIA was beyond her. Probably because Clark and the others before her couldn't be bothered to replace him. Just as she hadn't.

There was a whispered conversation in the background.

"Oh. It will apparently need a new photo. We'll send you the photograph to use right now."

Clarissa waited, but Miranda didn't say anything else. Finally, Clarissa pulled the phone away from her ear to look at it.

Miranda had disconnected without another word.

Then her phone buzzed sharply.

Clarissa tapped to open the image—and was staring at the face of Colonel Vicki Cortez.

She had to sit down on the toilet before she fell to the delicately inlaid tile. What was it about men and sex on cold tile? Maybe Rose would know, because it certainly seemed to be a male fantasy and Rose was an expert in those.

She knew it was just shock that was sidetracking her.

Clarissa forced herself to look at the picture again.

Early in her career, when she was still a field agent, she'd crossed General JJ Martinez. He was just Air Force, after all. She was fast-tracking her way into the hierarchy of the CIA.

In response, he'd sent no note.

No report to her supervising officer—she'd been ready for that.

Instead Clarissa had received a visit from then-Lieutenant Vicki "Taser" Cortez. Not once had she raised her voice. Hadn't said a goddamn word other than introducing herself. The little Latina looked like she was twelve and didn't even come up to Clarissa's armpit.

She'd been about to ask how the fuck Cortez had gotten through security at Clarissa's CIA black site in the heart of Afghanistan.

Before she could, the Taser had pulled out a phone, snapped a photo of Clarissa faster than she could blink, tapped a few keys, then turned the phone for Clarissa to see.

It was Clarissa's face. And she was standing in front of a torture victim. She twisted around and saw the bastard Javan's battered face close behind her. She'd looked back at Cortez's phone.

Clarissa's face.

A high-profile torture victim on full display.

A simple caption: *Black Site operator, CIA agent Clarissa Reese.*

The address of her safe house. Even the license number of her car.

It was an e-mail, addressed to the Al Jazeera news site.

She'd be dead within hours of it being sent. Assuming her CIA bosses didn't get to her first.

Still not saying a word, Cortez had simply turned off the phone—without sending the email—and walked away.

It was the only time in her entire career that Clarissa had stared Death directly in the face, and it looked exactly like the woman's image now on her phone.

In Ramson's hotel suite bathroom, Clarissa managed not

to puke up the plank-grilled Pacific Northwest salmon with baby asparagus, though it roiled in her gut. Mostly she resisted because she was suddenly too weak to stand up from the toilet and face it.

Clarissa could deal with Miranda. But Taz?

She knew two things for certain.

One, Colonel Vicki Cortez *was* absolutely and positively dead if anyone thought to ask her.

And two, that Clarissa was going to expedite the passport for one "Tasia Flores" as fast as the CIA could manage, with no questions asked.

By the time she returned to the living room, Senator Ramson was gone.

Rose shrugged, "I think it is going to just be us ladies tonight. He was called away."

"Did he say why?" Clarissa sat back at the table. It was always a pleasure to have some time alone with Rose Ramson. It was just what she needed tonight.

Rose sipped at her wine before replying. "He was being a little more cryptic than usual. Something about a meeting with the Chairman of the Joint Chiefs and the President about Taiwan."

Clarissa wished she was still in the bathroom so that she could put her head between her knees until at least *some* blood had returned to her brain.

54

Taz still held her intercom headset in her lap after Miranda took her picture and sent it to whoever. She turned to Mike, who slid one ear of his own headset aside and leaned close.

"How long does it take?"

"To do what?"

Taz glanced toward Miranda, "To stop underestimating her."

Mike laughed, "The twelfth of never."

She could believe that easily enough.

Mike's kind of skill with people or Holly's fighting speed could be underestimated. But, while impressive, they were the sort of skills that, once understood, ceased to dazzle.

Miranda? Maybe not so much.

Jeremy had some of that, but mostly because he was so humble that he was easy to overlook. Humble? Or maybe he simply didn't know how good he was?

There was no question that he'd saved her life at the airshow when the thick section of bullet-proof helicopter windshield had shattered her chair moments after he'd dragged her out of it. Yet he hadn't said a word about it, might not even realize how exceptional his reaction had been to sweep both her and Miranda to relative safety underneath that table.

Taz caught Jeremy's attention and tipped her head down the long cargo bay.

He didn't get it.

She held two fingers dangling down and made a walking motion.

She could see him say, "Oh," though she couldn't hear it without the headset. It made everyone who was still on the intercom turn to look at him as he unbuckled, stood up, and then was almost thrown to the deck by the cord of his headset.

He carefully removed it as others laughed, then joined her.

Not a whole lot of secrets in this crowd.

They walked toward the rear of the empty cargo bay on non-slip flooring along side-by-side tracks. Between them lay a slippery surface of large ball bearings for the cargo-handling system. It was the first time they'd been alone together since the short walk from Miranda's island hangar to her big house, and she didn't know quite what to say.

"Thank you for saving my life." It sounded awkward and stilted, especially as she had to practically shout it over the engine's roar, but she didn't know how to fix the way it came out.

"When?"

"At the airshow."

"I did?" Then he shrugged. "Okay, you're welcome, I guess."

If he hadn't done it consciously, that meant that he'd tackled her and Miranda to the ground from instinct.

"You're a very odd man, Jeremy Trahn."

"I've been told that before." His grimace said quite how often, but she hadn't meant it that way. She couldn't think of how to fix that either. Nothing in Taz's history had taught her how to deal with a "nice" person.

They reached the back wall of the cargo bay, a blank vertical surface.

Turning, they walked back toward the group.

"How does everyone know the Zhang Ru guy?"

"It was part of a classified mission, our first one with Miranda."

"Classified?"

"Yes, everyone on this team is cleared Top Secret or better. That's why we get the really strange military crash stuff."

"You're cleared Top Secret?"

Jeremy just nodded. As if that was somehow normal.

Then she looked again at the group they were approaching. Andi and Holly were both former Special Operations, so they made sense. Miranda had mentioned her parents had been in the CIA. Mike must have some strange background that she knew nothing about. And Jeremy...

"What do your parents do? Are they still alive?"

"Sure. Engineers at Microsoft. Sister, too."

That didn't strike her as a group that needed high levels of clearance; then she remembered some of the flight simulation software the Air Force used was written on top of Microsoft Flight Simulator, so maybe. Jeremy's comment that he might be able to fake it and fly her away from

Miranda's island because he'd flown flight sim games so much, actually fit.

"Back to Zhang Ru."

"I never saw him before, but I think that Miranda solved a crash for him once."

"For a general on the Chinese Central Military Commission?" She came to a stop at the big cargo door just forward of the wing. She peeked out the tiny circular window set in the door. Nothing much to see except the sun sparkling off the Pacific Ocean. Blue. "Why was he here?"

Again a Jeremy shrug. Wherever Miranda said to go, Jeremy went without question.

She would never... Except she'd done precisely that for nineteen years for General Martinez. He'd taken her anger and honed her into a weapon.

Miranda had taken Jeremy's...what? His passion? And honed it into...excellence?

Sure, right up to the moment when Taz had crushed it out of him aboard the Ghostrider.

He'd been Miranda's supporting Chinook helicopter until, as Mike said, Taz had broken one of his rotor blades.

At least that was Mike's version. Taz was less sure. She might have hurt Jeremy, but he was the one who'd solved the MH-47G Chinook's crash at the airshow—almost as fast as it had happened.

Somehow Jeremy had...grown up.

That was it! Matured from the overeager boy she'd met, but still so reliable that Miranda utterly depended on him.

But it was as if Mike and Holly couldn't see that.

So, Jeremy was Miranda's right hand. Mike was her people skills. Holly and Andi, in addition to being her muscle, were her structural and rotorcraft experts.

"What the hell am I doing here?"

Jeremy quirked a half smile.

"What?"

"Well, a part of me wants to give you a real Miranda answer: You're standing in a FedEx 767's cargo bay."

Taz snorted at the joke. And once she'd started to laugh, she was finding it a little hard to stop. Of all the ludicrous reasons swirling through her brain from Holly and Mike's threats to the twenty-eight hours and nineteen minutes she'd spent with Jeremy, mostly aboard a stolen Ghostrider gunship, it was the only one that she could actually relate to.

"There's that laugh again," Jeremy's smile had changed, gentled.

"What laugh?" But she knew. The one she hadn't found until she'd joined the hotshots. "This one's a little different, Jeremy."

Her laugh before with Max had been a lot less close to the hysterical desperation she felt now.

"But thank you for the reminder. Every little bit helps." She reached enough over the ball bearing track to hug him briefly, but that was too strange. Too real. She pulled back.

When it became clear that neither of them knew what to say next, they returned to their seats.

55

Jeremy donned his headset into the middle of Holly and Mike telling Miranda about Mei-Li's information.

"I don't understand," Miranda spoke up. "What do we have to do with her plans to destroy either General Zhang Ru or the Central Military Commission?"

"They need to fucking go down for the things they've done! Purposely crashing a Chengdu J-20 is one thing, but threatening the lives of the pilot's family to force him to do it? That's just one of a hundred obscenities that Mei-Li told us about." Taz's laugh was nowhere in sight. She sounded viciously angry instead.

Jeremy was less comfortable with this version of her.

Mike made a patting motion and Taz threw herself back into her seat.

"Okay," he offered one of his smiles. "That's the opinion of our F-35 Lightning II fighter."

Taz's dark skin flushed even darker as she stared down at her clenched fists.

"Think of it this way, Miranda." Mike turned to her and

made a globe shape with his hands. "Think of your spheres of influence, except work them from the inside out."

"But that doesn't make any sense. A crash is best understood from the outside in. Weather and terrain first. Then define the outer extent of the debris field, thus restricting the scope of the investigation. Then, only after proceeding through the debris field and the crashed aircraft itself, do we approach your specialty of human factors. That's what makes sense."

Mike didn't have a quick answer.

Jeremy wondered why he would push against something they all knew so well; it was the way that Miranda *had* to approach a crash in order to understand it.

Oh, but not always. Jeremy remembered a few times when—

"Miranda, remember the outer meta-sphere concept. The one on which you can temporarily attach conjecture of plausible causes of a crash without confirming or discarding ideas until more facts were found to support or break the hypothesis."

Miranda's shrug looked more like a chill, despite the well-heated cargo space.

"I have never been comfortable with that methodology of investigation. But," Miranda sighed, "I understand your meaning."

"So," Jeremy played with the idea for a moment, "Ah! Rather than thinking from the inside out, what if we add one more sphere?"

"*Another* one?"

Jeremy nodded reluctantly. "It might be useful in situations like this. What if we add a 'Causal' sphere? One that exists outside the bounds of the factual inner spheres or the conjectural meta-sphere."

He could see Miranda's frown of confusion.

How else to explain it?

Mike's shrug said he didn't know either.

Taz was still staring at her clenched fists. Something about Mike's F-35 comment had really upset her. He'd likened Taz to an F-35, which didn't seem right at all. She was...

The card game!

He yanked it out of his pocket and fanned the deck as well as he could. Not all pretty and even the way Mike would, but it was close enough.

"These are all airplanes."

"And rotorcraft," Andi chimed in.

"And rotorcraft," Jeremy conceded.

"Though inside the Night Stalkers, we often refer to them as airplanes anyway. Just don't call them choppers, those are motorcycles for riding across the American West."

Jeremy waited to see if Andi had more to say. He hadn't known that about rotorcraft also being called airplanes.

She flapped a hand at him to continue, but he was less sure about her smile.

"Some designs..." he paused, but Andi didn't add anything more "...are better, some worse. Some are better at one thing than another. Have more or less crashes. And so on."

Miranda nodded for him to continue.

"What if we had another deck? Call them...Missions for now. Like solving Zhang Ru's Gyrfalcon crash. Stealing that satellite. Stopping Taz and General Martinez."

Taz glanced up at him through her thick hair.

"There are even types of missions: crashes, combat, and I guess that you might call this one diplomatic. The 'causal sphere' is the sphere of the world out beyond the crash—*but* related to the crash. And we've just been dealt a diplomatic mission by Zhang Ru. He is effectively giving us a J-20 for reasons I don't begin to understand. But Mei-Li's information tells us that there's way more behind this. I have no idea what, but it will probably be important before this is all done."

"So...there are...causes, beyond the scope of any mechanical failure or pilot error, that are nonetheless relevant to the crash."

"Right! The hacker who attacked all those Thunderbolts that—"

"Wait! *What?*" Taz sat bolt upright and shoved her hair out of her face. "I never heard those crashes were related."

Holly just pointed at him. Jeremy could feel the heat rising to his own face.

"You did that?"

Holly snorted. "Oh yeah. Because there are so many vicious bones in Jeremy's body. Oh, no, wait, there aren't *any*. Those are all mine. Jeremy's the one who *fixed* it."

56

TAZ HAD NEVER BEEN SO OUT OF HER DEPTH BEFORE. THE LOSS of so many A-10 Thunderbolts in just twenty-four hours was a disaster of epic proportions that the Air Force had covered up so deeply that she didn't even know they were related.

Jeremy was blushing fiercely. "I just did the software. Miranda's the one who—"

"Just shut up and bow, young Padawan." Holly laughed and punched his shoulder hard enough that only his seatbelt kept him from launching out into the cargo bay. The cards he'd still been holding flew into the air and fluttered down all around them.

"But—" Taz didn't know "but" what. Jeremy hadn't just been involved, but had *stopped* the devastation?

Jeremy unbuckled, carefully removing his headset to avoid throttling himself with it again, and began picking up the cards.

"It really was mostly his doing." With Jeremy temporarily out of the circuit, Holly's tone was suddenly completely serious. "He has a truly exceptional mind. Me?

I'm just really good at blowing shit up or seeing how it *was* blown."

"He's just full of surprises," Mike's smile was all-knowing. As if he enjoyed that they were messing with her head.

"You people are a bad influence!"

Mike just grinned when she snapped at him.

"We are?" Miranda sounded worried.

Shit! She'd forgotten about the intercom connecting all five of them. Six, Jeremy was back in his seat with his headset on and counting the cards.

Taz handed him the three that had landed in her lap, then he looked very relieved as if his cards were as important as saving manned jets.

And Miranda...was looking both confused and upset.

Get your shit together, Taz. "Sorry, Miranda. Your team is making me feel exceedingly small."

"But you are small. Even smaller than me. How do you think that affects your world view? I've often wondered about being taller, but I never thought to consider the ramifications of being shorter." Miranda had pulled out a small notebook and appeared ready to take notes. In fact, Taz could just see her own name in front of a question in Miranda's neat printing.

"That wasn't exactly what I meant," but Taz had dealt with enough engineer-types to know it was better to answer their question before trying to move forward. "I find the main advantage is that people discount me."

"I don't," Jeremy looked up at her.

Which was also an odd truth. From the very first moment, he'd *seen* her as if she was a person, without her having to prove herself.

She stretched out a foot to press it momentarily against

his knee across the gap between the two rows of seats, but couldn't quite reach.

"And there's a disadvantage."

"What?" Miranda's pen was poised.

"It's harder to play footsie with someone."

Holly stretched out her forever long legs and rested them easily on Mike's thigh. Her smile said she was enjoying showing off. Taz had always wanted legs like that, not that they'd fit the rest of her.

Then she saw that Miranda was actually writing down her footsie observation. If she hung around with these people, she'd have to remember how literally Miranda took everything. Nothing was of more or less importance. One moment they were trying to analyze international political gamesmanship, and the next what it was like to be short.

"Miranda," Taz waited until she had her full attention, or at least her left ear did. "Being as short as me versus being as short as you or as tall as Mike and Holly isn't all that different. I'm still me. Some things, like kitchen cabinets, are designed for taller people, so I use a step stool, but otherwise I don't notice it much. It's the size I've been since I was fifteen and joined the Air Force."

And that required a whole explanation she hadn't meant to give about her multiple identity and name changes as she'd aged at crossing the border illegally, and then lost those years and more after her supposed death.

"So you're not Vicki Cortez?" Oddly, everyone, even Miranda, had simply accepted all of it—except Jeremy.

"Are you Jeremy Trahn?"

"Since the day I was born."

Taz nodded. "I've been *me* since the day I was born. My name hasn't changed me: Vicki Cortez, Tanya Roberts—"

Mike snorted out a laugh at that one, then left it to Taz to sidetrack into the topic of tall, redheaded 1980s Hollywood sex kittens.

"And now Tasia Vicki Flores," she finally returned to the point. "Those are all still the same me."

Except they weren't.

Consuela, the child always afraid. Vicki, the teenaged lethal survivor in a street-level war. The Taser who'd spent two decades as an Air Force general's enforcer. Taz, briefly a hotshot. And now…

Who the hell was she, anyway?

She tugged out General Martinez's challenge coin and rubbed it in her fingers for a moment. For all its familiarity, it now felt foreign as well. If she was no longer that person either…

Well, this was no time to add to the confusion. Maybe, if all of the plates that were in the air stopped spinning for a moment, she could figure out who she was.

But not right now.

She stuffed the coin back out of sight.

"I think we need to focus on Jeremy's 'mission card' or, by another name, Miranda's 'causal sphere.' We need to understand what we're getting into before we land in Taiwan."

But for all of the debate that followed, they ended up little wiser.

57

PRIVATE SPECIALIST HUAN DE KNEW SHE'D BEEN GIVEN THE single most boring job in the entire Republic of China Air Force. When the People's Republic attacked, they'd be coming from the west, crossing the Taiwan Strait in overwhelming numbers.

Being perched at the tedious end of nowhere was *not* why she had volunteered.

Yes, someone must watch the east, but why did it have to be her?

And why from here?

Keelung City to the north had excellent clubs. Luodong Township to the south offered nothing except the only real town for a long distance.

But she was halfway in between and could not take easy advantage of either.

Nor was she down at Fulong Beach, where she could try out her new bikini during lunchtime or the long summer evenings. No, she was stuck atop Ling Jiou Mountain in an isolated shack. Her companions atop the mountain? Two Taoist temples and a Buddhist Monastery.

It was the highest point overlooking the easternmost tip of the country, but that didn't mean anything had happened here since the Japanese invasion of 1895.

She glared at the monitors, because there was absolutely nothing else to do except wonder if Shao Cai would finally introduce her to his older brother, rather than slobbering after her himself—Shao Yating was...delicious to look at.

Maybe this weekend at the beach, in her killer bikini, she'd find the confidence to introduce herself. Better yet, maybe her bikini would make him introduce himself.

This weekend when the annual Hohaiyan Rock Festival took over the beach, it would be a constant party. If she then—

A dark blip caught her attention on the Sandiaojiao Lighthouse camera. Too high to be a distant ocean freighter, but too low to be a flight descending into Taipei Songshan Airport thirty kilometers to the northwest.

Radar showed nothing, but the dot was definitely there.

And growing—fast!

She flipped up the protective Lucite cover and punched the alarm.

"Report!" A voice snapped out over her radio within seconds.

"A low-flying aircraft approaching Sandiaojiao Lighthouse at less than a hundred meters. Negative radar image."

"Repeat that last."

"Negative radar image. It's—"

It flashed by the lighthouse camera, clearing it by less than ten meters.

The image appeared to fracture, as if struck with a hammer.

Four seconds later the jet flashed over her lookout atop Ling Jiou Mountain with an earthshattering roar. Her small window was blasted into a thousand pieces, scattering glass over all of her equipment as De covered her ears.

Somewhere in the background was a voice demanding her attention, but it sounded faint and far away.

"Supersonic!" she called into the microphone. Careful of the glass shards, she scrolled back the camera recording from the lighthouse, and froze the image the moment before the jet had passed over, then smashed the camera's lens with a sonic boom.

The image was blurred, but she'd been tediously well trained in plane spotting, and knew it immediately.

Still, she checked the poster on her shack's wall.

"It's a Chengdu J-20 *Mighty Dragon.*" Then she swallowed hard.

If she said the next words, nothing else could matter. Not her new bikini, not Shao Yating. Nothing.

But she must.

For seventy years her country had prepared for only one thing: an invasion from the mainland.

She keyed the microphone.

"It has begun."

Her hearing was starting to return. A sonic boom could break glass above eleven pounds-per-square-inch overpressure, and the loudest ever recorded was a hundred-and-forty-four psi at such close range. Training had assured her that there would be no permanent hearing loss below seven hundred psi.

However, next to her observer's shack, a nineteen-meter

Fagus hayatae—Taiwanese beech—had been swaying from the hammer-blow of the massive wind pressure. For an instant, its future remained held in the balance by a thin root that had burrowed under a neighboring *Quercus myrsinifolia* —bamboo-leaf oak.

Unable to take the strain and right the beech, the root snapped.

The towering, multi-trunked tree gained momentum as it fell until it crashed through the shack's roof, shattering everything within.

The Buddhist monks of the Wu Sheng Monastery didn't find the only Taiwanese fatality of the attack for several hours.

58

"*Nǐ niú shǔn fèifèi húndàn, Zhang Ru!*" Captain Chen Bo cursed General Zhang Ru. The automatic cockpit voice recorder would pick that up, of course. It was the first words he'd spoken aloud since the message he had dutifully spoken aloud shortly after departing Mainland Chinese airspace.

Not that it mattered any longer.

Silently, he offered a few more words of imprecation, first upon Zhang Ru's many ancestors—may they roast on a fiery spit and be eaten by weasels—and then upon himself.

Bo bemoaned the day he'd signed up for the PLAAF. The People's Liberation Army Air Force, as if that was not some great irony that even the Buddha himself could never unravel.

Liberation? Not if it put his life into the hands of a man like Zhang Ru.

Zhang had promised that if Bo would do his bidding, he would be picked up by a quiet fishing boat just off the

Taiwanese coast after ditching the J-20 aircraft on Fulong Beach.

Except when he had tuned to the frequency, all he'd heard was the Voice of America shortwave broadcast from the Philippines.

Ru's idea of a grand joke.

Bo was fast running out of options. He'd circled back out to sea hoping to spot a fishing boat of any size, but all he saw were tiny local boats that wouldn't serve beyond a kilometer offshore, and ocean-going freighters.

He tried a call on the VOA frequency anyway.

Nothing except more propaganda about the grand nation's achievements, worse than the headlines on the *People's Daily* newspaper.

However, he had other problems. His long-distance radar showed two four-bird flights lifting out of Songshan Airport. They would be on him in under two minutes.

Ru had trapped him so perfectly.

If you do this, I won't send your wife and daughter to the Xinjiang prison camps as whores for the guards' entertainment.

If he tried to return, the government would do even worse to him. No amount of claiming he just wanted to "test their newest fighter against the weak Taiwanese defenses" would save him. Even without Ru labeling him as a traitor, which he'd be sure to do to protect himself.

And without rescue, he'd never leave Taiwan alive.

If he landed the J-20 intact as a bargaining chip, then claimed political asylum, perhaps—

A new blip on the radar, closely followed by two more, told him that option had just been closed off.

If he had merely crossed the midline of the Taiwan Strait, the Taiwanese Air Force would merely have threatened him or tried to crowd him back over the line. He'd flown enough authorized "system test" missions across the Strait that the PLAAF now had an accurate map of Taiwan's tactics and response times.

But that wasn't what he'd done.

Under Ru's orders, he'd circled the island, and crossed over their land as well. That would be unforgivable in Taiwan's mind, as the trio of blips showed only too well.

They were closing at Mach 6. That meant they were Sky Sword II air-to-air missiles with a range of a hundred kilometers. His window of opportunity had just shrunk from two minutes to twenty seconds.

The Chengdu J-20 was a stealth jet in more than one way. Not only did it have an incredibly low radar profile, its exhaust also had an extremely low heat signature. The Sky Sword II was an infrared tracker.

Bo turned once more for the land, pointing his exhaust out to sea and aiming for the beach.

The missiles overshot, picked up his heat signature again, and turned to follow. They were even better than reported. That was *unbelievably* bad news.

As the first missile closed within five seconds of contact, he released a cloud of chaff and flares. His plane had plenty of glide, so he killed the J-20's engines as well, removing his heat signature entirely.

The leading Sky Sword II reached the infrared heat of the flares. Reading the chaff as a close-proximity range, the pulse doppler radar ignited the warhead, exploding harmlessly behind him. The second missile targeted the explosion of the first, but the third twisted to follow him.

Bo hit the fuel dump—not much left to spill. Definitely not enough to return home.

General Zhang had ordered that the plane not be flyable after the crash, but neither could it be utterly destroyed. The final missile seemed determined to negate that. Knowing he'd been tricked, Chen Bo didn't care, except the explosion might kill him even as he ejected.

The final Sky Sword II was less than two seconds behind him.

A thousand meters to the beach, Bo armed the LS-6 bombs and pressed the emergency release on all four of them.

They plunged into the waves.

Two thousand kilos of high explosive ignited on impact, launching a massive fountain of water close behind him. Hopefully the last of the Taiwanese Sky Sword II missiles would fire its warhead upon reaching it, or drown.

Either way, it never came out the other side. He was safe—from that.

Skimming the waves, Bo waited until he was sure that the jet would impact the beach hard enough to be broken apart without being destroyed.

Then he pulled the emergency handles on the ejection seat and braced himself.

Nothing happened.

He pulled them again.

The beach lay less than three seconds ahead.

Again.

Ejection seats didn't fail.

It just didn't happen.

Unless...Zhang Ru didn't want him telling his story to anybody.

Bo reached for the control stick to ease the nose up,

perhaps smooth out the landing and make it survivable, but there was something in his way.

"Ó, xióngmāo niào." It was the last thing he'd ever say.

A massive, temporary bandshell stood on the beach directly in his path. It towered six stories high. He couldn't climb fast enough without his engines. He was too low to turn aside without catching a wingtip in the water that would send him cartwheeling and guarantee his death.

The Chengdu J-20 *Mighty Dragon* skimmed onto Fulong beach traveling at four hundred and seventeen kilometers per hour.

It plowed into the scaffolding that formed the bandshell, ripping off both wings.

Whatever Zhang Ru had done to sabotage the ejection seat was knocked loose by the impact.

The cockpit canopy bolts fired. The canopy drove upward, creating a momentary bubble in the collapsing structure. Four milliseconds later, the seat's rocket fired. Because the seat's independent altitude-sensing system determined that the aircraft was at ground level, it fired with its full force to lift the pilot to a safe altitude before the parachute opened.

Captain Chen Bo was launched upward with a force of fourteen gravities. Normally, the g-force would permanently compress his spine by as much as two inches, making him that much shorter.

Instead, he was launched through the center stage point of the platform. The impact pulverized every bone in his body above his solar plexus. The trajectory of his body and, after the first point-six seconds, his body parts impacted eighty-three separate elements of the stage's structure. His remains would not be recognized as such until his boots were found three days later.

Without its canopy or pilot, the J-20's fuselage continued through a channel formed by the scaffolding's structure and out the far side. After teetering for a long moment, the bandshell folded in on itself and collapsed into the area that would have been crowded with tens of thousands of concert-goers tomorrow night.

The support for the above-stage camera, attached at the very top of the structure, drove down from the sky like a javelin. It embedded deep in the sand after punching through the corner of the blanket that Shao Yating had spread with his latest girlfriend—who looked amazing; there was nothing he liked so much as a pretty girl in a skimpy swimsuit. His physical fitness routine guaranteed an endless supply of them.

The J-20's fuselage exited the far side of the bandshell's wreckage, rammed into a dune, and stopped abruptly.

The rear fifteen meters of the twenty-thousand-kilogram airplane crumpled close behind the cockpit. Pivoting on that point, the tail lifted until it stood three stories tall, then continued over. Separating from the cockpit still buried in the sand, the entire rear of the plane flipped end-for-end, first planting its tail in the sand beyond the nose of the plane before finally slamming down once more on its belly.

The fuselage broke between the midframe bomb bay and the rear engines.

It finally came to a rest on the backside of the dune, right-side up, parked tail-to-nose with its own cockpit.

59

"It's here," Taz pointed at the sky as they were deplaning. The 767 freighter only had a small crew door that even Taz had to duck a foot to clear. She and Miranda were first out onto the metal stairs.

Miranda shaded her eyes against the late afternoon sun. "How can you be sure?"

She pointed to the two diamonds of jets launching off the end of the runway.

Miranda squinted, "Four Taiwan-built IDF fighter jets in the first group. Four American F-16s in the second."

"Yes, they're the F-16As, upgraded to Vs, because that's all we could sell them before the PRC threatened violence if we sold them more jets. But they're all on full afterburners. They're headed somewhere in a hurry. I'm guessing that would be Ru's J-20 scaring the crap out of them." They turned to watch them as they disappeared to the west behind the 767's tall tail.

Suddenly three bright streaks flashed past the far edge, closely followed by the eight jets.

"Missiles. They're trying to kill the J-20."

"If they do, there will be little for us to recover," Miranda pointed out.

"I can think of worse situations." As they reached the bottom of the ladder with the others close behind, Taz eyed the approaching Taiwanese officer. The man beside her had to be a customs official. And here was one of those "worse" possibilities.

"Hello," the woman saluted sharply, her English was almost accentless. "I'm *Siōng-hāu*...apologies. I'm *Colonel* Zhao Tung-Mei. I was asked to place my Black Hawk helicopter at your service for the duration of your visit. I was also asked to hand this to you."

Miranda took the brown envelope, glanced inside, then passed it to Taz. Taz pulled out the American passport tucked inside. When she opened to the picture, Holly glanced over her shoulder.

"Hey, it even looks like you."

"That's convenient, isn't it?"

"It is."

Taz handed it to the customs official.

He handed it back with a pen. "You must sign it, please. And add your address." The wonders of traveling at this level, officials merely overlooked irregularities like magically-appearing passports.

She signed it. But didn't know what to do with the address. "I don't have—"

Holly took it, filled out something, then handed it to the official. He noted down the number, stamped it, and returned it to her.

Taz inspected the address, one she didn't recognize.

"The four of us, not Miranda, rent a house together

there. It's close by her private NTSB office. It will do as well as anything else until we decide if your final address is swimming with my friend's salties or not."

"Gee, thanks."

Holly slapped her hard on the back. "Anything for a *mate* of Jeremy's." She even offered a wink as if the broad Aussie accent wasn't enough of a giveaway about her double meaning.

Taz tucked away the passport in her under-clothes belt pouch and ignored her.

But it did raise the question, was she helping Jeremy? Or was she his worst nightmare? He still believed the former. She still leaned toward the latter.

Once they were all checked off, the customs official strode away. Taz would wager that whoever got him next would be in for officious hell; nothing a bureaucrat hated worse than circumventing his own job under someone else's orders.

Once he was gone, Colonel Tung-Mei led them toward a Black Hawk helicopter.

"I offer greetings from the general of the Republic of China's Air Force, Tsai Jui-en. I have been asked to expedite your aircraft recovery."

Taz knew it wasn't that simple. "Do you know why?"

Tung-Mei smiled. "I look forward to your Senate releasing our latest purchase request for twenty new fighter jets and an equal number of Black Hawks. Though I'm unclear which aircraft."

"Let's follow those fighters we just saw go aloft."

Apparently General Drake Nason had been busy during their FedEx delivery across the ocean.

Even as Tung-Mei's Black Hawk climbed and headed

west, a call came in on her radio about the location of a downed jet. During the five-minute flight eastward as they climbed over the rugged forests of northern Taiwan, everyone just watched out the windows. It was an island with twenty-four million inhabitants, she hadn't expected there to be any wilderness. But in those thirty kilometers, they overflew no towns and only one or two roads.

Other than people milling on the beach, they were the first to arrive on the scene.

As they soared over the reported downing, all she saw at first was the massive wreckage, as if a giant C-5 Galaxy cargo jet had crashed on the beach instead of a small fighter jet.

A ridiculously small wingtip stuck out of the monstrous pile of twisted metal.

"This is going to be a real mess."

Then Jeremy tapped her on the shoulder and pointed beyond the wreckage. How had she not noticed when he took the seat close beside her?

Beyond the mound of toppled scaffolding lay a small tube in three sections. It took her only a moment to see that the main fuselage of the plane had somehow ended up beyond the wreckage.

Tung-Mei pushed back the gathering crowd with the down-blast of her rotor blades. People huddled, or raced away to get clear of the windblown sand.

While the men all wore board shorts, the standard attire for Taiwanese women was apparently skimpy bikinis. She saw only two women in one-pieces, so the sand must really sting; they certainly raced away fast enough.

As they were landing, she saw that the sections of the fuselage were out of order.

She had no doubt that Miranda and Jeremy would solve

how it was even possible for the parts of the plane to be so jumbled up.

No, what bothered her wasn't the layout of the plane in neat little sections. It was Jeremy's causal sphere. General Zhang Ru wouldn't sacrifice a hundred-million-dollar jet just to show "good will" to General Drake Nason.

60

TAZ DID WHAT SHE COULD.

Along with Tung-Mei's Black Hawk crew, they quickly organized a security perimeter. Several policemen arrived and were instantly recruited by the colonel.

Unlike Americans who would push closer and closer when asked to step back, the Taiwanese simply did. They still ran their smartphones, just like an American would, but otherwise they were far more civilized than she was used to.

When the bandshell crew approached, they were upset about the destruction of so much work and worried about tomorrow's concert—at least until they realized that the crashed jet wasn't theirs, but rather an attack from the Mainland. She assigned them the task of making sure everyone was accounted for on their team and that no one had been caught in the wreckage.

With them occupied, she turned to watch the NTSB team.

Miranda was leading them on a walk along the edge of the debris. On the smooth sand, they barely had to pause for

Jeremy to jab a small orange flag into the ground, marking the outer edge of the debris field. It extended past the fuselage in only a few places.

As if that wasn't obvious in the first place.

Miranda started heading toward the wing section sticking out from under the edge of the bandshell's remains. Clearly she was preparing to do a complete crash investigation, even though they already knew the cause.

And then Taz saw something that completely erased any patience.

A Taiwanese Army truck arrived and a stream of soldiers unloaded. Their first action was driving back the crowds even further. That was fine.

But there was an itch that worried her.

Tung-Mei was nearby. "Did you get notification to your Army as well?"

One look at Tung-Mei's face told her the answer to that.

"Why not?"

"Your general told my general that we were told to keep it most secret. We did not expect the crash on a public beach."

"How many more Black Hawks do you have available?"

"Four in my squadron."

"Good. Get them here, with lifting cables. Now!"

"But—"

"Then get aloft and get a cable on the cockpit section yourself. That's the most important. Get it back to Songshan airport. Have them grab the other sections as fast as they can. We're leaving."

"Why—" But she was already nodding and pulling out her radio.

"Tell them to ignore anything, and I mean *anything* that is happening here on the ground. And see if your general can get these guys to stand down. Meanwhile I'll do what I can." Then Taz raced across the sand toward Miranda while Tung-Mei sprinted for her helicopter as she called the rest of her squadron.

"We have to go, Miranda."

"What do you mean? We haven't finished mapping the debris field's extent yet."

Taz recalled Miranda's spheres of investigation. No matter that the debris field was little more than a few torn bits of metal, Miranda would study that until it was complete before even thinking to look at the plane itself. It was the plane that was the prize.

Taz made sure she had Holly and Andi's attention, then she simply pointed.

Behind the Army truck, a steel-gray Mitsubishi SUV rolled up. And the man who climbed out of the passenger seat had all of the markings of a midlevel popinjay, swollen with his own importance. She knew the type just by his walk —the Pentagon Strut. Officious as hell.

"Bloody hell," Holly's mutter confirmed her assessment.

"The next step is for me to identify the perimeter of the debris field around the wing." Miranda's tone was sharp. Not with anger. Almost...with fear.

Taz took a grip of both of Miranda's hands—remembering Mike's advice just in time, she made it a firm grip.

It forced Miranda to focus on her. Not quite look at her, but it definitely locked her attention on Taz rather than the edge of the debris field. Most of which was buried under the unsafe collapse of the bandshell anyway. Though Taz would wager that wouldn't stop Miranda for a moment; perhaps she wouldn't even see the danger.

"We have two choices, Miranda, and only two."

"I thought you said you had no choices."

Taz wanted to laugh, and to cry. Miranda connecting the word "choice" across two completely different conversations, most of two days and an entire ocean apart, only served to illustrate how bewildering her world must be.

"At the moment, we have two. If we act quickly, we can secure most of the key pieces of this aircraft, load them aboard the FedEx 767, and get them safely back to the US. Then you can inspect them at your leisure."

"What's the second choice?"

"If we hesitate, that man coming toward us will claim the rights to the aircraft, and by the time he's done, we'll get none of it. Remember the possibility that you told us Ru mentioned. Agents from the Mainland would blow it up. It could be one of those people who just arrived."

"Drake wouldn't like that. He told me as we boarded the Black Hawk that he wanted this plane badly, but we must be careful."

"Do you trust me?" The words were out before Taz realized it. No one had ever been naive enough to trust her—except her general who was now dead. And Jeremy.

Before she could take the words back, Miranda turned to look at the others.

Mike spoke first, "On this, Miranda, I would trust her absolutely."

Taz looked at him in surprise.

"Gamesmanship at the top levels of the military? Way out of my league, Taz. Yours too, Holly, just in case you were getting some crazy ideas."

Holly just held up her hands defensively; for once, not saying a word.

Mike turned back to Miranda. "Taz is your expert on this."

"Okay." And that easily, it seemed she had accepted it.

Taz couldn't believe it, but now was not the moment to consider the implications.

"Mike. Jeremy. You two get Miranda onto that helicopter and get her back to the FedEx plane. If it looks as if they're going to try and stop you, just go. The rest of us can always catch a commercial flight."

"I'm staying with you," Jeremy didn't make it a request.

"Jeremy—"

"Tough. I'm sticking."

Mike gave him a one-armed hug before rushing Miranda off to Tung-Mei's helicopter.

Holly actually ruffled Jeremy's hair rather than punching his arm. His swat at her hands was wholly ineffective. She headed over to help the cable team on the ground.

Bizarrely, they appeared...proud of him. Later. Another thing to think about later.

"Follow my lead," she headed over to cut off the strutting peacock before he could reach the Black Hawk—they were rigging lifting cables as fast as they could but still needed more time. Then she side-shifted a step to walk close beside Jeremy, "And you keep quiet. You too, Andi." Taz didn't know why she was tagging along, but it was too late to argue.

"But—"

"Shh!"

And then they caught up to the popinjay.

61

"Lieutenant," Taz greeted the man she'd pointed out.

Jeremy wasn't sure why he himself was a problem.

The officer reminded Jeremy of his seventh-grade math teacher. Mr. Bantam had controlled twenty-seven unruly thirteen-year-olds with all of the military precision and perfect posture of a Marine sergeant.

"Major," the man snarled out and tapped the gold five-petal plum flower on his collar point.

"Sorry...Major."

But Taz would know that. Colonel Zhao Tung-Mei had explained the triple plum flower of her own insignia. Why would she intentionally antagonize the man?

Then Jeremy saw, behind the man, Miranda and Mike taking off aboard the Black Hawk. Moments later, they'd taken up the slack and lifted the cockpit away.

The Taiwanese major spun to stare aghast at the departing helicopter.

He turned to the orderly at his side and snapped out a command while pointing at the helicopter, ordering it to be stopped. At least that's what Jeremy hoped it was, rather than orders to shoot them if any of them moved.

Andi said something in Mandarin that stopped the orderly as he reached for his radio.

The major spun to glare at her.

"You don't want to be interfering in this, Major," Taz said it as calmly as she'd ordered pizza at JBLM.

Miranda and the front section of the aircraft were well away, but Jeremy knew it was a ploy that would only work once.

"And why not!" he was practically spitting fire. He stepped close and glared down at Taz.

For lack of anything better, Jeremy slipped his favorite screwdriver out of the side pouch on his field pack and tucked it out of sight along his forearm in case he needed a weapon.

Taz reached into her belt pouch. She slipped out a card and handed it across.

Jeremy knew a CAC—Common Access Card military ID —when he saw one. He wondered why Taz hadn't thrown it away.

"I'm Colonel Vicki Cortez of the US Air Force. I'm here on a highly classified special assignment for your General Tsai Jui-en. He, the Pentagon, three-star General Jorge Jesus Martinez, my commanding officer, and I appreciate your cooperation."

Jeremy was careful to keep his expression neutral, since the last two of them were dead, even if only one was dead in reality.

The man eyed her suspiciously. He was just Jeremy's height, but that was still eight inches taller than Taz. She was dressed in the wildfire t-shirt that she'd worn to the JBLM airshow, jeans, and boots.

"And who are these people?" The major was far from convinced.

Jeremy caught Taz's attention, then glanced upward. Three more Black Hawks had just come over the horizon of trees and were already settling toward the remaining parts of the jet spread across the beach.

She slanted her gaze sideways.

He knew what she wanted, to get him out of the way by going over to coordinate with the Black Hawks. Instead, he watched until he saw that they knew exactly what they should be doing before he turned back to their small group.

Taz glared at him briefly.

"This," she waved a hand at his chest, "is a civilian contractor here to liaise with your Air Force. Captain Andrea Wu is an aircraft specialist and Staff Sergeant Holly Harper is our structural specialist. We're all cleared Top Secret or better. Now I must ask you, Lieutenant—"

"Major!"

Out of the corner of his eye, Jeremy saw someone walking over from the newly arrived helicopter, but he didn't dare look away. Things were getting tense, and the major was armed. The screwdriver tucked in his own hand offered little comfort.

"Sorry. Major. Are you cleared for this operation? It has been code-word classified, and I'd appreciate the code before I can let you or your men proceed onto this site."

"I— What are you talking about? This is a Mainland Chinese military aircraft and—"

"And we have the situation completely under control. Now, I would appreciate it if you and your men could help us extract the wing that's pinned in the wreckage there. Then we'll need you to make up a search team to comb the wreckage for any injured citizens."

Jeremy had to bite his tongue not to laugh. The major was looking down at Taz as if she was a giant hand grenade about to explode in his face.

Then his expression shifted, and he looked suddenly dangerous.

Jeremy clutched his screwdriver more tightly.

"Well?" the man spoke from behind them, making Taz actually jump in surprise. "You heard the woman. Snap to it, Major!"

The man wore a full uniform.

"What the—"

The man tapped the two stars on his jacket's shoulders, a lieutenant general.

"Yes sir!" The major looked absolutely furious as he saluted sharply. Then he turned and screamed at his men to head toward the wreckage.

The general smiled. "I arrived as quickly as I could. Sorry for the delay. I was busy addressing a perceived invasion, until I was informed that your team had landed. General Chang, at your service."

"Much appreciated, sir."

"I'll just go keep the major out of your hair. I would continue to move quickly. Word is spreading rapidly."

"Thank you, sir."

He headed toward the wreckage.

Andi and Holly hurried away to help the Black Hawk crew that was presently rigging a lift cable to the engine section.

"Next time I tell you to do something in a situation like

that, Jeremy, you've got to just do it. And a screwdriver? Really?" She tugged it out of his hand and stuffed it back into his pack's pocket.

"You were *magnificent!*" He couldn't keep it in any longer. "The way you handled Miranda was so perfect. She always needs to know the truth and that's exactly what you gave her so that she could make her decision. You were so cool with that general, too; they always make me nervous when I have to speak to them. And then that major. Ugh! He reminded me of this Air Force general the day I met Miranda. Though you were even scarier than he was."

"Who was that?"

"General Oswald Harrington."

"Oh, Oswald wasn't ever an officious prick. Though he wasn't the smartest man ever."

"Well, I'm glad General Nason threw him out of the Air Force."

Taz stopped and eyed him. "Is that what happened to him?"

"He pulled a gun on Miranda and was running an illegal drone operation for the CIA. That's how we got connected to Zhang Ru...kinda."

"I'd like to hear that story in order someday."

"I probably shouldn't have said anything, that mission was code-word classified too, just like this one. By the way, what is the code word for this? I must not have been paying attention."

Taz shoved him up against the fuselage of the J-20 and kissed him hard.

He didn't understand why, but he wasn't dumb enough to hesitate.

He wrapped his arms around her and remembered what

it had been like to make love to her in the heart of the Baja desert.

She broke off long before he was ready. In fact, the kiss had only lasted moments, which was probably best under the circumstances—in danger on a Taiwanese beach.

"What was that for?"

Taz just grinned up at him. "There *is* no code word on this mission, Jeremy. I was making it up as I went. And the next time I signal you to leave, you leave. It was all coming apart. If that general hadn't stepped in, we'd have been in deep shit. I wanted you clear."

"Oh." He still didn't get why she'd kissed him. "Well, I wouldn't have left you alone even if I had understood. Besides, you made it up pretty amazingly well," he nodded toward the wreckage. "I almost wish the general hadn't showed up. I'll bet you could have pulled it off. You're amazing!"

A Black Hawk was hovering over the wing sticking out of the wreckage. The major's men were leveraging back pieces of the bandshell's structure using other scraps as levers. Using a cargo winch, the Black Hawk was able to tug the wing free with only a minimum of damage, and then soar aloft.

Holly and Andi came hustling toward them.

Together, the four of them climbed into the last Black Hawk. In moments, it too was aloft, carrying the last section of the shattered fuselage.

62

THE INTERIOR OF THE 767'S CARGO BAY WAS AN IDEAL SPACE for studying the wreckage of an airplane. Miranda would have to remember that if such a situation ever came up again.

The parts of the Chengdu J-20 were laid out on tracked pallets that were secured to the cargo deck. There was plenty of room to circle around each section because, even in pieces, the jet didn't begin to fill the vast cargo bay. The lighting was bright and even, as would be appropriate for handling cargo.

If she had any complaint, it was that the pieces were not in order. The cockpit was at the rear, next came one of the wings. The heavy twin engines were at the center of lift over the wings for balancing purposes. And then close behind their pallet of seats was the midsection that included the bomb bay, engine intakes, and the attachment point for the canard wings that they hadn't been able to recover from the wreckage.

"I don't know where to begin."

"With a little sleep?" Holly stretched.

Miranda looked at her watch. "It's eight a.m."

"Miranda! That was so fifteen times zones ago."

Which was an inaccurate statement. They'd only crossed nine time zones to reach Taiwan and were through no more than one on their return to JBLM, where they'd refuel and offload the team before continuing to Groom Lake and offloading the Chengdu.

"I can't. This is probably my only opportunity to study the plane. Once it arrives at Groom Lake, I doubt they'll want our help. Do you realize that this aircraft has the Xian WS-15 engines? Everyone thinks that they're still in development. With these engines, the J-20 is capable of fuel-conserving supercruise at Mach-plus speeds. Have you ever studied the configuration of a supercruise engine?"

"New one on this girl. Okay, you've convinced me. Sleep is for wimps and dipsticks anyway. Let's start there."

Miranda extracted her new camera and a fresh notebook from her pack.

Mike and Andi were still in their seats. They would have very little to say about the J-20. Yes, Andi was right, they each had their expertise.

Jeremy, being the systems specialist, had started in the cockpit. Taz was with him.

Miranda had thought that Taz knew very little about crashes, but at Fulong Beach, she had acted as if she knew a great deal. On the helicopter flight back to Songshan Airport, Mike had assured her that Taz knew exactly what she was doing. And sure enough, the remaining pieces *had* arrived in quick succession.

Perhaps that she was inspecting the cockpit with Jeremy proved the point.

Yes, Miranda would focus on her own specialty, learning as much as she could about this aircraft in the next eleven hours.

There would be time to learn more about Tasia Flores later.

Miranda knelt to peer at the midsection of the fuselage.

Holly knelt beside her.

"Let's work the engines from front to rear. First we'll image the shape of the underbelly air intakes, at least where they weren't damaged too much by impacting the sand."

"What's that?"

Miranda held up her new camera. "It's a hundred-and-thirty-four-megapixel 3D camera by Matterport. It is really intended for creating true 3D images of a room for creating virtual tours and the like, but I wanted to test it on a crash. If we could accurately record the damage in 3D for later inspection, that could be interesting."

"Goodonya!" Holly offered what Miranda had assessed to be her highest praise—it consistently topped the chart in her notebook of Aussieisms.

Miranda liked the feel of that.

63

Jeremy sat in the hole left by the ejection of the pilot's seat. The scorch marks of the rockets had turned the floor black, so he'd tossed down an in-flight courtesy blanket to keep his pants clean. His nose was even with the edges of the cockpit. It made him feel munchkin tall.

He could identify all of the instruments, even if they were labeled in Chinese. Most were lifted from Russian designs, which in turn had been lifted from Western designs. All of the stealing from each other did offer a layer of translation.

Without the engines running, the console was dead and inaccessible.

Or was it?

The engine throttles were pulled back to shutdown. If this was even loosely based on the Russian Sukhoi Su-35 *Flanker,* then the switch at the lower right would be the fuel dump. Which was pressed. That would explain why the jet hadn't exploded on impact, the pilot had dumped the fuel before beaching the aircraft.

Once he had the general flow of the fuel system figured out, he could see what logically must be the hydraulic system's controls.

That meant the electrics were—

"Hey!"

"What?" Taz was leaning against the plane with her arms crossed on the cockpit's edge and her chin on her arms. She'd been just standing there watching him.

Jeremy took a guess and stabbed a button.

The cockpit instruments lit up.

Taz peeked at them in surprise. "What did you do?"

"The battery. There would be a battery so that the instruments would work even if the engines weren't running. In fact, it's probably in the cockpit so that the radios would function in case there's a catastrophic failure farther back in the aircraft."

"A catastrophic failure like the fuselage being broken into three parts?"

"Yes, exactly like that."

He wasn't sure why she was suddenly smiling at him.

"What?"

She just shook her head in a flurry of hair, but her smile didn't go away.

He turned back to study the console before he did something stupid.

"I wonder..." A light stuttered at him. He clapped his hands; it blinked on, then back off.

"What now?"

"They installed a Quick Access Recorder. A QAR should record most of the airplane's data." He only had to poke around a little before he found where the memory stick was stored. He popped it out. And checked the interface.

"Can you read it?"

"Standard interface. No problem."

"So what does it say, Jeremy?"

"I don't know."

"I thought you said you could read it." She was squinting at him and that laugh was really close to the surface again.

"I can. With an adapter on my computer."

"Spoilsport."

Jeremy pushed to his feet and climbed out of the cockpit. "What are you talking about?"

"I assumed you were such a super nerd-boy that you could just *read* it. Like a book."

He was finally getting a feel for her sense of humor. The first time they'd met, she'd never shown a single hint of one...in fact, she'd rarely spoken except when he asked a direct question. But now...

"Well, I *could* just read it..." he headed toward his pack, which was still at the far end of the cargo bay up by the seats.

"But..." Taz was definitely teasing him.

He leaned in close, until he could feel the warmth of her cheek close by his, and her hair just brushed against his skin. "But I don't like to show off too much."

Taz's laugh of delight caused Holly to stand too quickly and bang her head on the engine's rear cowling. That would pay her back for all of those arm punches. Or at least a few of them.

At the seats, they pulled on headsets, then he fished out his laptop and plugged in the right adapter.

Mike and Andi were eating a meal of zapped burritos and a can of Coke. They had their microphones swung up out of the way.

Jeremy ignored the growl in his stomach and studied the

screen. He could make sense of many of the data streams just by their configuration. He began pairing them off with the software's labels: altitude, airspeed, engine temperature...

At some point, Taz must have left him because she handed him a too-hot burrito, which he almost dropped on his keyboard, and a can of soda. He took a bite—almost crunching down on his microphone—sucked in cool air, and went back to unraveling the data.

The number strings that must be global positioning didn't make any sense until he remembered this was a Chinese aircraft. He flipped his filter from GPS to BDS—the BeiDou Navigation Satellite System.

There.

He sent the feed to his course-mapping software, which quickly traced the path of the J-20's final flight.

"Weird flight path. Pretty slick, Mr. Trahn."

"Uh, thanks." Was Taz teasing him again? Hard to tell.

"What's that?" Taz was leaning so close to view the screen that her shoulder rubbed against his when she pointed at the data stream. She was very distracting or he might have noticed it sooner. Maybe not, the blip wasn't very big.

"A voice track. Voice-activated." That's why he hadn't picked up on it sooner, it only occurred in a few places in the timeline. He patched it into the intercom, isolated the peak Taz had spotted, and hit play.

A short bit of Chinese sounded over the headphones.

Andi snorted her Coke on a burst of choking laughter. "Play that again! Play it again!"

Jeremy could hear her despite her mic being off.

Andi laughed even louder the second time.

"Okay, what did we miss?" Holly and Miranda came over, donned headsets, and joined the group.

Jeremy just pointed.

Andi was still giggling as she swung her microphone down, which turned it back on. "Please tell me there's more."

Jeremy isolated the audio track from the other data streams. "Four bits." He hit play.

64

Taz watched Andi sober immediately before she started the translation.

"This is Captain Chen Bo of the People's Liberation Army Air Force. I have been ordered by General Li Zuocheng to test Taiwan's defenses with a solo intrusion of a Chengdu J-20. I am told that if they retaliate, the President says we are ready. I do this willingly to honor my country."

"Fuck me," Holly sounded as if she'd just had the air kicked out of her gut.

Jeremy paused it, "That's the first segment. He recorded that shortly after crossing the midline of the Taiwan Strait, though a hundred kilometers north of Taipei."

"His tone," Andi shook her head. "Play it again."

Taz just didn't know Mandarin. She had no ability to read the pilot's mood.

Andi looked impossibly sad after the second playing. "He doesn't sound honored. He sounds miserable. Who the hell is General Li Zuocheng?"

Jeremy did a quick search.

When Taz saw the result, it was her turn to curse.

"He's one of the vice-chairmen of the Central Military Commission. The second most powerful person in China," Jeremy told the others.

Miranda nodded as if pleased. "I thought his name sounded familiar. Good. Now I know why."

"He's also..." Taz felt as if she was going to choke, "...Mei-Li's lover's grandfather."

Mike tipped his head enough that Taz could feel his neck pop even if she couldn't hear it.

They all waited.

"There's the first piece," Mike was nodding to himself. "I was wondering when it would start coming together."

"It's coming *together?*" Taz wasn't the only one who was shocked.

"At JBLM, Chen Mei-Li said she'd been 'owned' by General Zhang Ru, apparently as a sexual slave. She worked out some sort of trade to get free of him, a trade which placed him on the CMC. And now it makes sense. She somehow connected Zhang Ru and Li Zuocheng, one of the vice chairmen. As a bonus, she gets rid of Ru and pairs up with Zuocheng's favorite granddaughter as a lover instead. And between them, they somehow have enough power to leave the country to attend the University of Washington. My guess is that it is far more about safety than about either of them needing an advanced education. She was incredibly smart."

Taz juggled the pieces in her head—and they fit. She should have seen it.

"Hey, Mike?" She waited until he looked at her. "Totally the A-10."

"Thanks." He'd got the compliment, of course. Not Mr.

Warm-and-fuzzy, *I'm-just-a-little-Mooney-passenger-plane.* He was totally the A-10 Thunderbolt II close-air-support jet fighter.

Holly, just out of Mike's sightline, offered her a firm nod of "You got it right, girl."

Surprising, but better than being fed to a float of salties.

"Play the next piece, Jeremy."

"Okay, this is after the pilot arrived just offshore from Fulong Beach, but hadn't overflown it yet." He hit play.

Everyone turned to Andi, who just nodded when it was done.

"It's not so funny now. The pilot is some kind of pissed. The literal translation is: 'You cow-sucking baboon's ass, Ru.'"

"Ru, not Li?"

"It's definitely Ru he's angry with."

"That fits, too," Miranda was nodding. "At the table with Drake and Lizzy, Ru sent a text. He said he had ordered a crash as a token of good faith. He was giving the J-20 to Drake for helping him to stop the Chinese President from invading Taiwan."

Taz felt the shock down to her boots. Miranda had been at the center of a piece of global politics. Did she even understand that?

No one else looked surprised, as if Miranda did that all the time.

Holly just slouched in her seat and grinned at Andi. "You Chinese people have very weird curses. You shoulda been an Aussie; you'd fit right in."

Andi barely smiled at Holly's attempt to lighten the mood. "The reason I laughed so hard the first time is that it's from this great, one-season science fiction show called

Firefly. The show's curses were all in Mandarin to get around the censors, but it's become a thing. Chen Bo must have been a fan because the curses weren't authentic Chinese. They were all made up for the show."

"Oh man," Jeremy groaned. "That's like the best show ever. I remember looking up all the Chinese words and phrases the first time I saw it. But that was a while ago; guess I forgot them."

By his tone, Taz knew that if she herself hung out with Jeremy long, she'd be watching it, too. Binge night with Andi. She was surprised that Andi and Jeremy hadn't become a couple, but what did she know.

Taz glanced at Mike, but he was keeping his own counsel.

Andi looked beyond weary; as if the short bits of translation were ripping out her soul.

Miranda flipped open a small notebook, glanced back and forth between a page and Andi's face a few times. Then she reached out tentatively and rested a hand on Andi's shoulder. Just as Miranda was closing her notebook, Taz saw the page was covered in emojis.

She must have identified: *sad*. And then probably had a note of appropriate next action: *console*.

Taz remembered the Boeing engineer who offered her hot tea every time they met, even if they'd only parted ten minutes before. Someone had taught him that's what you did when you met someone, in addition to being a brilliant, if somewhat hyper-focused, engineer.

Miranda's lookup table was much more sophisticated.

The moment Miranda touched her, Andi clutched onto her hand like a drowning woman grabbing onto a lifeline.

Even with the support, her voice was shaky as she spoke.

"What are the last two pieces? Play them both. I don't know if I can hold it off long enough to do this twice more."

Mike released his seatbelt and tensed.

Something else was going on here besides the recording, but Taz wasn't sure what. She prepared herself as well as she could for the unknown, silently easing off her belt as well and tapping the inside of her wrist against her thigh to ensure that her knife was in place.

Jeremy hit play.

"He's calling for help," Andi translated in little more than a whisper. "Apparently there's a boat that was supposed to meet him, except there wasn't."

"The last," Jeremy whispered during a brief silence, "was less than a second before he impacted the bandshell."

The Mandarin phrase was short, and sounded resigned, even to Taz's untrained ear.

"It's another *Firefly* curse. 'Oh, Panda piss.' He knew he was about to die."

And then Andi simply folded up into a little ball.

Mike leapt from his chair, but hesitated when she landed with her head on Miranda's lap.

After a long hesitation, Miranda began gently stroking Andi's hair.

Mike watched them for a bit before reaching over and unplugging Andi's headphones without removing them, taking her out of the circuit.

He must have seen her puzzled expression after he returned to his seat.

"PTSD. Crashes are really hard on her. She drove herself into an episode—for us. Holding it off by sheer force of will to help."

Taz didn't think that was quite right; not based on where Andi had curled up for safety from her memories.

She hadn't done it for *them;* she'd done it for Miranda.

Just as Mike and Holly had both threatened her, in their own ways...for Miranda.

And she didn't want to take any bets about whether Jeremy's instincts would have chosen to protect her or Miranda at the JBLM helicopter crash, if he'd only been able to save one.

Though she still didn't understand what Miranda did to garner such loyalty, Taz could feel it working on her as well. And it wasn't the blind, unthinking loyalty she'd given to General JJ Martinez. She had, past all reason, given him her soul. Miranda made no such demands, which made her so much harder to understand.

No, she would stay focused on what General Zhang Ru was up to.

65

Leaving Mei-Li in a taxi to go to her school, Ru had been one of the last to board the flight from SeaTac to Beijing.

He should have forced her to tell him what she'd said to the Americans at the other table. But he didn't think of it until they were at the airport's curb, and he'd run out of time. Besides, she could play her hand very close when she chose to.

Ru didn't dare miss his plane in case Drake had some idea about keeping him here or exposing him. That's why he'd purposely chosen a China Airlines flight; once aloft, they wouldn't turn around for any foolish American demands.

He kept an eye out the window until they passed out over the Pacific Ocean.

Once they had, he snapped his fingers at the first-class attendant, who trotted over in her tight little red-and-gray blazer and skirt. "Scotch. American."

Yes, his plan was coming together very nicely. He would celebrate, a little. It wasn't done quite yet.

Drake would get his J-20.

Ru assumed the Americans had already stolen the plans, so it wouldn't make much difference as long as they couldn't fly it.

As to the half-billion-yuan financial loss? If that sycophant Chen Bo had done his job properly to save his family, then it would land squarely on Li Zuocheng's shoulders.

Yes, it was sad that Zuocheng was one of Ru's old war buddies, and had elevated Ru to his current position, but he was now getting in the way of the future.

Ru counted again; the numbers still added up.

Mei-Li had done exceptional research. He could directly control the votes of two of the CMC's seven members. And with the sudden removal of Zuocheng, he could use fear to guarantee at least one more. That would give him a majority.

Trading a J-20 for the seat of one of the vice-chairmen of the CMC was a small price to pay. Especially because Zuocheng would be the one paying for it with his life.

Installing a replacement for his old seat with someone he could absolutely control would make his majority an overwhelming five of seven.

And with Zuocheng gone, Mei-Li's little lover would lose all her favoritism and protection. Her on-going safety would come under Ru's control. What he could do with two such women stretched the imagination.

As much as he'd enjoy returning them both to Mei-Li's former role as a mistress (that he could lend out when he needed leverage), Mei-Li had proven that she could help in other ways...if she was willing. Her deep stubbornness was most unexpected. Sadly, he knew that he must forego the carnal pleasures she was such an expert at providing.

But his price for their freedom would be both girls working to solidify his complete control of the CMC. From there, the Presidency was not such a great step.

There lay the true power. It was dangerous and care would be needed, but the President, as Chairman, could overrule them all.

After he deplaned at Beijing Capital International Airport, a secure alert pinged onto his phone. It would never be mentioned in Chinese media, but a rogue J-20 jet had crashed in Taiwan, killing the pilot.

Excellent.

And he'd enjoyed sticking it to Drake right in his own backyard. Crashing that MH-47G Chinook, the newest addition to their Special Operations Night Stalkers, during an airshow had been a joyous sensation. It had also been payback, which had been even better. He knew that Drake must be behind embarrassing him in front of the vice-chairman of the CMC.

Now if he could just stick it to that pretty little general-wife of his, life would be very good indeed.

Just ten minutes later, Ru found what he was looking for so easily that it must be a sign of good fortune direct from the gods. Too bad he didn't believe in any of them.

She was just finishing her shift at the VIP passenger security kiosk.

A hundred and sixty centimeters and not a gram over fifty kilos, even in her Army boots. A technical sergeant, which placed her in her mid-twenties. Older than Mei-Li, but she still had the look of youth.

Most importantly, she was mixed-blood Japanese.

The other part of the mix was Chinese rather than American like Drake's *xiao riben guizi*, but she had the same look: the longer and wider face, the up-slanted, larger eyes. Just enough Chinese showing to not be distasteful. Probably the great-granddaughter of one of the comfort women from the Japanese Army's occupation during World War II.

Yes, he could work with that. She would have been ostracized by many of her peers for her obvious mixed blood and her clear reversion to her great-grandfather's Japanese features. Probably even passed over for promotions.

His guess proved accurate over a simple, late-night dinner of noodles with soybean paste and pork dumplings: just turned twenty-seven, she'd been given an undeserved poor review rather than a promotion.

It took only a phone call to fix that, which he made while at the table. Her commanding officer would be transferred to the Tibetan wilderness, and her promotion to master sergeant would be signed by tomorrow. Over a dessert of *aiwowo*—sticky rice cone cake with a sweet bean paste center and a red fleck of sugar jelly perched like a nipple atop the perfect white ball—a quick e-mail fixed the trivial matter of the advanced health care needed by her ill mother.

In his in-town apartment that night, once he had coaxed her out of her uniform, he decided that even more than her face, her body was *exactly* as he'd imagined General Elizabeth Gray's to look.

He turned her to stand in front of the mirror so that he could see all of her at once, and still she didn't disappoint. He wouldn't have to pretend at all, they must be very alike. Perhaps they shared an ancestor. That was a *most* pleasing thought. Her hair would need to be trimmed to match Gray's shoulder-brushing cut. Or perhaps he'd leave it long, tantalizing as it was along the upper curve of the girl's small breasts.

Coming up behind her, he lifted those two hands, just as fine fingered as the American general's, to brace against the mirror. He would find out how skilled she was with them —later.

This time...

He grabbed her from behind, and took her.

Her cry of surprise was so perfect, so sweet.

Yes, Lizzy Gray would cry out just like that for her general—if Drake had the balls to take her properly, which Ru doubted.

In the mirror, the comprehension first showed in the further widening of her already oversized Japanese eyes until they seemed larger than her whole face. As he surged deeper into her, a blush radiated from her brow all the way down to her breasts.

So unblemished a soul.

Yes, that had been the problem with Mei-Li. Any illusions had been driven from her by the man who had enjoyed her while she was still a gymnast. There had always been a feisty edge to Chen Mei-Li, as if a man just might be about to tangle with a dragon. It had been very invigorating.

Not this one.

Her meekness was utterly charming. Added to already being an outcast from Chinese society for her mixed-race Japanese features, and not daring to lose the new-found health care her mother needed so badly, he'd be able to count on her cooperation.

He rode into her hard, forcing her to keep her hands braced against the glass. When she tried to look down and away, he released her breast to clamp a hand around her chin and force her head up to watch herself and him over her shoulder.

Yes. She was timid enough to not fight his control. And so perfectly tight.

It didn't matter whether she was skilled or not. He would keep her—add her to his military security detail as a cover. She and his wife Daiyu could service him together while he thought of Drake and his little Jap devil. And Daiyu wouldn't dare complain when he told them to service each other, while he watched and thought of Chen Mei-Li and her lover Chang Mui.

With General Li Zuocheng gone, Ru's own path to the presidency was as firmly in his grasp as this girl's crotch.

And if that didn't work, he'd help the president do to Taiwan what he was doing to the young tech sergeant right now—together they'd fuck that troublesome little island properly as only true men could. It should have been done seventy years ago when that bastard Chiang Kai-shek was still alive to watch his own dick shrivel as he lost everything.

Of course, if Mao had done what was needed, then Ru wouldn't have this opportunity. Though there were many very satisfying paths to power, opportunities as good as this were beyond rare.

He could taste that edge of perfect power as he probed her depths so completely that the girl's arms gave out and she collapsed forward to lie pressed against the glass. Driving her against his hands now pinned between her body and the mirror, his explosion inside her was the most glorious since his final time with Mei-Li.

Yes, she would do very well.

66

"Wait! Wait! Wait!" Taz waved her hands until everyone shut up. A single intercom channel made everyone speaking at once impossible to understand, and the engine noise of the cargo bay didn't allow for talking easily without it.

Well, everyone except Andi, who still lay curled up in her seat with her head resting on Miranda's thigh. Though she finally appeared to be sleeping.

Holly had scared up a blanket, and showed a surprisingly gentle solicitude as she spread it over Andi. Taz hadn't known she had it in her.

"Just," Taz held out her hands once more, "wait. There's a scenario here that no one's considering."

"And what's that?" Mike was trying to act as referee, but between Miranda's inability to see any bigger picture, Jeremy's knee-jerk support of her emotional blinders, Holly's attacks, and—Taz sighed—her own assumption that they were all adversaries, he had a tough job.

She pointed at Jeremy's computer. "We have a recording

here that blames both Li Zuocheng and Zhang Ru. They're both bastards."

"How do you know that?" Jeremy asked as if he didn't actually understand.

Maybe she understood why Holly occasionally patted Jeremy on the head.

"First, General Li Zuocheng. You can't get to be the second most powerful man in China by being a nice guy. Chen Mei-Li said she had dirt on him a mile deep. And General Zhang Ru? Mei-Li told us enough to make Li Zuocheng look sparkly clean. That's aside from his predilections for rape. It's the most unforgivable crime there is."

"Sure," Holly nodded. "If you don't count murder or—"

"Were you ever raped, Holly?" Something inside her snapped and she shouted out, "Were you?"

Holly hesitated, then shook her head.

"If you're murdered, you just end up dead and it's over. If you're raped, it lasts for-fucking-ever. You want to know why I was nicknamed Taser? Trust me, it had almost nothing to do with my being the general's right-hand weapon."

Jeremy put a hand on her thigh, and all Taz could see was Miranda's little book of emojis: *upset,* with the note to then: *console.*

She slapped his hand aside—hard—and turned back to Holly.

"Before I got good with a knife, it happened a couple times. I was eleven the first time, and my mother was forced to watch. Part of the price of coming to America. But when I got into the Air Force, I thought I was done with that and dropped my guard. I was sixteen, nineteen by my ID papers, when my commanding officer came after me. General Martinez walked in on us."

Taz kept her head up. She swore she'd never be ashamed by this moment; *she'd* been the victim.

But she couldn't look at Jeremy. He saw her as somehow perfect. She knew that was horseshit...but *he* didn't. He saw her as so much better than she was, and she hated losing that.

However, she knew the anger would eat her alive if she tamped all of it down even one more time.

Instead, she continued glaring at Holly, which placed Jeremy out of her peripheral vision.

"My clothes were in shreds and his dick was out in the wind. The general didn't even hesitate. He shot my commander in the back. Instead of us both dying, as I expected from a through-and-through shot, he twitched like he had epilepsy and collapsed to the floor. The general looked at the weapon in his hand as if pleasantly surprised."

"A Taser," Mike said softly.

Taz nodded. "A prototype of the X26. The whole idea of a Taser as a military-grade weapon was still brand new back then. All he said was, *I was given this for evaluation as a less-than-lethal weapon. It seems to work.* When I told him that I wanted one, he pulled out a fresh cartridge, showed me how to load it, and handed it over. I wore that prototype next to my sidearm for my first five years as his assistant. I only had to use it twice before word got around to never touch even my ass without an invitation. Soon, *I* wasn't going to some meeting, 'The Taser' was."

And not once had the general looked at her nakedness. She'd followed him and never questioned his requests from that day until his last. Over the last forty-eight hours—

seeing what she'd done to Jeremy, starting to think about the choices she'd made in her life—she'd become much less sure about her decision to do that.

"Every time someone calls me Taser, or even Taz, it's a reminder of power versus helplessness, a reminder of *not* being raped. Do you think Mei-Li gets to have that? She deserves to see Ru go down."

"No, she doesn't," Jeremy spoke softly, but it was like a roar in her ears.

"Why the fuck *not?*" She turned on him.

He was still nursing his hand; she *had* hit it pretty hard. Great! She was back to hurting him.

She waited until even the headset-muffled roar of the engines seemed to fill her head to bursting.

"Miranda said—"

Taz was going to lose it if one more person cited the preeminent Miranda Chase of the NTSB as the ultimate authority on everything.

"—that their President wants to invade Taiwan."

"Oh-kay." Not quite the direction she'd thought that sentence was going to go.

"Zhang Ru also said that he must be stopped. If this leaks out and damages the CMC, the President's power becomes unquestioned. If he attacks Taiwan, thousands, perhaps millions will die. He'll attack the island, we'll send in aircraft carriers, they'll target our carriers with hypersonic carrier-killer missiles like the DF-ZF that we don't think we can block. This is major, Taz."

It was. "That doesn't mean men like Li and Zhang don't need to be taken out."

Nobody argued the point, but neither did they offer any other ideas.

"This isn't what we do," Miranda spoke softly.

"What?"

"We investigate crashes. We do not cause them. We do not attack, invade, or harm others. We now have six hours and seven minutes left of this flight to learn what we can from this aircraft. Jeremy, have you copied the contents of the QAR?" And just that simply the conversation was apparently over.

"I have."

"See if you can find a black box flight recorder. If the Chinese systems are like ours, it will carry less detailed flight data than the QAR but it might contain more. After that, check the systems' layouts. Holly, I want you to switch focus to an analysis of the aircraft structure. It appears to have some dynamic flexibility that I expect enhance maneuvering at velocities over Mach 2. It would be nice to understand those. Especially look for their quality of manufacturing as I've never cataloged a Chinese jet before. Mike, assist Holly. Taz, you may assist me in analyzing stealth modifications of surfaces and configuration."

Then Miranda eased out from supporting Andi as Mike slipped a folded blanket under her cheek. Andi showed no sign of noticing, though her rate of breathing said she wasn't asleep either.

Taz waited until everyone except Jeremy was off the headset system.

He too seemed to have something to say.

She spoke first, "We're not done with this. Though I guess it will have to wait until we're back on the ground."

Jeremy nodded but didn't speak. He definitely wore an emoji *sad* face.

"I'm sorry about your hand."

He nodded again. And again didn't speak. *Sadder* face.

It was—

Oh shit!

"No, Jeremy. Tell me you're not going there." Why did men always get so weird around women who'd been violated?

He nodded a third time.

"Say something already."

"I'm sorry."

"For what? You haven't done anything to me."

"For what those men did to you. For what they made you have to do." Then he brushed his fingers so lightly on her cheek that she barely felt it.

A moment later, Taz was the only one still in the seats other than Andi.

Kindness. Of all things, she'd never expected him to respond with kindness. Even an entire summer with the hotshots hadn't prepared her for Jeremy.

67

THE FLIGHT FROM JBLM TO TACOMA NARROWS AIRPORT IN Miranda's Citation jet took less than three minutes in the air.

Only when everyone else was off the plane and she was airborne again and headed for her island did Miranda feel she could breathe.

For fifteen glorious minutes, she raced north in silence. She stayed down at five thousand feet so that she didn't have to talk to anyone, not even air traffic control.

It was just her and the few other fliers enjoying the beauty of being aloft during a summer sunset. She considered extending the flight, perhaps circling up over the Olympics to watch the sun slide into the ocean. That such a flight would also pass over where the first Chinook had been felled by a wildfire was a good reason *not* to go there.

Besides, it had been so long since she'd slept that she probably shouldn't be flying in the first place. They'd left JBLM to fly to Taiwan over thirty hours ago—but staying in Gig Harbor tonight with the others hadn't been an option.

Over the island, she dialed the frequency of her runway

lights, then clicked the mic transmit button three times. The relay flipped closed and turned on the lights. They were on a ten-minute timer.

Her wheels kissed the grass of the Spieden Island runway just as the sun kissed the distant ocean. The long summer evening of the San Juan Islands was still rich with reds and golds by the time she'd shut down and hangered her jet.

The first thing she did was turn off her phone. If there was a crash, they'd have to launch some other team. She'd only done that once before in her seventeen years with the NTSB, but this time it was necessary.

The walk back to the house was a luxury as well.

But it wasn't the cloister it usually had been.

She could feel Holly and Andi at the table. Miranda straightened all the chairs and put away all except one of the placemats.

Mike and Taz, getting to know each other as they cooked together in the kitchen. Only when she had reordered the spices properly and emptied the dishwasher so that every pot, plate, and mug was in its designated place could she relax.

Even after putting fresh sheets on the bed, she could still feel Jon's presence. As if, even now, he had some question for her about why she behaved the way she did. Even when he didn't give voice to them, she could hear the thousand tiny corrections just the same. She tried to conform, but it was hard. He made it impossible to come to rest beside him. Miranda enjoyed his company and liked the sex. She liked that they were both crash investigators.

She showered and lay down, but it didn't last. She could still feel Jon.

Finally, she went to the big couch in the library at the end of the second floor. Taking Tante Daniels' quilt, *Storm at Sea,* she sat where she had spoken to Jeremy and looked out the big window at the silhouetted islands and the dark water.

The last of the evening's deep blue gave way to the black of night. The deer and sheep would have settled by now, tired by the disturbance of her landing and a busy day of foraging.

As Miranda watched the darkness, she could feel the three crashes.

The fiery death of the first Chinook and the sabotage of the second.

Perhaps she understood some of Taz's anger at...everything.

The sabotage of the Chinook was unforgivable. And the crashing of the J-20 jet by General Zhang Ru, just throwing away an amazing machine and its pilot. Having only studied the plans for America's two fifth-generation fighters, it was incredible to inspect one of the only other ones in the world so closely.

But the waste.

Unlike Taz, Miranda had never been attacked personally; most men went out of their way to avoid her. But she could feel some of Taz's hurt when she thought of those needlessly destroyed aircraft. It was a violation of all that was right.

Miranda sat up and clutched the quilt tightly as she stared out into the night.

The second Chinook and the J-20.

Both "felt" the same, not that she'd trust her own feelings...but they did. What if they were somehow linked?

Zhang Ru had ordered the crash of the Chengdu J-20

Mighty Dragon. He'd also been present at the crash of the Boeing MH-47G Chinook. Had he been responsible for that as well? Taz made it sound as if the man had no morals at all and was capable of anything.

She should tell somebody. Holly? Drake?

But she couldn't face anyone right now.

Couldn't face turning on her phone.

And there had been a fourth crash. One that she could presently empathize with—Andi.

Miranda slowly sat back against the couch.

When the world became too much, Andi had collapsed. Miranda had heard Mike's judgment that she'd driven herself there to help them understand the crash. Yes, it *was* a great gift, given at such a painful cost.

She'd still been pale and shaky when they had roused her for the landing at JBLM.

Andi didn't have the luxury that Miranda did. Her PTSD attacked her from the inside, from which there was no escape. Miranda's own problem was with the external world, and escaping to her island had always been a solace.

Would tomorrow be easier?

Yes. She'd had no sleep for the two nights in a row with the house full of guests. And then another sleepless night and day spent in the long flight to and from Taiwan.

Sleep was the answer. Then maybe in the morning she would call someone.

Or the next day.

68

Taz stood in the living room of the team's Gig Harbor house. The waterfront lights were just enough to outline a body of water, but the darkness was too complete to see more.

The décor was IKEA, unadorned IKEA. It looked as if the team wasn't here for much other than sleeping. The open-plan kitchen was the only real exception, it was well-equipped and laid out. She opened a random cupboard and discovered a wide variety of canned tomato products, but no jarred sauce. Another cupboard revealed the spice rack of someone who cooked from scratch. Mike.

"That's my room," Holly pointed. "Andi takes the spare bed, except the rare nights Miranda joins our merry band, then she gets the couch. I'll be in with Mike tonight, so you're welcome to my lay-down. That room is Jeremy's."

"And you'll decide about killing me in the morning," Taz kept her tone dry.

"Too right," Holly offered with her normal cheerfulness, then unsuccessfully tried to stifle a big yawn. Her grin was a little sheepish. "Besides, it's bad form to off someone when they haven't had enough sack time." With that, she and Mike were gone into one of the bedrooms.

Andi had already gone to bed.

Now it was just her and Jeremy in the IKEA model living room.

He was again doing one of his not-speaking things. That had definitely been a major change since the first time she'd met him six months ago. Getting Jeremy to shut up had been the real challenge then.

"What are you thinking, Jeremy?" Taz was thinking that there was no way she'd be sleeping in Holly's bed, so it was the couch for her.

Jeremy looked at her for a moment, asking, then blushed brightly and looked away.

"No way. Sorry, I don't mean that as in *no,* I'm just surprised. Are you deranged enough to think that we can just pick up where we left off six months ago?"

Jeremy shook his head.

Out of other options, Taz decided to try waiting him out.

"I..." he swallowed hard, then looked directly at her and spoke in a rush. "I'm not...*deranged* enough to think that we are who we were back then, when we were who we were before who we are now. I'm not stupid. I mean, I get that all that's changed and that twenty-eight hours shouldn't mean so much but—"

"And nineteen minutes," she couldn't resist adding in.

"—and nineteen minutes," he smiled for half a moment. "But I've never met anyone like you. I'm not talking about when we made love down in Baja, though that was incredibly, uh, incredible. I mean your understanding of Miranda, the amount you care about Mei-Li, that trick you pulled on the Taiwanese Army major to get Miranda to safety *and* salvage the jet. She even said you had great insights about the stealth configuration."

"I was General Martinez's liaison with the defense contractors for eighteen of my nineteen years in the Air Force. He was deeply involved in the aircraft design branch of the service. When learning is part of my survival, I do it very well."

"Is that all you ever get? Survival?"

Taz didn't even know how to respond to that. Until this last summer, that was all there had ever been. Before she could think of what to say, Jeremy continued.

"I guess I was kind of like that, but in a different way. You know, before I met you. I was always focused on the next cool thing to the exclusion of all else. You made me see that there can be so much more. Then I thought I lost all that when you died in the crash. Uh, I'm really glad you didn't, by the way. I just think I should say that because, you know..."

"You know they could arrest me tomorrow and throw away the key?"

Jeremy shrugged uncomfortably, then tried to shake it off like a wet dog, which made her laugh.

"And you have the greatest laugh I've ever heard," his voice was barely a whisper as he took her hand and rubbed a thumb over her knuckles.

No one, absolutely no one had ever seen her the way Jeremy did.

Out of all other ideas, Taz used their connection to lead Jeremy toward his bedroom. She closed the door behind them and led him toward the bathroom.

"One thing is certain though, I definitely need a shower first."

Jeremy stumbled to a halt at the threshold, almost pulling her over backward because of his tight hold on her hand.

His eyes looked a little wild.

"Haven't you ever showered with a woman, Jeremy?"

He only shook his head.

"Well, you start by getting naked."

His eyes widened even further, then he gave her the biggest smile since her return.

"I think he likes that idea."

"He does." Jeremy reached out and began tugging her t-shirt out of her pants.

"You're supposed to be kissing me while you do that."

His response was equally enthusiastic.

69

Taz's hair still lay damp across his chest. He made a mental note to purchase a hair dryer to keep in his bathroom.

In the shower, Taz had smoothed over all his nervous apprehensions.

"How do I know if I'm doing it right?"

"I'll tell you if you're doing it wrong," had been her simple answer.

"But that's only if I'm doing it wrong. How do I *know* if I could be doing it *right?* You know. Better?"

She'd laughed merrily. "Gods you're so sweet. I'll give you pointers."

And she had. Sometimes they were as simply nonverbal as shifting against him or riding her hand on the back of his. Others it was a quick gasp begging him to do that more.

For him? Well, he'd always thought he had a fairly vivid imagination about sex, perhaps in compensation for having had so little of it. Taz quickly proved him wrong. Both in the shower and again in bed.

Just as she had in Baja, she'd knelt over him, but it couldn't have been more different.

Rather than sweating in the heat of the desert sun during a stolen moment, they'd generated enough heat to peel back the blankets and welcome the cool air of the room on their skin. Instead of seeing her body in the stark daylight, in his shadowed bedroom their lovemaking had become entirely about touch. He'd never been so aware of every single shape that passed beneath his fingers as he did tracing the outlines of Taz's body. She was glorious to hold.

He'd managed to scoot the covers back over them as she now lay half tucked at his side and half sprawled across him.

But even wrung out as he was, he couldn't stop touching her. Tracing the lines of her cheek and jaw. Studying the shape of her ear. Was this what lovers did? He hoped so, because he never wanted to stop.

"Jeremy?"

"Uh-huh," he let his fingers sweep over her shoulder and ribs to brush against the side of her breast where it was squeezed sideways by being pressed against his ribs.

"What are we going to do about Zhang Ru?"

He could just reach her hip and brush along where her thigh lay over his waist.

"Jeremy?"

"Uh-huh."

"As much as I hate to stop you doing that, because yes, it feels just as good for me as it probably does for you, can you kick that brain of yours back into gear?"

"Does it mean I have to stop thinking about how incredible you are?"

Taz's sigh sounded like a contented one. "No. I like that you think that. That's new for me too."

"Okay." He tucked his hand over her knee and leaned his cheek on her damp hair. "Okay. Zhang Ru."

"Yes. He deserves to die. To be put down like a rabid dog."

"But if we do, it destabilizes the CMC. It will give the president an excuse to exercise his powers as one of the chairmen, appoint a replacement to his liking, then force the Taiwan issue. The fact that Ru was promoted to the CMC *by* the CMC means that he probably isn't the president's yes-man."

"All I can see is that Ru has to go down."

"I'm not all that great at people, this is more Mike's thing."

"Are you suggesting I should be in bed talking to Mike?"

Jeremy had to laugh, "I don't think Holly would be very amused by that."

"At least then she'd have a real excuse for killing me." He'd never get tired of Taz's laugh, even when it was gentle and wry like this one. Taz could express a thousand emotions with that laugh.

"Why do you only think with anger?"

"What are you talking about?" Taz pushed up enough to look at him in the dark.

He took advantage of her position change to slide his hand back up to cradle her breast.

"Jeremy!"

"You said I could think about both you and Ru."

She thumped her forehead against his shoulder, "I did. Fine. Cradle my breast like you've never felt one before."

"Well there was only the one other, and yours are much nicer."

"Thanks. Now, Ru?"

"No, we were talking about anger. You're letting your anger at Ru block you from seeing what else is possible."

"It has to do with his raping—"

"No!" Jeremy let go of Taz's breast because it *was* really hard to think of anything else when he was holding it. He pushed up until they were both sitting cross-legged, facing each other in the dark. "You're...Ah! You're thinking like a playing card."

"I'm *what?*"

"You're being an F-35 fighter jet, just like Mike said. Your first thought is always to attack. What if you were...an E-3 Sentry AWACS?"

"Then..." her silhouette tipped its head in the dark as she puzzled at that.

"Remember what an AWACS does. It has that big radar dome on top to make early observations of distant events."

"...I'd be thinking about the big picture and how to turn it into a win for everyone?"

Jeremy loved the sharp agility of Taz's mind. That was at least as exciting as her body. It made him want to push her down atop the covers and start all over again.

"So, now that I'm an AWACS. The air is pretty thin up here and I'm not used to it. The right question would be... How do we stop China's president and save Taiwan?"

"The only way is to keep the CMC stable," though Jeremy knew that meant leaving Ru in place.

"No, that won't be enough." Unlike Mike, who looked around for an idea, he could feel Taz's thoughtful glare boring right into him. She took her problems head on.

"What would Miranda do?" He asked himself that all the time when he was—

"Goddamn it, Jeremy! She's not some magical queen.

She's a woman who's just as fucked-up as the rest of us. Maybe more so. You've got to get her off the goddamn pedestal. Yes," she held out her palms to stop his protest before he could make it, "she's a fucking genius when it comes to an air crash. The things I thought I already knew when we started going over that J-20 together weren't a hundredth of what she knows. But she isn't why this team works, even though you all worship her like a goddess. It's the three of you. Maybe it'll be the four someday, but Andi's even more of a mess than Miranda is right now."

Jeremy opened his mouth, but couldn't think of what to say and closed it again. Maybe Andi wasn't trying to push him out, instead just trying to survive. But the team worked even partly because of him? There was no way that he—

"I can *feel* your brain churning, Jeremy. I saw you side-by-side with her on the CH-47D crash at the fire. You solved the MH-47G's sabotage completely on your own."

"Only because I happened to see it occur."

Taz growled deep in her throat. "And you did nothing on uncovering the story behind the J-20's crash?"

"She trusts me to—"

"Exactly. *Trusts!* Touchdown plus field goal! You just lost all future right to argue with me. Mike pegged you exactly when he said you were just like the Chinook: dead reliable, and able to lift heavy loads for Miranda. And before you deny it, remember that your goddess agreed with the metaphor."

He didn't… He wasn't… "That's not how I see myself."

"Well, it's true."

"And the way you see yourself is all backward, too. You know, this gives me an idea."

"What idea?"

He grabbed Taz's hand and dragged her out of bed.

"This isn't about more sex, is it?"

He paused just long enough to kiss her and hold her breast again for a luscious long few seconds.

Taz almost stumbled into him as she tried to draw out the kiss when he moved away.

"Regrettably, no. Get dressed."

"What?"

"We have to go see someone."

70

Mei-Li lay happily tangled in Mui's arms.

She'd spent the last day and a half in terror that Zhang Ru would find some excuse to block Mui's departure from China. The instant Mui had appeared at the head of the escalator into SeaTac's baggage claim area was one of the happiest moments of her life. Exceeded only seconds later when Mui had spotted her and run into her arms.

Now they were in their own bed, in their own apartment, in America!

It was as impossible as it was perfect.

Until a year ago, Mei-Li's life had been about surviving hell—every single day.

Mui had taught her more. Mui had taught her that sex didn't have to be about power, that it could be about fun. And she'd taught Mei-Li about love, which had previously only been a lie in ridiculous movies.

Yet she loved Mui.

Mei-Li held her more tightly as Mui slept upon her

breast. It was terrifying, too. As if a piece of her heart, Mui, was out walking around in the world.

But Mei-Li would keep her safe. She'd keep her—

At the knock on their studio apartment's door, Mei-Li almost screamed.

Zhang Ru or his minions had come!

They would tear everything apart!

Her heartrate exploded as Mui slowly sat up and rubbed at her sleepy eyes.

The knock again, and Mei-Li could see the fear slip into Mui's eyes where it should never be. Where it had *never* been a year before. After a most privileged upbringing, Mei-Li had taught her fear, and hated herself for it.

She slipped up to the door and almost yelped again, this time in surprise, when she saw who it was.

They both quickly pulled on robes.

Then Mei-Li answered the door.

"We're, uh, sorry to bother you so late, but we need to talk." Jeremy's eyes traveled from her to Mui to the unmade bed, then he blushed brightly. "Maybe we should come back later."

Taz rolled her eyes at Jeremy. Taz's hair was a mess, and she wore no bra despite her figure. Jeremy's hair was neatly combed, but his shirt was misbuttoned. There was little question what the two of them had also been doing recently.

Mei-Li invited them in. Their furniture so far in the spacious studio was two desks with chairs and the bed; she and Mui sat next to each other on the bed with their thighs touching while the Americans took the chairs.

Jeremy didn't spend any time on pleasantries. He barely waited until she'd introduced Mui. Thankfully, Mei-Li had already told Mui about the strangeness of the airshow yesterday during the taxi ride home.

Home? Such a strange word to use automatically. Yet this small studio, when their rank and privilege could have afforded them so much more, was perfect because it was all theirs. Mui's grandfather had purchased it for them and given them the deed.

"You should know that the pilot who died in the J-20 crash in Taiwan left a recording that implicated both Zhang Ru and Li Zuocheng."

Mui tensed beside her. She was too well trained to show it, but Mui was her lover and their bodies had no secrets from each other.

"My grandfather would not do such a thing," Mui finally found her voice. "I know what he is, but he is also a man of honor. He would not sacrifice a man's life that way."

"Well, unless we come up with a different solution, I would bet that recording will leak. When it does, they will both be removed from the CMC. Your president will then have the power to order the military to annex Taiwan. There will be a war."

Let them die! Mei-Li would gladly let that happen.

But again, Mui's body betrayed her. She wouldn't.

Taz spoke for the first time. "I think Zhang Ru should be crucified for what he's done to you—slowly, painfully, while being forced to chew on his own testicles."

Mei-Li let herself smile. She had been right to trust Colonel Vicki Cortez.

"But Jeremy said there must be a better solution. A way to stop the war before it happens."

"No one," Jeremy nodded at the two of them, "knows

more about the seven members of the CMC than you two. Do you have any ideas?"

Let them die! Again, Mei-Li kept the thought to herself.

She looked at Taz, who shook her head. "No. I'm not able to see it. Jeremy says that I only think from a place of anger. I know...something of what you went through too well."

Mui stroked a hand over Mei-Li's hair so gently she could almost cry.

"Mei-Li knew only pain," Mui concurred. "She has now learned there is more, I offer her all I know how to."

"It is more than I ever dreamed of," Mei-Li kissed her briefly before turning her attention to the Americans. "She is the blessing of my life." And it was true.

Mui turned to Jeremy. "Until they learn to leave the anger aside, we must be their guides. Yes?"

Jeremy looked thoughtful, then offered Mui a slight bow of respect. Mei-Li now knew that Taz had chosen her lover well.

Taz looked at Jeremy in such surprise that both Mei-Li herself and Mui laughed.

She grimaced, then shrugged. "We don't even know if we get to stay together tomorrow."

"None of us do," Mui nodded to the door. "Mei-Li assumes that every knock will be the entire Chinese military marching through the door to drag her back into her nightmare. Even though we are finally in America, our visa *can* be revoked at any moment. I often tell her that the only answer is to live every day very completely so that we do not regret as much if there is no tomorrow."

"So, how do we make sure there is a tomorrow?"

Mui smiled at Jeremy's question, "I have an idea on that."

71

TAZ'S HEAD WAS STILL SPINNING WHEN THEY ARRIVED BACK AT Tacoma Narrows Airport.

Jeremy had called ahead and the others were waiting by the Mooney. Mike had already rolled it out of the hangar.

"It's only a four-seat airplane."

"Andi and I are barely enough to make up a whole person together."

"This had better be worth it." Andi did look a little better for having gotten some sleep.

After a little juggling, Holly sat behind Mike. Andi ended up in the back seat as well. Taz was on Jeremy's lap in the front passenger seat, slid all the way back against Andi's short legs, and held close by a seatbelt extender.

"If she'd just answer her phone..."

"Well, she didn't. So we've got to go find her. Just don't crash." Taz draped an arm over Jeremy's neck and pressed against him to not bump the copilot's control wheel.

He rested his head on her shoulder and she tipped her cheek onto his hair.

"Aw, aren't you two just the sweetest thing since Vegemite."

"Vegemite is as bitter as hell," Taz glanced back at Holly as Mike got them into the air.

"I didn't want to get carried away."

Was it a warning? Not to get too carried away about Jeremy? Taz couldn't tell. It's not as if there was really a place for her on this team. Her car and most of her personal gear were still parked down in southern Oregon at the hotshots' base. Her future was probably parked in Leavenworth prison.

Twenty minutes later, they were circling over Spieden Island, and she had no more answers than when they'd first taken off.

72

MIRANDA WOKE TO THE SOUND OF AN AIRPLANE BUZZING through her dreams.

She knew the sound of the plane, but couldn't place it.

All she could hear was the heavy beat of a Chinook's shredding rotors as Zhang Ru chased her across the sky in a shattered Mighty Dragon jet—shedding parts as it raced ever closer.

Flying through her own—

She was still on the couch.

Under the *Storm at Sea* quilt.

Out the big picture window, she saw that the plane was real. It circled one last time, switched on a bright landing light, and turned final. The light was glaring right at her, so she couldn't make out any details.

When she looked aside, she saw that her runway lights were on. Very few knew how to turn those on, and she couldn't imagine who it would be.

Then she finally came fully awake.

She hadn't recognized the sound because it was *too*

familiar: a Continental TSIO-550 engine driving a Hartzell Scimitar three-bladed prop.

It was her Mooney.

Her watch said it was almost three in the morning.

What could be so important?

She dressed carefully and waited for them in the garden by the back door.

The last thing she wanted was visitors. Even if the visitors were her team. She wished they would go away, but that wasn't a polite thing to tell a visitor.

If she'd been younger, she'd definitely have thrown a tantrum. But she wasn't a child anymore. So she stood in her garden, breathed in the night air, and breathed it back out again.

It took longer than she expected for them to arrive. Perhaps she should have gone to get them with the golf cart instead of leaving them to walk down from the hangar. Except the golf cart was still parked at the hangar; its keys were in her pocket. But she didn't want them here anyway.

She could hear their approaching footsteps.

They weren't conversing.

Without a word, she led them inside and started to make tea.

Mike shooed her out of her *own* kitchen and began to make it himself. He would put the tea away wrong and disorganize her mugs once more, but he left her little choice.

She sat at the table and waited.

"I'm sorry, Miranda," Jeremy spoke first. "We tried calling you, but you didn't answer."

"My phone is off."

"Oh, well, we want to call General Nason."

"Why do you need to call Drake?"

"We have an idea on how to stop the Chinese president from starting a war over Taiwan, and nobody gets killed."

"Who's we?"

"These two jokers," Holly indicated Jeremy and Taz. "As far as we can tell, they had wild sex, went to talk to that Chen Mei-Li girl and her lover, and together the four of them cooked up something. It sounds good to us."

"But," Mike began distributing mugs, "you get last word. And we don't know how to call Drake."

"Oh," Miranda pulled her phone from her pocket and turned it on.

The instant she did, it rang so sharply that she almost lost it to the floor.

73

"Hi, Miranda, I'm sorry to wake you."

"Well, that's convenient," Taz kept her voice low as she recognized Drake's voice over the phone, as apparently everyone else did.

"We're not asleep," Miranda observed in the perfectly logical way of hers.

"We? Your team is there?"

"Yes." There was a small chorus of agreement from the others. Taz still didn't know what she was, so she kept her mouth shut.

Miranda continued. "I'm sorry, Drake, but we won't have even an initial report on the J-20 for you until tomorrow—"

Holly held up her wrist as if looking at her watch.

Miranda checked her own. "—or rather later today."

"That's not why I was calling. I'm here with the President."

"Good morning, Roy," Miranda continued without missing a beat.

Taz glanced at Jeremy and whispered, "Roy?"

"He asked her to call him that."

"And she does?"

Jeremy just waved a hand toward the recent proof. Maybe Miranda deserved at least some of the pedestal this team had her up on.

Drake continued, "He wanted to hear from the team on the ground why you think the Chinook MH-47G was sabotaged. If it really was, could it have been related to—"

Taz jumped in, "Oh, it was sabotaged, Mr. President. We also know that it was done by General Zhang Ru blackmailing a Night Stalkers' mechanic."

"What the hell? Who is this and how do you know?" the President's voice was even deeper over the phone than on the television.

Shit! Taz really should know when to keep her mouth shut. "This is..." she took a deep breath "...Colonel Vicki Cortez, former aide to General JJ Martinez. And I know because a Chinese national witnessed the blackmail and informed us."

"Cortez? I thought you died with Martinez."

"So did I, Mr. President."

"This Chinese national Tweety Bird told a dead colonel about blackmail they just happened to witness being done by one of the top seven Chinese military generals?"

"Yes, sir. She told myself and Jeremy Trahn." And then Taz looked around the table and realized that neither of them had thought to mention that piece of Mei-Li's information to the rest of them.

"Do we have any idea why?" the President's growl sounded lethal.

"We were told that it was payback for a person. A connection that our informant uncovered about the timing of a phone call made to General Zhang Ru's private personal number. I'm sorry, sir, but that was all of the detail I was given."

"A *Persona?*" Miranda asked softly.

Jeremy smacked his forehead, Holly looked ill, and Mike just folded his arms on the table and slumped until his face rested on them. Only she and Andi were left in the dark.

"Fuck!" was Drake's assessment over the phone.

Then Taz remembered a tiny news item. It was about the crash of an AN-124 Ruslan Condor in Siberia last year, and the loss of a three-billion-dollar *Persona* spy satellite during its delivery to an eastern Russia launch site.

The reactions around the table said that it wasn't a crash at all. And somehow both Zhang Ru had become involved, and knew that Drake Nason was a part of it.

Again, glancing around the table, they all looked like normal people, though she was becoming convinced that they weren't.

"Okay. I think we're done with that topic," the President's tone put a definitive end to it. "Thank you and your team for their time, Miranda."

"Of course, Roy. Though we were calling Drake with a question of our own."

"Fire away, Miranda. Anything I'd be interested in or can I get back to my day job?" The President was actually teasing Miranda.

Miranda waved a hand at her.

Taz had no idea why she was suddenly the one on deck. Other than there hadn't been time to bring Miranda up to speed with the latest.

"Well, Mr. President, it turns out that China's loss of the

J-20 was an opening move about starting a war in Taiwan. And we think we have a way of stopping it."

The silence at the other end of the line was deafening.

"Is that of interest, Roy?" Miranda asked in that perfectly rational way of hers.

74

ZHANG RU LAY BACK ON THE COUCH WATCHING THE WESTERN news. CNN was one of the many privileges of rank. Daiyu and the new girl were talking quietly over tea on the other sofa.

Ru had thought about calling the girl Lizzy, but it would be too sweet a nickname and he didn't want her getting any romantic ideas. Daiyu had done that when he'd first married her; thankfully that phase hadn't lasted long.

He knew the news release must come sometime today because the West must explain the crashed J-20 jet to the Taiwanese and the world, before another night fell. Crashing it on Fulong Beach the day before a major music festival had been perfect. The media was still covering the removal of the destroyed bandshell, and their lame attempts to still hold the concert on the sand.

Half his attention remained on the television, but half wandered to the two women. They'd gotten past the initial jitters since he brought the girl to the house.

He'd considered fucking Daiyu to convince her that she

still had a place here, and wasn't being discarded. But the girl had proved to be most agile this morning at his city apartment, and, while not yet particularly skilled, had proved herself to be very open to suggestion. Yes, he would wait until their usual time to reassure Daiyu of her place.

Sitting side-by-side, they did make an exceptionally attractive pair. The contrast of Daiyu's athletic build and the girl's slight one made them much more beautiful together than either was apart.

How best to use them was the question.

The other vice-chairman of the CMC who sat beside Li Zuocheng was completely the president's man. Mei-Li's research...

Ah! That was it! How perfect everything was.

Her research had uncovered that the vice-chairman had a single vice, but one that ran deeply—a fetish for mounting lesbian women. In couples. Very roughly. As if he could only be aroused while proving his male superiority over them. He kept it very well hidden, but Mei-Li had proven it with hospital records and pictures.

By the latter, it was clear that the man had no taste at all. He wasn't a connoisseur of women; he was a greedy pig.

Perhaps, after Ru had replaced Li Zuocheng, he could invite the man to visit. Maybe for a quiet dinner—new vice-chairman seeking advice of the sitting vice-chairman.

Then he would happen to be called away, and leave his wife and...her younger half-sister. Yes, that was a good explanation for the *xiao riben guizi* girl in his household.

His wife and her half-sister would then "entertain" the commission member in his absence.

Until Ru himself stormed in, too late to stop his dastardly deed. And before he damaged Ru's women, of course.

They would cry rape, and he would be justified in having the man executed and his family shamed, perhaps confiscate his fortunes as well. The bastard was even better off than Ru himself.

Ru would make sure to have his phone out under some pretext to undeniably capture the evidence. Better yet, a hidden video camera. He could enjoy the seduction himself as often as he wished, and use the footage of the attack and rape to damn the bastard to hell.

Yes, once Ru himself had replaced Li Zuocheng, that would be his next move. Then, as sole (surviving) vice-chairman, he would be able to influence exactly who would take the other vice-chairman's seat. With his own man in place, he would control five of the seven who—

The news flashed to an aerial view of the on-going cleanup at Fulong Beach. The jet was long gone, of course, taken to America. The Miranda mouse woman had been an awkward way to guarantee that the pilot's recording fell into their hands, but the Americans wouldn't be able to resist the bait once they'd heard it.

A news anchor cut in with a "Breaking News" banner.

"We have a new development in the matter of the Mainland Chinese J-20 *Mighty Dragon*—a fifth-generation stealth fighter jet—that crashed on The Republic of China's eastern shore, destroying the site of the annual Hohaiyan Rock Festival. It seems that a recording the pilot made moments before his death has survived. We'll play it for you now."

This is Captain Chen Bo of the People's Liberation Army Air Force. I have been ordered by the President of my country to test Taiwan's defenses with a solo intrusion of a Chengdu J-20. I am told that if they retaliate, the President says we are ready. I do this willingly to honor my country.

The anchor returned, "It appears that the president of the People's Republic of China is declaring to the world his personal intention to start a war. World leaders are already condemning this. An immediate and total trade embargo has been threatened by over seventy countries if there is not an immediate retraction. Many are offering to mobilize their forces if—"

"No! No! No!" Ru shouted at the anchor. "That's not what you were supposed to say, you dirty little bastard! Just because you're dead, don't think your wife and daughter are safe. I'll—"

His phone rang.

His personal phone, from a blocked number. It could only be one person.

He turned off the fucking television and answered it.

"You goddamn bastard!" He screamed into the phone. "You changed it, didn't you? It was supposed to be fucking Li Zuocheng, not the damned President who said that."

"Yes," Drake's voice was completely calm. "Now know this! If you threaten or so much as touch an American citizen ever again, *our* President has said to expect retribution to the *fullest* abilities of the American military. That includes any relatives of Staff Sergeant Bob Wang, whether they are in America or China. And if you personally ever set foot on US soil again, in any capacity, you will be arrested and incarcerated as an *agent provocateur*. In other words, I will own your ass."

"What's to stop—"

"Your President has just been shamed on the global stage. He will not dare to move against Taiwan now. And if you yourself attempt to push forward an attack, I will make sure that he learns precisely who shamed him. Do we understand one another?"

Ru knew he was shaking, but that bastard and his little Jap bitch had twisted this. They had him by the balls and knew it.

Unable to contain the fury...he heaved his phone at the television, hard enough to shatter the screen.

It had all failed.

Li Zuocheng was still in place as a vice-chairman of the CMC.

Ru himself still controlled only three of the seven votes including his own. Far from a majority.

Ah! His eyes alighted on the two women huddled together on the opposite couch.

But!

If he used them to eradicate the other vice-chairman as he'd just been considering, that would get him four votes. And Li Zuocheng would be thankful to have that thorn removed from his side; the two vice-chairmen did not get along.

Oh, friend Zuocheng. I had tried to make peace with the bastard to help you, you know I am always your humble servant. Instead he rapes my wife and beats her half-sister. She's just a poor mixed-blood Japanese, but I take a broader view and don't hold her rapist Japanese ancestor against her.

For that favor, Ru would be able to turn who had the controlling vote in naming the replacement of his vacated seventh seat when he became the second vice-chairman. He could get his man in place without having to kill his friend. That was four votes of seven. And he'd be in the perfect position to influence Li Zuocheng's vote if it was a crucial decision. Excellent.

"Mei-Li, you and your little lover are safe for now," he told the room. He wouldn't need them to aid in shifting the balance of power in the CMC. At least not until he reached for the presidency. For now they would be his secret weapons, his sleeper agents.

Then he turned to Daiyu and the girl who still clung as close to Daiyu as if she was already protecting her, as a younger sister. That too was very good. They were as natural together as sisters should be.

Now to make them appear as lovers; lovers able to entice the second vice-chairman to his doom.

"You two. We are going to practice something until you both have it perfectly right." And he was going to enjoy the practice almost as much as he would catching the vice-chairman with his dick buried in Daiyu's ass.

The girl's ass, that was strictly his.

75

MEI-LI AND MUI SAT TOGETHER ON THE BED AND HELD HANDS. They could manage no more than that.

Classes started tomorrow, but neither of them had dared to leave the apartment, not even to purchase textbooks.

They'd seen the news broadcast.

Rather than Ru climbing onto the top of the CMC's pile, his actions had caused the president of China to be shamed.

Publicly shamed—about Taiwan!

Ru would be beyond furious.

Their visa would be revoked. They'd be returned to China, and Mei-Li couldn't begin to imagine the horrors she'd suffer. Even worse, that Mui would suffer.

Their attempts to make love a final time had offered little solace. Instead they were left with no satisfaction but tears.

"I *hate* the danger I've put you in." Mei-Li held Mui's hand tighter.

"It is not you who intends to kill my grandfather."

"I must expose Zhang Ru. If only I knew how to do it in time, and without getting you killed."

It was a conversation they'd had a hundred times since Jeremy and Taz had visited them in the middle of last night. And many more times since seeing the news.

The Americans' ploy had stopped a war, but for her and Mui?

Nothing.

Ru was still in power.

The CMC was stronger than ever.

And for them?

No answer was satisfying.

She would sacrifice herself in a heartbeat for Mui. That must be what love was. So little she understood, so late.

This time at the knock on the door, they both cried out. If they were to die, clothes wouldn't matter. They pulled on robes and Mei-Li answered the door without bothering to look first.

"Sorry if I surprised you. Mei-Li Chen?" A man in a FedEx uniform held out an electronic device.

She could only nod.

"Sign here please," he waggled the device at her again.

Was it her own death warrant? A new way to deliver secret poisons?

Not knowing, Mei-Li signed anyway.

He handed her an envelope with a bright orange "Small Critical Pak" on the outside of the envelope. He tapped his hat brim and was gone.

After carefully re-locking the door, she and Mui sat together once more on the edge of the bed.

The return address was some building in downtown Seattle—meaningless. A time stamp said it had been sent less than an hour ago.

"Is it a bomb?" Mui's voice was barely a whisper.

How big did a bomb need to be to kill two people? *Not very* was the only thing Mei-Li could think.

She should send Mui away before she opened it, but she knew asking would be useless. Mui had long since taught her that they were in this together.

Finally, they slid a hand around each other's waists.

Mei-Li held the envelope.

Mui pulled the tab to open it.

When nothing happened, they peered inside together.

What she saw made no sense. Tipping the envelope, some paperwork and two blue passports landed in their laps.

American passports.

Hardly daring to look, Mei-Li eased one open to the picture. There was a decent picture of Mui, with an embossed stamp, and the incomprehensible words under Nationality: United States of America.

Mui was looking at the photo of her that had the exact same words.

They traded, but her own didn't make any more sense than Mui's had.

She set it down carefully, just in case it did decide to explode, and unfolded the paperwork.

"These are certificates of citizenship," Mui breathed out as they studied them together.

They were. Mei-Li peeked inside the FedEx envelope; there were two cards. She gingerly tipped them out.

The first one simply said, "Thank you." There were three names: Drake, Lizzy, and Roy.

Mui traced them with a finger. "You told me about the first two..."

"I think the third one just might be the American President."

"Wild!"

The second card had a Mandarin ideogram for "Welcome to the USA." It had been reasonably done with a ballpoint pen.

"Who *are* all these people?" Mui pointed at the six signatures. Colonel Vicki Cortez's was by far the most prominent.

Mei-Li held the card to her chest for a moment, then set it carefully aside with the other papers and passports.

"You met two of them last night. If we're incredibly lucky, you'll get to meet the others someday."

"It's all real." They opened their passports again to stare at the pictures together.

"It is real," Mei-Li confirmed. It was impossible, but it was real.

Mui's squeal this time wasn't fear, it was purest delight. She threw her arms around Mei-Li's neck and kissed her soundly.

"And if you are very, very lucky," Mui whispered against her lips as she slipped her hand inside Mei-Li's robe, "you will survive what I'm about to do to you."

"I don't know. I may be invincible. I'm a US citizen now."

"I'm one, too. Thanks to my perfect lover. Let's find out if you *are* invincible."

And as Mui strove to prove them both right, Mei-Li really did feel it.

Together they had shamed the Chinese president, causing him to lose massive respect. Forced to change his rhetoric and leave Taiwan alone.

Zhang Ru had been caged, at least for now.

And, against all odds, she had freed them both.

Mui had told Jeremy, *Until they learn to leave the anger aside, we must be their guides.*

Mei-Li had, as much by luck as skill, led them this far. They were free and protected as US citizens.

Perhaps she *would* set anger aside and let Mui be her guide for whatever happened next.

Mei-Li's breath caught. She couldn't suppress the groan and the deep shudder that followed.

Indeed, Mui *had* found something new in her infinite supply of creative ideas.

Maybe she wouldn't survive. But if not, it would definitely be worth it.

76

"WHAT ARE YOU THINKING?"

Taz had become accustomed to asking Jeremy that, not the other way around.

The others had all finally gone to sleep in the big house just as dawn was shading the sky.

Miranda, who'd been so carefully rigid when they'd arrived, had relaxed completely after Drake and Roy—Christ, now *she* was doing it—after General Nason and President Cole had agreed to Mui and Jeremy's plan. She'd even been...cheerful.

After everyone else had retired, Jeremy hadn't taken her to a bedroom.

Instead he led her outdoors. In some mix of peace and exhaustion, they followed the one dirt road that headed south. It eventually led to a tiny harbor.

"Well, now we know how she gets her major supplies onto the island." Jeremy pointed. In the softness of the predawn light, they could see two parallel piers that supported an unloading crane, big enough to pick up a container.

"She's a one-woman machine," Taz was trying not to be impressed by the sheer scope of one woman living alone here.

Never mind trivial things like her being a lead crash investigator and all the other details Taz had learned about her in the last three days.

"Three days?" It couldn't be so little.

Jeremy offered one of his shrugs that didn't argue the point.

She went to follow the road toward the big boat house and the small floating dock.

"We'll check it out some other time." With their interlaced fingers, Jeremy continued to lead her south, off the road.

They disturbed a few grouse and a very sleepy looking deer as they climbed through the deep grass and up onto a rise.

"It's called Green Point." Jeremy tossed down a blanket she hadn't noticed he was carrying.

But Taz stayed on her feet to admire the view. Their perch was perhaps a hundred feet in the air and offered a nearly three-hundred-and-sixty-degree view of the San Juan Islands. Only to the northwest did the narrow spine of Spieden itself block the vista. Islands covered in soft grasses and towering pines dotted the water like gumdrops.

"They say it's a drowned mountain range from the ice ages. The water is actually incredibly deep around the perimeter of the island group."

"It's gorgeous." Even in their short walk, the soft pink had become rich golds reaching around the entire horizon.

"Personally, I think the view just got a whole lot better."

Taz turned to look at Jeremy, who was making a point, eyebrows raised, of ignoring the landscape in favor of her. When she laughed, his smile just grew.

"So, what are *you* thinking?" Now he was asking her.

"I'm thinking you have some kind of magical skills. Something way beyond what we mere mountain-fairy evaporating hotshots can begin to understand." She pushed against his chest and he landed on his butt on the blanket.

"Such as..."

"You mean, other than averting a major war?" She straddled his legs to pin them as she undid his belt.

"Other than that," he agreed.

"Other than the President granting me a full pardon as a courtesy for helping save the nation?"

"Well, Drake did insist that you take an honorable discharge and leave the Air Force."

"He did." She raised herself up enough to shuck off Jeremy's pants. "But I think that may have been General Lizzy Gray's doing. I think she was tired of dealing with me from the old days."

"Could be. Could be." Jeremy made agreeable noises as he sat up just enough to drag off his shirt. "I wonder how she'll feel about Miranda's offer."

Taz stopped what she was doing and rubbed at her face, trying to make sense of it all. Fifteen years as a street kid. Nineteen more under the absolute control of General Martinez. Six months that had felt like freedom, and now?

Miranda had offered her a place on the team.

Taz had thought hotshotting had been the good bit. But just maybe *this* would the even better bit.

It hadn't even seemed like Mike's idea.

Andi says that I need to keep people around me who are good at the things I'm not.

Taz had agreed that made sense. The others around the table had remained quiet.

Mike is good at people, but he isn't military. Holly and Andi are military, but not nearly so good at understanding people. You are exceptionally good with military people. You also were involved in the design of dozens of different aircraft, which proved particularly useful in advancing my understanding of the J-20. Since military investigations constitute most of what we do now as a team, I think you should join us as a military liaison.

That was the part that General Lizzy Gray just might hate.

But if she approached her role as Taz, rather than "The Taser"—and checked her anger at the door—maybe. Just maybe...

Before Taz even had a chance to glance over for Jeremy's reaction, Miranda had gone into the kitchen and begun straightening the mugs in the cupboard.

"I still don't know what I think." She looked down at Jeremy lying on the blanket. "Incredibly lucky? Like maybe she just gave me a chance to finally have a life."

Jeremy's nod confirmed the feeling for himself as well.

"I have to remember to thank her; I didn't do that properly. But I think I'd be foolish to look any further." Because at no moment in Taz's life had there been one that felt as good as this.

As she rose enough to remove her own jeans, Taz felt General Martinez's challenge coin tucked in its little pocket. She pulled it out as she set her jeans aside, and looked at it carefully.

He'd made it a simple design. Plain, uncolored bronze.

One side simply read, General Jorge Jesus Martinez. The other was a waving American flag. He'd been a patriot in every way that mattered, and the coin was a simple statement of that fact.

But there was nothing else there.

There was no...heart to it.

It was the coin of a warrior and nothing more.

She turned it over again and again as Jeremy watched her silently, but she couldn't find anything else there.

Not even any sign of herself.

With a quick turn and flick, she heaved the coin high and hard.

It arced through the dawn light, plunging down, until it disappeared into the dark waters off the point of Miranda's island.

Then she tugged off her shirt, and once more straddled Jeremy.

"What are you thinking?" Because she didn't want to think about the past anymore.

The first rays of sun washed over them from a cleft in the distant Cascade Mountains.

"I think seventy-two hours."

"What about seventy-two hours?"

He turned his watch so that she could read it. "Seventy-two hours and no minutes. That's how long ago I met you for the second time. Up on Hurricane Ridge at sunrise three days ago."

"So our record now is way better than twenty-eight hours and nineteen minutes?"

"Way better," he slipped his hands onto her bare waist.

"So, maybe I should stick around at least seventy-two more. You know, just to keep you people out of trouble."

"I'd like that," Jeremy was looking at her eyes, not her chest. "I'd like that a lot."

As Taz lay down upon him she decided that she'd like that a lot too.

77

MIRANDA SAT ALONE, CURLED UP ON THE LIBRARY COUCH WITH the *Storm at Sea* quilt pulled over her.

She'd watched Jeremy and Taz walking together south across the island until they were out of sight.

After tucking the quilt more warmly around her feet, Miranda let the dawn fill the room while she thought about how she felt.

Taz was a good addition to the team.

Miranda had taken to heart Andi's maxim: *being wicked smart about aircraft doesn't mean that you get to know everything.* Then, she'd added a corollary of her own: what *didn't* she wish to become an expert at?

Dealing with people like Zhang Ru.

When Taz had proven that she understood people like him, and could even handle Jeremy's new outermost Causal Sphere concept, it became an easy decision.

All she'd ever cared about was the crash.

And now that her team was in place, almost as neatly as Mike's playing cards, she could finally see the metaphors.

Jeremy, Holly, and Andi helped her see different aspects of the crash itself.

The others had tried to explain how Mike was like the A-10 Thunderbolt II—the close-air-support specialist. But she still liked the Mooney. He was good with people, just like her Mooney.

And Taz? Taz was the world-class fighter jet. Perhaps needing a little tempering by Jeremy, but she flew high and fast, and knew where to attack.

Herself and her F-86 Sabrejet?

Miranda pulled the quilt up under her chin and let her eyes drift closed.

She wasn't like Taz, even if they were both fighter jets. But just maybe she was like the Sabrejet anyway.

It was the first of the swept-wing fighters; the most successful military jet in history by almost every measure. And everyone insisted that she was the best crash investigator in the NTSB.

Even though neither of them were a weapon of war, they each, in their own way did do one thing incredibly well.

They both, in their own way, really flew.

HAVOC (EXCERPT)

IF YOU ENJOYED THAT, BE SURE YOU DON'T MISS THE NEXT TITLE IN THE MIRANDA CHASE SERIES!

HAVOC (EXCERPT)

Seattle-to-Sydney Direct
600 miles southwest of Hawaii
39,000 feet
Seat 57A

HOLLY DID NOT APPRECIATE THE IRONY OF THE MOMENT.

Not even a little.

She'd been sitting one row from the very rear of the Airbus A330-900neo jet. If she didn't hack off her legs to get away from the muscle spasms soon, it would be a Christmas miracle—too bad it was October.

Tall people were *not* meant to sit in economy on fourteen-hour non-stops. But National Transportation Safety Board investigators also knew better than to sit in the front of airplanes.

Statistically, the rear rows of modern jet liners were

marginally enough safer that she couldn't quite bring herself to sit forward, no matter how safe airplane travel in general had become. Far and away the safest form of transport—except when it wasn't.

And her job as a crash investigator was all about when it wasn't.

The very tail of all wide-body jets had a motion that seemed disconnected from the rest of the aircraft, and, at the moment, the vibration was almost as annoying as her legs.

Only six hours into fourteen, for a flight she didn't want to make. It was lucky for whoever wasn't there that the seat beside her remained empty; it was best that her need to vent her frustrations to someone, *anyone,* had no ready target.

Hell, at the moment she'd even vent to Mike, though their parting at the airport hadn't gone smoothly.

Are you sure you don't want me to go with you? And Mike had even insisted on driving her to SeaTac for her flight. As if he somehow *knew* how hard this trip was going to be for her—despite her not telling anyone anything about why she was going. Of course it was Mike, so he knew even without being told.

Which was almost as annoying as how comforting his presence had been on the drive.

But the *last* thing she wanted was her past touching any part of her present.

It was a completely rank horror-show that she herself had been given no choice.

Then at the curb he'd gotten all clingy, like he was going to miss more than having her in his bed most nights. Like he...*owned?*...some piece of her?

So not her.

She'd already been with him longer than anyone before in her life. Maybe it was time they were done—just to avoid his getting *too* attached. Soon, maybe he'd be wanting more than she was willing to give.

The period of the vibration shifted.

Rather than the slightly annoying slow sway of the airplane's butt—like riding in a big old 1970s station wagon that desperately needed new shocks—it took up a distinct rhythm.

One that accelerated fast.

With a periodicity that, in all her experience, should never happen to any airplane.

She opened her left-side window shade to glare out. Her eyes ached as they adjusted from the dim you-should-be-sleeping-now interior to the glaring dawn over the Central Pacific.

There was the source just at the edge of her view—the Number One engine was shaking visibly.

Shaking hard.

It didn't explode or shatter like an uncontained turbine failure. Those happened in milliseconds; things occurred fast when meter-wide titanium fans shattered at thirteen thousand rpm.

This engine was swaying side-to-side on its mount.

She'd never seen that before. Or read about one doing that. Or even heard of such an event. Holly barely had time to wonder if Miranda ever had.

Three seconds later it broke free of the left wing.

Shit! There was an event she could go a lifetime without witnessing herself.

Just as the engine mount's shear bolts were designed to

do, rather than letting the engine destroy the wing, they sheared.

The suddenly disconnected Rolls-Royce Trent 7000 turbine— unburdened from doing its half of dragging the two-hundred-and-fifty-ton twinjet across the ocean—shot forward, then climbed up and over the wing. As it passed safely above the wing, the engine did finally fail. It shattered spectacularly, before disappearing aft faster than she could track.

Holly cringed and dug her fingers into the arm rests, but no metal pinged off the main fuselage.

She held a deep breath for maximum blood oxygenation before exhaling with the abrupt hull decompression.

But there wasn't one.

No oxygen mask suddenly dangled inches from her face.

Apparently the hull was still intact. The engine failure was directed downward from the inverted engine's top, pummeling the wing with a single loud bang. The well sound-insulated plane muffled it to little more than the noise of retracting landing gear.

Holly's fingers ached as she released the padded armrests, even though it had only been seconds.

She tried to remember the last aircraft she'd heard of suffering a complete breakaway engine loss, but she wasn't Miranda Chase. Her team's IIC—Investigator-in-Charge—carried the entire encyclopedia of aircraft accidents around in her head. It was only one small part of what made Miranda the best IIC in the entire National Transportation Safety Board.

Herself, not so much.

Holly took a slow deep breath before she dared to look again.

The engine was definitely gone.

She focused on recalling her military training to remain calm in a crisis—because crisis was just the normal state of operations.

Then she looked down and lost the bit of calm that she'd mustered.

That was definitely the vast emptiness of the world's largest ocean seven long miles below.

She looked over her shoulder at the two flight attendants. Still chatting quietly in their seats.

A glance up the long aisle revealed that most people were asleep, except for a few diehards watching movies. It was seven a.m. back in the flight's origin city of Seattle—after a one a.m. departure; sensible people *were* asleep just the way any airlines wished their passengers to be. Always. She was surprised they didn't just drug the coffee and be done with it.

The aisles were empty, and there was no splash of light from any other open window shade revealing the pile-driver sunrise pounding in her window.

She knew that from the angle of the cockpit it would be impossible for the pilots to check the engine visually. However, their instruments would certainly be reporting the loss with several catastrophic tones. Trained pilots would now be ensuring the integrity of the Number Two Engine.

But someone should be coming out to look out a window that could actually see the engine. Or at least a flight attendant should have been asked by the pilots to inspect it for them if they were too busy with alarms.

She would count to ten.

Holly made it to five before she punched the call button.

One of the flight attendants behind her, a male, reluctantly unbuckled and came up to her seat.

"You really should keep the shade down, miss. Others are all catchin' a bit of shut-eye." While she enjoyed the Aussie accent—it was a real relief after spending the last year in the US—she had other priorities.

"I didn't want to alarm anyone, but you just lost an engine." She kept her voice down and her tone even.

The attendant hadn't started out looking friendly and now was looking less so. "I'm sure the pilots have everything well in hand."

Holly grabbed the attendant's pretty two-tone tie by the back strap, used her thumb to slide the knot tighter to make sure she had his full attention, then dragged him across the empty seat beside her and her lap to mash his face up against the window.

His choked-off squeak of alarm sounded ridiculous coming from a guy, especially an Aussie.

"We've lost a bloody engine, mate. See?" She thumped his face against the plastic a few times to make her point.

"Don't move!"

Holly looked up and into the muzzle of a Glock 19, the new Gen5 which she'd been meaning to check out. An air marshal must have been sitting in row 55 directly in front of her. He now knelt on his seat and had aimed his sidearm at her over the seat back.

Her former training as an operator in the Australian Special Air Service Regiment kicked in.

The air marshal held it one-handed, and with his finger outside the trigger guard. He was making it too easy.

Keeping one hand firmly on the flight attendant's tie, she swung her other hand up from where the marshal wouldn't be able to see it over the seatback. Catching the barrel in the Y-shape between her extended thumb and hand, she grabbed on and rotated it upward away from her face, forcing his finger to slip completely off the trigger guard and below the weapon.

If he'd been doing a two-handed hold, she'd need a different, more difficult technique, but he didn't even get that right.

Continuing the motion, she peeled the gun completely out of his hand.

Then Holly tossed it in the air just enough to flip her hold from barrel to handgrip and jammed the barrel up his nose.

Her finger was inside the trigger guard.

"You! By law, air marshals are required to flash their badge and give a warning before wielding a sidearm. So you're in serious trouble there, mate. Now sit down and behave unless you want your brains to finish the flight with a free upgrade to First Class."

He made a tiny nod of acknowledgement—about as big as could be made with a 9mm pistol rammed up one nostril.

She hit the magazine release, dropping it on the back of the flight attendant still pinned across her knees. He flinched and gagged a bit.

Racking the slide back against the edge of her folded tray table, Holly saw no round in the chamber. He hadn't been a real threat at all. She pulled the trigger on the empty chamber, tugged down the paired slide release levers midway down the barrel, nudged the slide against the tray table again, and, with a quick shake, the gun fell into pieces.

The air marshal started to move, but not the right motion to turn and sit.

She dropped the rest of the parts on her temporary tray table built from the choking flight attendant's back—she eased up his tie a bit—and grabbed the air marshal's windpipe with her free hand. Holly pinched hard enough that he wouldn't make a sound that could alarm other passengers.

"And if you reach for your bloody baton, you wanker, I'm going to use your own handcuffs on you and leave you face down in the thunder box." Not an airline toilet in the world didn't reek after the first six hours of a flight.

She shoved him away, gathered up the Glock parts from the flight attendant's back, then hauled him off her lap.

"You! Call the bloody cockpit and tell them they've lost the Number One engine." She glanced out the window and saw it was even worse than she'd expected. "And that the wing isn't looking so pearla either."

***

First Officer Quint Dermott slid into the empty seat next to the golden-blonde staring out the window. She was a serious treat. If she had the face to go with that hair and body, she'd be a stunner.

If this was an airport bar, he think some thoughts. But they'd just carked a bloody engine in the middle of the Pacific Ocean. If the flight attendant hadn't been freaking, he sure as hell wouldn't be here—it was hard to spook one that much.

"I'm the copilot. What seems to be the issue here?"

"Well, mate. I'd say you're the one having a serious issue." She didn't bother turning to face him as she spoke. Her Strine was so broad it was like being home.

"Fair dinkum?" Quint could have a good time calming this passenger down, not that she looked upset. Long blondes with legs to match and who spoke like they were from the heart of the Outback, was something he hadn't run into in far too long. Maybe *never* a Sheila of this quality. Too bad he had to hustle back to the cockpit.

Twice he'd been blocked from the left side of the aircraft by some doddering fool getting out of the seat, so he'd just hustled down the right side without getting the outside view he wanted to check the engine's status. They'd hit the fire bottle, but there were no readings at all which they should have from even a crippled engine.

She waved out the window.

This wasn't the best angle to see the engine but it was better than nothing. He leaned in. Close enough to see the wing out her window and feel—his heart skip the next three beats.

An ES—Engine Separation. *Shit!* No wonder there were no readings coming back to the cockpit.

"I'm seeing some serious flexion at rib number nine," her accent slid away as she continued at a volume barely louder than a cozy whisper in his ear. "Directly above the engine pylon is where it seems to be doing the worst of it. You're already getting enough buckling in top panels eleven through fifteen that I think the rear spar is FUBAR as well."

"Uh, where?"

She pointed.

He leaned in again. He was a pilot not a mechanic, so how in the world would he know which skin panel was which? But practically lying in her lap, he could see what she was talking about. There was a crinkle in the aluminum skin directly above where the engine had been. Like a fist had punched down on it from above—a damn big fist.

Fucked Up Beyond All Recovery was a depressingly accurate assessment.

"You'll also want to switch off any cross-tank transfer pumps or that leak is going to empty the plane of fuel faster than a possum up a gum tree."

Now that she'd pointed it out, he could see the dribble, okay, the fair gush of petrol going the wrong way.

"Oh, one more thing." She dumped the parts of a handgun into his lap, then reached forward and patted the head of the man seated in front of her.

He cringed as if he'd just been whacked by a hammer—a ruddy farrier's one. For shoeing Budweiser Clydesdales.

"I didn't really want to give that back to your air marshal. He seems inclined to want to shoot me."

"Happen much?"

"Not anymore." She offered a luminous smile.

"How—"

No time for finding out how she knew any of that.

"You—"

Nor how she'd disarmed an air marshal.

"ATSB structural specialist on loan to the NTSB," she answered his first question at least.

On the Australian *and* the Yanks' Transportation Safety Boards? That explained a hell of a lot.

Definitely time to get back to report to the captain.

"You're with me." He shoved to his feet.

Or tried to.

She hooked onto his belt and used it to slam him back into the seat before he was half out of it.

"What?"

"Don't want to scare the B&S unless you're into a dog's breakfast," and her broad Strine was back.

He looked up the long aisles.

A Bachelor and Spinsters Ball was a common dance party in rural Australia—a fun and typically very big gathering. Maybe not as many as were presently on the plane but on a good night...maybe. It wasn't only singles who came out for a B&S Ball dance.

And a dog's breakfast was always a proper mess.

Right-o, he'd leave the passengers to their quiet sleep and free-movie pacifiers.

He did his best to smile at the blonde and rose as normally as he could.

She smiled back like she hadn't a care in the world.

***

"Dani. It's me. I have a tag-along," he looked at the pieces of the air marshal's gun that he'd carried up the aisle. "I'm the one with the weapon. We're good as Vegemite."

He ignored the blonde's snort of laughter.

It was today's agreed-on safe word. Without it, Captain Dani Evers wouldn't have opened the door.

There was a sharp snap as the cockpit door's three heavy bolts unlocked.

He swung it open and flinched when he saw the captain's sidearm aimed to just behind him. Quint hadn't known that Dani was one of the thirty percent of airline pilots who now flew armed. He showed her the gun parts, not that he had a clue how to put them together, then moved for his copilot's seat and dropped them into a cup holder.

Dani lowered her aim just enough to center on the blonde's chest as soon as he was out of the way.

"Clean as if I showered just last Thursday." The blonde didn't flinch. Instead, she did a slow turn with her hands out, like she was a runway model for airplane disasters, then shut the door behind them.

"Who is she and why is she in my cockpit? And how bad off is my engine?"

"Bad. Gone."

"Explain."

He just waved a hand at the woman.

She sat in the jump seat located just behind and to the left of his own righthand seat. She slipped on a headset, then propped her feet up on the end of the central radio console that ran between his and Dani's positions as if she was kicking back at home to view a program on the telly.

Dani offered the blonde one of her patented Looks of Death.

The feet went away. Experience had taught him that Dani Evers' Look of Death could scorch a pushy guy in a pub right down into a puddle on the beer-stained floor. He could almost feel the blonde shrug as if it was no big deal.

However, in keeping with her stated background, she launched into her observations, explaining the status to Dani in a way that was detailed, concise, and rattled off like the professional she claimed to be.

Quint buckled in and cut the fuel flow to the left wing.

Dani looked at him in question when she described the damage to the wing.

He nodded that it looked exactly as bad as the assessment made it sound.

Dani's semi-eyeroll was her version of a violent curse—not something you did when the cockpit voice recorder was listening. It was one of the many reasons he liked flying with Captain Dani Evers. No games; there was never any question about what she was thinking.

He watched the fuel gauges for a minute to make sure the flow had stopped, and tried not to feel incompetent just listening to the passenger.

"You've got an ETOPS-330 rating on this jet," she reminded them as she finished her analysis. "Three hundred and thirty minutes of Extended Operations flying time on a single engine. All that right ripper ability won't be doing you a spec of good if the wing comes a cropper first."

"We're eighty minutes past Hawaii," Quint checked the charts. Then glanced back at the blonde.

She was staring at the Escape Rope cubby beside the overhead breaker panel. There was one on each side so that, in the event of a crash blocking the cockpit door, he and Dani could open a side window and descend safely.

It had always been an academic bit of knowledge from training—maybe not anymore.

After a long study, she turned back to him.

"I might just be chucking a wobbly," she was perhaps the least berserk person he'd ever seen, "but I don't think you have reaching-Hawaii kind of time. And eighty minutes past Hawaii means that Howland Island is the next nearest watering hole, two hours the other way—that's if you want to be landing on a deserted sandy beach and curling up in a watery sleepout with Amelia Earhart. Howland's the place she never reached in the end. Leaves you but one squat to plant your tush." She stopped, not telling him where, of course.

Quint had to search around a bit until he found Johnston Atoll. The island was abandoned and the runway closed, which was why it hadn't shown up right away as an alternate field. It was less than twenty minutes away. It would take them that long to descend seven miles—unless they lost the wing, then it would be much faster. More like ninety seconds, which wouldn't end well.

Technically, Johnston wasn't available for any kind of landing. But nine thousand feet of decommissioned US military-grade runway compared with crashing into the ocean when their wing fell off wasn't a contest for him. He'd argue with the Yanks' FAA *after* he'd survived. Better, he'd let Dani do it; she was the Captain after all.

"How sure are you?" Dani asked as Quint put Johnston on the center screen, then flipped the radio to the satellite frequency for their airline's emergency mechanic.

"Personally, I'm surprised we're still aloft." The blonde recrossed her legs the other way as if she had nothing better to do. He did notice that despite her apparent ease, she'd put on the jump-seat's full five-point seat harness: lap belt, shoulders, and the crotch belt from the front edge of the cushion to the central clasp that any mere tourist would have missed.

"Who the hell are you?" Quint felt as if he should know. But even thinking about her being in a totally unexpected place, he couldn't account for her.

"Sergeant Holly Harper, retired from the Oz Special Air Service Regiment. At your service, mate. Wondered when you were going to ask."

Quint could only stare at her.

Couldn't even blink.

SASR were the elite special operators of the entire Australian military. Which explained why she was so calm in a crisis.

What it didn't explain was...*Holly Harper?*

"Christ. I thought you were dead."

"Close a few times, maybe more than a few, but not yet. Why were you thinking that?"

It would take far too long to explain.

He turned to Captain Evers.

"We're going down, Dani. We need to get on the ground fast."

Because if there was anyone who knew about surviving, it was Holly Harper.

ABOUT THE AUTHOR

USA Today and Amazon #1 Bestseller M. L. "Matt" Buchman started writing on a flight south from Japan to ride his bicycle across the Australian Outback. Just part of a solo around-the-world trip that ultimately launched his writing career.

From the very beginning, his powerful female heroines insisted on putting character first, *then* a great adventure. He's since written over 60 action-adventure thrillers and military romantic suspense novels. And just for the fun of it: 100 short stories, and a fast-growing pile of read-by-author audiobooks.

Booklist says: "3X Top 10 of the Year." PW says: "Tom Clancy fans open to a strong female lead will clamor for more." His fans say: "I want more now...of everything." That his characters are even more insistent than his fans is a hoot.

As a 30-year project manager with a geophysics degree who has designed and built houses, flown and jumped out of planes, and solo-sailed a 50' ketch, he is awed by what is possible. More at: www.mlbuchman.com.

Other works by M. L. Buchman: *(* - also in audio)*

Action-Adventure Thrillers

Dead Chef

One Chef!
Two Chef!

Miranda Chase

*Drone**
*Thunderbolt**
*Condor**
*Ghostrider**
*Raider**
*Chinook**
*Havoc**
*White Top**

Romantic Suspense

Delta Force

*Target Engaged**
*Heart Strike**
*Wild Justice**
*Midnight Trust**

Firehawks

MAIN FLIGHT

Pure Heat
Full Blaze
*Hot Point**
*Flash of Fire**
Wild Fire

SMOKEJUMPERS

*Wildfire at Dawn**
*Wildfire at Larch Creek**
*Wildfire on the Skagit**

The Night Stalkers

MAIN FLIGHT

The Night Is Mine
I Own the Dawn
Wait Until Dark
Take Over at Midnight
Light Up the Night
Bring On the Dusk
By Break of Day

AND THE NAVY

Christmas at Steel Beach
Christmas at Peleliu Cove

WHITE HOUSE HOLIDAY

*Daniel's Christmas**
*Frank's Independence Day**
*Peter's Christmas**
*Zachary's Christmas**
*Roy's Independence Day**
*Damien's Christmas**

5E

Target of the Heart
Target Lock on Love
Target of Mine
Target of One's Own

Shadow Force: Psi

*At the Slightest Sound**
*At the Quietest Word**
*At the Merest Glance**
*At the Clearest Sensation**

White House Protection Force

*Off the Leash**
*On Your Mark**
*In the Weeds**

Contemporary Romance

Eagle Cove

Return to Eagle Cove
Recipe for Eagle Cove
Longing for Eagle Cove
Keepsake for Eagle Cove

Henderson's Ranch

*Nathan's Big Sky**
*Big Sky, Loyal Heart**
*Big Sky Dog Whisperer**

Other works by M. L. Buchman:

Contemporary Romance (cont)

Love Abroad

Heart of the Cotswolds: England
Path of Love: Cinque Terre, Italy

Where Dreams

Where Dreams are Born
Where Dreams Reside
*Where Dreams Are of Christmas**
Where Dreams Unfold
Where Dreams Are Written

Science Fiction / Fantasy

Deities Anonymous

Cookbook from Hell: Reheated
Saviors 101

Single Titles

The Nara Reaction
Monk's Maze
the Me and Elsie Chronicles

Non-Fiction

Strategies for Success

Managing Your Inner Artist/Writer
*Estate Planning for Authors**
Character Voice
*Narrate and Record Your Own Audiobook**

Short Story Series by M. L. Buchman:

Romantic Suspense

Delta Force

Th Delta Force Shooters
The Delta Force Warriors

Firehawks

The Firehawks Lookouts
The Firehawks Hotshots
The Firebirds

The Night Stalkers

The Night Stalkers 5D Stories
The Night Stalkers 5E Stories
The Night Stalkers CSAR
The Night Stalkers Wedding Stories

US Coast Guard

White House Protection Force

Contemporary Romance

Eagle Cove

Henderson's Ranch*

Where Dreams

Action-Adventure Thrillers

Dead Chef

Miranda Chase Origin Stories

Science Fiction / Fantasy

Deities Anonymous

Other

The Future Night Stalkers
Single Titles

SIGN UP FOR M. L. BUCHMAN'S NEWSLETTER TODAY

and receive:
Release News
Free Short Stories
a Free Book

Get your free book today. Do it now.
free-book.mlbuchman.com

CPSIA information can be obtained
at www.ICGtesting.com
Printed in the USA
LVHW031622150321
681595LV00029B/376